Copyright ©2021 by Bella J
All rights reserved. This book or any portion thereof may not be reproduced or used in any manner whatsoever without the express written permission of the publisher except for the use of brief quotations in a book review. This is a work of fiction. Any resemblance to actual living or dead person, businesses, events, or locales is purely coincidental.

AUTHOR'S NOTE

The Villain is a dark romance and COMPLETE STANDALONE that contain scenes that might offend sensitive readers.

Possible triggers:
- Child abuse
- Drug abuse
- Violence
- Kidnapping/Stalking

PROLOGUE
CHARLOTTE

Present

Silence.

It was a precious sound. A sound so many took for granted. A sound no writer or poet could put into words. It could only be experienced. Appreciated. Longed for.

People claimed to know what silence sounded like. But to most, silence was merely the absence of noise. To others, it was that time when you were finally able to hear your thoughts.

To me...it was this. This moment. This point in time when there was nothing, not even the sound of a single breath. The few seconds of peace when my mind was free of every thought. Free of the troubles that stirred the disquiet in my soul.

Free of the pain.

I settled my feet flat on the ground, my body relaxed yet posture firm. For thirteen years, every muscle was trained to release the tension so nothing hindered my pursuit of perfection. And no matter the chaos that surrounded me, or the pain that crippled me, there was nothing more important than that.

Perfection.

I held the bow between my fingers, leaned my head a little to the left as I focused on the smooth touch of the wood and the scent of rosin. That pine smell alone had the power to calm a thousand storms that raged in my veins. So familiar. Calming.

During these moments, I never thought about what would come next. The road ahead was always dark, unknowing, and uncertain. But that was the part I loved the most. The mystery, the excitement of wondering what perfection would look like this time. It was never the same. Constantly bending and shaping differently than it did before.

I let out a breath and slowly moved the bow across the strings, the first note causing chills to flow down my back as the anticipation started to build. The deep yet soft sound reached inside my chest, allowing me to feel it—to feel the music that escaped my heart only to echo off the strings and create the most beautiful melody that had the power to make souls weep. Even the cruelest and wickedest couldn't resist the seduction of music.

With every move of my fingers along the neck of the cello, the sound, the vibrato swept me away—out of this room, out of this world, far away from the pain.

Far away from...him.

Soon the music entranced me, the cello and I moving as

one. Note after note, I laid my every fear, my every dream out on the ground beneath my feet, because there was no place for anything but the resonating tenor of the instrument that rested against my heart.

With my eyes closed, I moved the bow flawlessly across the strings, the music filling the room, touching the walls as it built—louder, stronger, more powerful. I would solely exist to help it find its way toward the crescendo it deserved. And once it did, it would explode into fragments of unsurmountable splendor.

This was my life. This was what defined me.

Music.

As the final note played, I lifted the bow away from the strings and exhaled. Silence slowly smothered the sound until there was nothing left of the music I had just played.

My chest rose and fell, my skin electrified and sweat beading at my temples. I opened my eyes and stared out in front of me, straight at him.

The man who demanded I play for him.

The man who took me.

CHAPTER ONE

ELIJAH

A few weeks earlier

It was a splendid piece, a musical composition that had the power to make you feel the grief and loss even if you had no reason to experience either. The Mass of the Dead was an offering so the departed souls could be laid to rest. On nights like these, such an offering was the only mercy I allowed.

Mozart's *Requiem* blended with the pitter-patter of raindrops against the windows. The early-autumn rain, along with the scent of blood, enhanced the unavoidable fear of the one thing none of us could ever escape.

Death.

The sobs of a man knowing he was standing at the gates of hell disturbed my enjoyment of the music. I turned up the volume to drown out his miserable weeping. He begged. He cried. He cursed. But it was all in vain. I had never shown any of these fuckers clemency. None. My lack of empathy ensured that my work was done mercilessly.

"You're him, aren't you?"

I ignored him and glanced at my wristwatch. *One more hour.*

"You're the man everyone talks about, yet no one has ever seen." My latest victim raised his voice so he could be heard through the music.

With my back turned toward him, I smiled. "That's because no one who has seen me lived to tell."

"Why are you doing this? Why am I even here?"

"My job is not to answer questions or to tell you your transgressions." I picked up my knife and gently eased my thumb along the sharp edge. "My job is to make sure that fuckers like you no longer walk the streets." I turned to face him, and his complexion paled instantly.

"Jesus."

"I'm afraid Jesus isn't here." I stepped closer. "Not today, and certainly not for you."

"Are you that guy, the one everyone whispers about? The killer who carves weird shit on his victims' chest." He struggled against the ropes which tied his hands to the chair, his eyes wide and filled with terror. "You're the—"

"If you've heard the whispers about me, then you'd know how this will end."

"Who is it? Who put a price on my head? Whatever they're paying you, I'll double it."

"Careful, now. Desperation will only make you look more pathetic. Besides," I touched the tip of the blade in my hand, "it doesn't matter who's paying me since I have my own reasons."

"What? What the fuck did I do to you?"

I approached him, one slow step after the other. This was the part I loved the most. The role where I played God, prolonging the inevitable simply to fuck with their minds. There was nothing more torturous than waiting for that which you feared more than anything else.

Sweat ran down the back of his neck, soaking his collar and leaving the ends of his hair wet, clinging to his skin. He reeked of aftershave, perspiration, fear, and piss. One would have thought that for a fifty-two-year-old man who had been a part of our society his whole life, he'd be wise enough to know not to fuck with the wrong people. But yet, here we were.

"Please!" His sobs grew louder, and it became increasingly hard to hear the music through his pathetic crying. "I'm sorry. Whoever it is, whatever they want, it's theirs. Just don't kill me."

"Even if by some miracle your death is no longer required by my employer, I'm afraid due to personal reasons I cannot show you mercy."

"I didn't do anything to you. Fuck, I don't even know who you are."

"It's not something you did *to me*."

His eyes narrowed, confusion clouding his expression. "Then what the fuck is this about?"

I placed the tip of my knife at the side of his neck against the pulsing vein, and he jerked his head to the side.

"Please stop. Don't do this."

"You thought you buried all your secrets," I dragged the blade down toward his throat, "but I found them."

"Jesus Christ," he whined. "I don't know what you're talking about!"

I pressed the knife harder against his jugular. "Eleven years ago, the night of November second." He stiffened. "Ring a bell?"

If it weren't for the music playing in the background, this moment would be accentuated by a crushing silence as his mind traveled back in time, back to that one night he thought could be erased from history. A night he buried his sins.

His chest rose and fell, his cheeks wet with cowardly tears and pale with fear-stricken regret. "Please don't do this. Please don't fucking do this. I have grandkids. A family."

Anger simmered, and I pressed the knife so the tip pierced his skin. "What about their families? Those two children?" I pulled the blade down, slicing a thin line in his flesh, blood oozing out as his screams hit the roof.

"Stop! Please!"

"Save your breath, Mr. Rossi. Your begging is futile."

"I'll pay you. I'll give you all the money you want."

"Money?" I scoffed, lifted the blade from his throat, and walked to stand in front of him. "I can assure you I have enough money of my own. I don't need yours."

With a swift tug, I ripped the sweat-soaked shirt down his front. His fat belly and abundance of gray chest hair only added to the disgust I felt for the man. "I bet there's a special corner in hell for men like you. In fact," I leaned closer, "I'm sure you'll recognize a few fuckers when you get there."

"Don't do this. Please don't do this." His uncontrollable sobbing continued, spit and snot dangling from his open mouth. It was never a pretty picture seeing a grown man sob like a baby and pissing his pants.

I reached out and turned up the volume of the music, drowning out his incessant cries and pleas. This wasn't my first rendezvous with a despicable man like him. It amazed me how easily these men who claimed to bask in so much power would shed their regal skin and show what cowards they truly were once a little pressure was applied.

I placed the cold blade against his skin and looked him in the eye as I moved my wrist, allowing the steel to cut his flesh. His screams were deafening. It could peel the goddamn paint off the fucking walls, blending with the splendid music I had playing in the background. To others, it would sound horrendous. To me, it added a powerful echo to the orchestra filling every open space around us.

For the next ten minutes, I carved through the skin of his chest. He sobbed, screamed, jerked, and fought against the pain. But I was too lost in the moment—the music, the blood, the parted flesh. It had to be perfect. I thrived on the pursuit of perfection, which was why every curve, every cut had to be precise and in place. The perfect treble clef.

The orchestra neared the crescendo, and I closed my eyes, enthralled by the deep and distinct tune of a cello that dominated every other musical instrument. Some wouldn't even be able to distinguish between the different sounds, yet I could. I had listened to this exact composition a thousand times—maybe more. It was a part of my soul, part of who I was and what I did once the sun disappeared in the west. Some said the darkness cloaked the wrongdoings of sinners. It gave them the shadows so they could purge themselves of the evil that festered inside them. But it wasn't like that for me. The night brought me peace. It gave me the freedom to be who I truly was. It allowed me to shed the skin of a man society demanded I be once the sun peeked over the horizon in the east.

I stood back and leaned my head to the side as I looked at the carving. "Perfection," I murmured.

"You fucking psycho! Jesus Christ, what the fuck is wrong with you?" More screams. More cursing. More reasons for me to send him to hell.

My sobbing victim tried to look down to see my handiwork carved in his flesh, but his double chin kept him from seeing the whole picture. "What did you do to me, you motherfucker!"

"I carved weird shit—as you put it—on your chest."

"What the actual fuck?" he cried, more piss running down his legs, the vile stench getting more awful by the second.

I plucked a handkerchief from my pants pocket and wiped the blade of my knife, all the while keeping my eyes on the sick fucker in front of me. "Don't worry," I started, placing the knife down and reaching for the gun behind my back. "Soon, the devil will feast on your wretched soul."

I extended my arm and stepped closer, aiming the gun at his face.

His eyes pinched closed, tears running down his cheeks as he recited a prayer in Italian. A prayer that was of no use to him now. It was too fucking late for him. It was too fucking late for all of us.

"You were right." I placed my finger on the trigger. "I am him."

His eyes opened. "You're the…the—"

"Say it."

The music ended, and silence settled while he kept his horror-filled gaze locked on mine.

"Say it!" My voice slammed against the ceiling, and he flinched. "Who am I?"

He took a breath, his eyes bewildered and fat cheeks pale.

"Say. It."

"The Musician."

I smiled. "That's right. Now that you know who I am," I pressed the nuzzle harder against his forehead, "say hi to my mother for me."

CHAPTER TWO

CHARLOTTE

I glanced around before slipping the key into the lock. It was just after midnight, and staff had already left, leaving the Alto Theatre empty and silent. This was wrong, maybe even borderline trespassing. But since this was technically my workplace, sneaking in here after hours wasn't *that* bad. I promised myself I'd stop as soon as I got caught—which would probably be a given, anyway. But I hadn't gotten caught yet, so I'd taken that as a sign to continue my midnight rendezvous' here at the empty theatre.

"What do you think you're doing?"

"Jesus." I yelped and slapped my hand against my chest, taking a deep breath when I recognized the familiar voice. "Chase, you fucking asshole."

He smirked and placed his hands in his pants pockets. "You shouldn't be lurking around here alone at night."

"First of all," I tucked a stray curl behind my ear, "I'm not lurking. And secondly," I let out a breath, "I bet being alone here is much safer than at my apartment."

"You're probably right. Your place is kind of a dump."

I slapped his arm. "My place is not a dump. The neighborhood, however, that's a different story."

Chase slipped on his jacket and pulled a beanie over his light blond hair. "I'm serious, though. You should be careful. You know there are all kinds of monsters in this city."

"Oh, yeah?" I narrowed my eyes. "Like who?"

"You've heard of The Musician, right?"

I balanced the cello case in both hands. "Oh, please. The man's a phantom, if he even exists. More like a folktale, a scary story parents tell their kids to keep them off the streets at night."

"Well, I've heard some of the orchestra girls say he roams the halls of this theatre some nights."

I grimaced. "And they would know, how?"

"I dunno. But my dad always says, where there's smoke, there's fire." Chase shrugged. "Let me give you a ride home."

"I'm fine, really."

He glanced at the cello case in my hands. "Ever thought about joining the orchestra?"

"What?" I shifted from one leg to the other. "No way. My stage fright is debilitating."

"Bullshit. I've heard you play, Char. You're good. You should totally audition."

"No." My cheeks burned. "I can't. Maybe someday."

He shot me a lopsided grin. "Okay. Well, are you sure you don't need a lift home?"

"Positive."

"Cool. Just don't stay too long." He walked down the corridor but turned back around. "Oh, and if you get caught, I know nothing about this."

"Of course, you don't." I shot him a half-smile.

As Chase disappeared around the corner, I took a final look down the halls before carrying the case through the door and closing it behind me. This goddamn case was hanging on its last thread, and I expected it to disintegrate or fall into tatters on the floor any day now. It used to be my mother's before she passed two years ago. Cancer stole her from me, and her death and my father's continued absence throughout my life had left me an orphan at eighteen. It had always just been my mom and me.

Now it was just me.

I turned on my small pocket flashlight and slowly walked down the stairs toward the stage. Excitement popped inside my veins. There was no pain tonight, which meant the next hour had the potential to be excellent. Just me and my cello, without the worry of failure and the judgment of the crowd.

By now, I knew there were precisely twenty-four stairs before I reached the front of the theatre, my pumps silently moving across the floor. Gently, I placed my cello case on the stage, hoisted myself up to sit on my ass, and straightened. It smelled like freshly polished wooden floors, and my shoes made that squeaky sound as I lightly stepped across the stage to switch on the light. The bright stage light blinded me for a second, and it took my eyes some time to adjust. Only then did I notice the single chair placed in the middle of the stage, a white cello case resting against it.

I froze. My shoulders tightened, and the blood in my veins ran cold. I'd be lying if I said that white cello, which seemed to have come out of nowhere, didn't spook the shit out of me.

I remained still, fisting my hands at my sides, my body as

stiff as a fucking log. I didn't know what rattled me more—the fact that I might be on the verge of getting caught or the fact that I might not be alone in here as I thought.

"Hello?"

Silence.

I narrowed my eyes, glancing from the chair to the darkness and back to the chair. The apprehension that coated my clammy skin made it hard for me to decide whether I wanted to look at the object in front of me or if it would be safer to look away. To run.

The corner of a white card caught my attention, neatly placed on the seat of the chair. I leaned a little to the right and saw my name written in elegant calligraphy. As I read it, the hair at the back of my neck stood up, my skin instantly cold and palms sweaty. But curiosity was far stronger than caution, and with every step toward the chair, my mind kept trying to convince me how utterly stupid this was, reminding me that it was always the curious and naïve girl who got killed first in scary movies. Yet I continued and picked up the card, the texture smooth between my fingers.

Charlotte.

I sucked my bottom lip and scanned the theatre as far as the shadows allowed me to see. My hands trembled, my fingers nervously toying with the sharp corners of the card. As someone who wasn't supposed to be here, seeing an envelope with my name on it as if whoever wrote it expected me was a whole different level of creepy. But the mind's first line of defense against fear caused by uncertainty was to find a logical explanation.

"Chase, is that you? This isn't funny."

Chase and I worked together at the theatre for the last

few years, cleaning other people's messes after every show. He was known for his annoying skill at pranking everyone when they least expected it.

"Chase?"

My gaze swept around one more time before drifting to the white cello case. I'd be a goddamn liar if I said I didn't feel the tiniest amount of excitement at the thought of what was inside it. Of course, simply because it was a cello case didn't mean there was a cello inside. It could have been empty. Or maybe there was a bomb inside. A severed limb, or the head of a slaughtered pig.

"Jesus, Charlotte. Ease up on the horror movies," I muttered to myself, straightening my shoulders and taking a breath as I stared at the card, which had nothing but my name written on it.

I licked my lips, my throat dry and fingers itching to open the case even though there was this loud warning knocking against my skull. I couldn't deny it. A part of me was curious, but I tried to push that part way down—curiosity killed the cat and all that.

"Okay, pull on your big girl panties and just open it." I leaned down and reached out, the sound of popping locks echoing through the empty theatre. As I lifted the top lid, keeping one eye closed, a soft gasp slipped past my lips. "Oh, my God."

An antique spirited varnish cello was proudly displayed and placed on black velvet. It was the most beautiful instrument I had ever seen. A hint of pine rosin wafted around me, the scent stirring a deeply rooted excitement.

Countless hours I had spent browsing the internet staring at images of new cellos, my heart bleeding to be able to afford one. But my job here at the Alto Theatre was barely enough for me to survive on.

I leaned back on my legs, my eyes glued to the flawless, brand new cello—a piece of art, in my opinion. Why would someone leave this here for me and not say who it was from?

A chill trickled down my spine. No one besides Chase knew I was here, and he sure as hell couldn't afford a cello like this.

Who else knew?

"Shit." I shot up to my feet, the ice-cold chill sinking to the soles of my feet as I rapidly glanced around the theatre. Someone knew I would be here. How?

Adrenaline blasted through my veins, and I grabbed my cello bag before rushing across the stage. My feet couldn't carry me fast enough, and paranoia clung to my skin as if a thousand eyes stared at me.

Every breath became deeper, more labored as I took two steps at a time and ran out of there. I reached for the door, but the second I touched the brass knob, a low, husky whisper echoed from the darkness. "Charlotte."

A scream tore my throat as my heart turned fucking inside out, and I jerked around. "Who said that? Who's there?"

Silence.

"Who is out there?" Fear tightened around my throat, and I was sure my heart would tear out of my chest. "Chase, this isn't funny."

I yanked the door open and rushed out. But the door slammed against my cello case, lodging it against the door-frame. I kicked at the door and pulled the case free, but as it dislodged, I stumbled and fell, my cello case skidding across the floor.

Without a second's hesitation, I righted myself, grabbed the case, and ran out of that damn theatre hall as quickly as humanly possible. There were no words to describe the cold fear that possessed me, the thousand thoughts of horror that swept through my mind all at once.

I rushed to the exit door, the one I could always sneak in and out of, and stormed down the stairs to the underground parking lot. Every few steps, I'd turn to see if I was being followed, gasping for air. But no one followed—at least not that I could see. The second my feet hit the pavement, a crowd passed by, singing, laughing, most of them drunk off their asses.

Immediately, I fell into step behind them and didn't dare glance behind me. My heart raced even though the New York nightlife gave me a slight sense of protection. If judging by the traffic, one would never think it was past midnight in this city.

It was only when I managed to get on a bus and safely took a seat that I allowed myself to take a breath. Sweat trickled down my spine, perspiration clinging all along my hairline, and the farther the bus took me away from the Alto Theatre, the more my pulse started to settle.

"Jesus," I whispered, leaning my head back, my body literally feeling like it became one with the goddamn seat. I had only ever felt this kind of crippling fear once before—the kind that wrapped around your chest with its icy tentacles, slowly suffocating you, your lungs fighting for air as you drowned in reality. It was the night my mother died. The night I sat next to her bed listening to her breathe, praying that each breath she took wouldn't be her last. I knew she was suffering. I knew she was done fighting. But the selfish daughter that I was prayed so damn hard that she wouldn't be taken from me. Not yet. Because even though she was ready to leave this world, I wasn't prepared to let her go.

Every single second that I remained by her side, the fear of losing her crippled me to a point where I was sure I'd die alongside her. God, there was a time I wanted to die with her because thinking about a life without her just didn't make sense. It was a thought I couldn't wrap my head around, the idea of living in a world where she no longer existed.

Tears stung my eyes, and I wasn't sure whether it was because of the adrenaline leaving my system, or if it was the memory of my mother reminding me yet again how much I fucking missed her.

I glanced at the cello case, too afraid to open it because I knew there was no way a forty-year-old cello could have survived being slammed in a door and falling on a tiled floor. It was probably nothing more than broken pieces of wood.

For the entire ride home, I had my jaw clenched as I held my tears, refusing to let my torn heart acknowledge the grief that always lingered.

I got to my apartment, still miraculously keeping my shit together. It was creepy as fuck knowing someone was there, at the theatre, watching me. I tried to convince myself it was Chase, or one of the other guys playing this twisted prank on me. But that voice. I didn't recognize it. Whoever was there wasn't someone I knew.

I locked the door and stared at the tiny living space I called home. Well, it wasn't home. Nowhere was home ever since my mom passed. This was just a shithole I cleaned up with my perfectionism and OCD tendencies. But there wasn't a magic wand in this entire goddamn world that could turn this dump into something worth living in—for others, at least. Me? I didn't have a choice. Thirty-year-old furniture that smelled like mothballs and soap greeted me every day, and my bedroom and kitchen were separated by a few inches of space.

If pathetic had a look, this would be it.

I placed the case on my bed, still not brave enough to open it and assess the damage. Deep down, I already knew what I would find. An old cello which had finally taken its last bow, never to be played again.

This time there was no keeping the tears from falling.

I hated this.

I hated my life. I hated the constant struggle to scrape by, to work two jobs so I could eat, pay for this crummy apartment, and afford the pain medication I needed merely to get through a single day's work. I hated that there would never be more to my life than this old and broken instrument—an instrument I could play with my eyes closed, yet I'd never be able to perform with.

All those nights sneaking into the theatre was the closest I'd ever get to even touching the dream of an eight-year-old girl who wanted nothing more than to perform on stage while a hundred people could witness her talent and love for the cello. But little did that girl know her dream would be crippled by a fear of failure as eyes were on her.

This was my life.

Mundane.

Unfulfilled

And completely alone.

CHAPTER THREE

ELIJAH

A week later

The inside of her apartment looked nothing like the outside of the building. It was clean, neat, everything perfectly set in its place. There was not a speck of dust to be found anywhere. The furniture was old and better suited to be burned than used, but the cotton sheets she had draped over it hid most of its horrendous appearances.

It wasn't the first time I'd been in the bachelor-sized apartment. I had stalked around the bedroom, living room, and kitchen, all in one tiny open space, numerous times before. I knew exactly where the filigree wallpaper had blanched from the sun shining through the only window in the apartment, and stared at the pattern, tracing a fingertip along the intricate curves. It must have taken her hours to glue the torn wallpaper back in place, the lines and edges easily visible when one stood so close.

The wooden floors creaked beneath my feet as I made my way across toward the single bed. The multi-colored floral sheets were neatly made up without a single crease, and I eased my palm across the cotton fabric. What kind of man was I for feeling envious of threadbare sheets, knowing they had been closer to Charlotte than I had ever been? Keeping her warm at night, maybe even comfortable since she had nothing else to compare it with. She had yet to experience the luxurious feel of silk caressing her skin while dreams stole her from reality.

I picked up the pillow and found an old picture hidden beneath it. It was a picture of her and her mother. *Clarissa Moore. Born in 1970 to parents Daniel and Cynthia Thompson. Married Thomas Moore in 1997, and gave birth to their daughter Charlotte Leigh Moore on May twenty-fourth, 2000—three months after Thomas up and left her to raise her daughter as a single mother.*

Died March twenty-first, 2019.

Cause of death, lung cancer.

Charlotte's life was like an open fucking book for me. There was nothing about her I didn't know.

Five-foot four. Considered a little underweight at a hundred and five pounds.

Worked two jobs. One as a cleaner at the Alto Theatre, the other as a waitress at some cheap-ass bar three nights a week when the theatre was closed.

Favorite food—pepperoni pizza, extra garlic.

Favorite drink—iced coffee, whether it was summer or winter. Sometimes during winter she'd opt for a vanilla and cinnamon latte, but more often than not, her love for iced coffee and brain freeze led her to order her favorite beverage.

I traced a finger along the edge of the picture. She had her mother's eyes—shades of gray framed with blue. Her eyes could speak a thousand words with a single glance, and tell tales of a girl who grew up loved. Cherished. Protected. But ever since she buried her mother, she lost that vibrant gaze. She lost the glint of contentment and now lived like she carried the world on her shoulders.

The day of her mother's funeral, I was there, leaning against a large oak tree, watching her stand beside the open grave. A handful of people attended the burial, everyone wearing black, the color of mourning. But not her. She wore this beautiful white lace dress, the hem touching just above her knees. The white heels she wore were ruined from the muddy ground caused by the rain from the day before. But she didn't care.

Her raven hair was pulled up in a tidy bun, the few curls framing her face gently moving with the morning breeze. Even through her heartache, through her grief, there was this elegant innocence about her. The more I watched her, the more she intrigued me, inspiring this overwhelming curiosity to explore every aspect of her.

While I watched her that day, I wondered about the grief she had to feel. It wasn't an emotion I could relate to, feeling sadness over the loss of a mother.

Charlotte didn't cry a single tear that day. She didn't speak. In fact, she didn't react in any way. All she did was stand there after everyone else had left...until it was only us. Her, me, and death between us.

The sun had started to set, the pink and yellow hues

painting her as a picture of broken beauty. I remembered how I couldn't tear my gaze from her, not wanting to miss a single moment. The music enthusiast in me wondered what kind of perfection she'd create if she had her cello with her, pouring that grief she hid so well into a solo performance that would excel past every other. Music, after all, stemmed from the soul, created by our emotions.

It was supposed to be a day where she'd expose the most vulnerable version of herself, but all I saw was strength and determination to not fall apart.

But I wasn't there to admire her or wonder about her thoughts and emotions. Charlotte Moore was a job, something I had to remind myself of whenever I watched her, documented her every move.

She was a contract. Not an obsession.

I brought the pillow closer to my face, clutching it tightly as I inhaled the familiar smell of jasmine mixed with a subtle hint of freesias. Her scent always lingered on the stage of the Alto Theatre whenever she left.

I remembered the first time I heard her play the cello. *Edelweiss*—a popular song known by millions and loved by many. But to me it was a beautiful music composition that held a piece of my soul. It was the first time I realized she and I shared the same passion for beautiful music.

I watched her from the shadows, the rich legato sound and distinct timbre of the cello singing to my blood. Listening to her play, watching her, witnessing how she and the instrument became one was like getting a glimpse of her soul. Her spirit. It was almost intimate, the moments she unknowingly shared with me. One could argue that I stole those precious moments, cloaked with darkness. But I didn't give a fuck how one looked at it. It was during those times that my demons were silenced, and the more I experienced the peace her music offered me, the more I craved it. It was a fine line I was treading on with the cellist. A line that, if I took one wrong step, the repercussions would be deadly...for both of us.

I placed the pillow back down, smoothing out the fabric, ensuring it was as perfect as I had found it, then opened the bedside table drawer, an unopened box of ibuprofen inside it. Her pain was getting worse, her trips to the pharmacy becoming more frequent. Charlotte had found herself in one of those unfortunate situations one could argue as an unfair curveball life liked to throw around at the innocent. It fucked with my head sometimes, thinking how rapists, pedophiles, twisted motherfuckers walked the Earth in their designer fucking shoes while the innocent suffered. Life wasn't fair—a cliché, but the truth.

I closed the drawer, my gaze drifting over a brush and two hairbands on the bedside table. A small bottle of perfume stood next to it, and I wondered why someone who earned minimum wage and lived in a crummy old apartment would splurge on an expensive bottle of perfume. It was probably the most expensive item in here, apart from the...

I glanced around. Where was her cello case? I watched her leave an hour ago, and she didn't have the case with her, which meant it had to be here.

The closet hinges were old and rusted, the doors hanging on the loose screws. She didn't own a lot of clothing, and her wardrobe consisted of torn jeans, two sweaters and a few t-shirts.

I looked back at the bottle of expensive perfume and

then cut my gaze to the half empty closet. The little cellist proved to be quite the enigma.

It didn't take me more than ten minutes to search through her apartment until I stilled in front of the bed, leaning my head to the side as I crouched and reached underneath to find the hidden cello. I'd be lying if I said I wasn't relieved. A cellist without a cello was like Romeo without his Juliet. Void and lost.

A truck passed the building, the loud rumble of its engine causing the windows to shudder. The traffic was utter madness, every second car honking down the street. No wonder she escaped to the Alto to get some silence so she could give her heart what it wanted. Music.

I took a breath and gently eased open the case, only to stare at a cracked and broken cello. There were no words to describe the sinking feeling in my gut when I saw the pieces. No wonder she never went back to the Alto after that night. She had no instrument to play. No reason to sit on the stage in front of an empty theatre.

And I had no reason to care. I *shouldn't* have cared. But I did.

"Fucking Christ!" I slammed the case shut. If only she had taken my gift. She should have taken the cello I left for her that night. Something I shouldn't have done because it compromised the job by making unnecessary contact.

"Fuck!" I roughed my hands through my hair, the voices growing louder, the memories becoming stronger.

"You're a fucking disease, little boy."

"You're nothing but a stray no one wants."

I closed my eyes, but instead of darkness, I saw red. Crimson. Liquid souls flooding everything in its path.

"You should have died, too."

"Do not make me choose, because I'll choose him. I'll choose him over you."

"Jesus!" I balled my fist and slammed it against the drywall, breaking clear through it. The filigree wallpaper tore, and I stared at the hole my fit of rage had caused.

She should be playing. Charlotte should be playing every minute of every hour of every motherfucking day.

"Fuck!" I cursed and pulled my fingers through my hair. This was supposed to be easy. But this thing with her was getting complicated—too fucking complicated, and I had no one to blame but myself. I got too close. Made it personal.

My phone vibrated, a text message finally confirming that which I knew would eventually come. Now, my little charade had to come to an end, this fucking fantasy I lived in now killed and drowned with one goddamn text.

I had three years to prepare myself for this moment, three years of tracking her, studying her, making sure I knew everyone she had contact with. Employers, colleagues, friends—even her fucking pharmacist. Every minute spent on this job, every move I made had led up to this exact moment.

The sound of keys resonated from the front door, and I darted toward it, pushing my back against the wall. Waiting. Anticipating. Breathing.

Charlotte walked inside and shut the door behind her with a kick of her boot, shrugging drops of rain off her jacket. With her back still toward me, she placed a brown paper bag on the tiny dining table, and my pulse raced, yet I controlled my breathing—controlled my thoughts. Control was the most crucial aspect of this job. Without it, stupid mistakes were made, mistakes that got you caught.

She turned and looked right at me—a single second in time that froze for what seemed like an eternity as I locked my gaze with hers.

I had no choice.

I had no motherfucking choice.

I had to do it.

I had to take her.

CHAPTER FOUR

CHARLOTTE

My eyes shot open, and I reached for my throat, remembering how fear sucked the air out of my lungs as he wrapped his hands around my neck. I tried to fight. Clawed at his hands, his arms, his face—anywhere so that he would let go so I could breathe. But he tightened his grip, fingers biting into my flesh, my lungs burning as he slowly suffocated me. I remembered wondering if this was how I would die—gasping for breath while staring the devil in the eye, trying to speak and beg for him to stop. But everything went dark, reality sucked away from my mind, my thoughts silent...until now.

I sat up and grabbed the unfamiliar sheets with my fists, scanning the room. Gray walls, white ceiling with dimmed lights, dark laminated floors, and large floor-to-ceiling windows that showcased the night lights of a city. New York City? God, I hoped I was still in New York.

I jumped off the bed and looked around, the furniture all sleek and modern, clearly decorated according to a minimalist's taste. I frantically searched through every drawer and cupboard, trying to find something I could use to protect myself. But everything was empty, as if no one had lived there.

The room sure didn't paint a picture of a dungeon, and neither did the white silks sheets I woke up on. But it was when I tried to turn the doorknob only to find it locked that I realized this was just a well-decorated prison cell.

The idea of breaking a window and jumping did cross my mind, until I walked over to the clear glass and saw how high up I was, my hopes of escaping that way diminished. At least the closer view confirmed I was still in New York since I recognized the iconic skyline.

The last thing I remembered was his face. His expression, hard and cold. Like stone. The moment our eyes met, his brown irises darkened with pure resolve. It took me a split second and one breath to realize what he came for.

Me.

Keys rattled by the door, and I leaped to the other side of the room, shoving myself in the corner as my heart simultaneously stopped and got lodged in my throat, causing me to hold my breath. Every horrible thought imaginable had crossed my mind as I stood huddled in the corner, watching the door as if death could come walking through it at any moment.

I pressed my back harder against the wall, trying to make myself smaller as the door slowly opened. Nausea slammed into the pit of my stomach as adrenaline crashed against my spine. I had never experienced fear of this magnitude before. The kind of fear that would make you gladly choose death if it meant escaping the crippling terror.

The moment he walked in, I stopped fucking breathing. The man looked like a powerhouse in a suit. Large frame, broad shoulders. Dark eyes.

Pure. Malice.

His eyes met mine as he closed the door, lines of disapproval forming on his forehead. "What the hell are you doing?"

The back of my neck tingled with the familiar tenor in his guttural voice. Low. Rough.

"Get up, Charlotte. You're not a fucking animal."

My name. How did he...

"Charlotte Leigh Moore," he said as if he could read my mind. His expression remained stone as he walked closer, his white shirt a stark contrast against his olive skin. My gaze dropped to the case he carried. A cello case.

"You'll find there's not much I don't know about you." He placed the case down on a black couch that stood against the adjacent wall.

His dark gaze pinned me in the corner, and I was too afraid to move. The expression on his face was hard, dark, void of any emotion. There was nothing there, his eyes empty, hollow, cold. The room chilled instantly, and every hair on my arms and neck raised.

"Who are you?" My voice carried a panicked pitch, and I hardly managed a breath.

"That depends."

"On what?"

He placed his hands in the pockets of his black pants, squaring his shoulders, standing regal and proud. "On who's asking."

"I'm asking."

He lifted a brow, his eyes orbs of cognac and venom. "For now, all you need to know is that I'm God...for you, at least."

"What do you want with me?"

A smirk curled at the corners of his mouth framed with a dark manicured beard as he glanced from me to the cello. "I want you to play."

"What?" My voice shook. I sounded weak, and I hated it.

"Play the cello."

Slowly, cautiously, I pushed myself up and straightened, my palms flat against the wall behind me. "I don't know what it is you think you want from me, but if you claim to know so much about me, you'll know I have nothing to offer you."

He roughed his fingers through his midnight hair, the longer strands at the front fanning over his eyes. "For now, let's just say all I want is for you to play the cello."

"What is going—"

"Just play the motherfucking cello!" his voice erupted, slamming against the ceiling and breaking through my chest. I jolted and turned to the side, pushing myself deeper into the corner as if it were possible for the wall to hide me from him, to swallow me whole and take me away. Tears burned my eyes, and my fingers trembled as fear consumed me.

"Please," I begged, and he launched at me, punching his fists against the wall on either side of my head. My eyes snapped closed, and there was a moment of heated urgency to relieve myself, panic shattering my insides. My veins burned, yet my skin was ice-cold as he brought his face close to mine, letting me feel the warmth of his angered breath against my cheeks. "Play. That's all I fucking want right now. Okay?"

Tears now freely streamed down my face, my soul

weeping with crippling fear. "Okay," I sobbed. "Okay. I'll play."

He stepped back, wiping his palm across his stubble beard, his expression nothing but angered lines and raging madness.

I wiped at my tears, and I could barely walk, my legs threatening to give way beneath me. But my desperation clung to every ounce of strength I had, strength he stole from me simply by being close.

Through the haze of tears, I stared at the cello in the case, unable to appreciate the instrument's majestic beauty and the familiar scent of rosin. If it were under any other circumstances, I would have gawked at it in awe while longing to feel the strings vibrate beneath my fingers. But this was different. This was life-threatening with the devil standing a few feet away, staring at me as if he wanted nothing more than to drag me down to hell with him.

My hand trembled as I reached out, my chest tightening around my lungs.

I paused. "Why are you—"

"Shut up and play, Charlotte." There was no negotiating, his demand as sharp a blade held against my throat.

I swallowed and wiped at a tear about to lap off my chin, trying my best to pull myself together. If I could only get through this, play as he demanded me to, maybe then he'd let me go. Just one song, and perhaps he'd let me run.

Gently, I eased the cello from its case, the wood smooth against my palm. It had been weeks since I held a cello, weeks since I played. I'd be lying if I said I didn't miss it. That I didn't lie awake at night imagining my fingers moving up and down the cello's neck, creating the perfect vibrato as I eased the bow along the strings. But I never would have thought that the next time I'd play would be while held captive.

I glanced at the man who watched me like a hawk from beneath thick, dark lashes—annoyance and agitation rolling off him in waves.

A chair stood at the other end of the room, and I slowly moved toward it, my feet heavy and cold. There was nothing but absolute silence as I sat down, positioning the cello between my legs. The chair was too high, so I reached down to adjust the endpin.

"Jesus Christ, woman." His words rumbled and cracked the silence. "Just fucking—"

"Play. Yes, I know. I'm trying," I snapped back. "I'm trying, okay?"

"Try harder."

I closed my eyes and took the bow between my fingers, trying to imagine I was anywhere but here. Trying to transport myself to a place where peace would set the music free.

The bow touched the strings, but I held my wrist all wrong, causing the most godawful sound. Everything was just wrong. My posture. The height of the stool. Even the cello felt wrong as I let it lean against me.

I took another deep breath and tried again, but the more I tried, the worse it sounded until I pulled the cello away and slumped my posture. "I can't. I can't play, okay?" Tears slipped free. "I'm sorry. I can't do it."

His nostrils flared. "You're not even trying."

"I am. I'm trying."

"Bullshit."

I launched up to my feet in a moment of angered insanity. "Don't you think I'd play if I could? I'm scared as fuck right now, fearing for my life because I have no idea what you're going to do to me. And right now, you're staring at me like you want nothing more than to tear my goddamn throat out. So, of course, I'm fucking trying."

As the last word poured from my lips, I regretted it immediately. He didn't look like the kind of man who would tolerate such outbursts, and I was sure there'd be repercussions. Punishment. Pain.

My body shuddered as I stood before him, his presence alone robbing me of air, making it hard to take a breath. Seconds ticked by, and he didn't say a word. He didn't even move. He just stared at me with a coldness that penetrated my bones—like an infection that has the means to make me rot from the inside out. The uncertainty of what he'd do next was worse than the fear of anticipating retaliation. By simply glaring at me in silence, he had me wishing I could take it all back and play him the perfect composition.

"I didn't mean—" I started, my voice nothing but a shaky whisper. "I didn't—"

He stormed out, his heavy footsteps as angry as the rage in his eyes. The door slammed shut, and I sucked in a breath as I closed my eyes, my pulse racing with heated adrenaline and overwhelming fear.

The weight of it all came crashing down, and I collapsed, a weakened version of myself sobbing on the wooden floors. This wasn't happening. This *couldn't* be happening. Why did it feel like my life would never be the same again? As if it all had now come to an end. Here. With him.

Whoever he was.

CHAPTER FIVE

ELIJAH

If I were any other man, I'd at least feel some twinge of sympathy toward the girl currently crying on the other side of that door. But I was too busy calculating every possible outcome of the events that were about to follow, of all the fucking things that could go wrong.

It had been hours since I brought her here, and while I waited for her to wake up, I had more than enough time to catapult myself into a frenzy of fucking madness, which was why I needed her to play. After all these years, her music became my outlet, my meditation to find calm so I could think without having to fight the insanity that constantly raged through my thoughts.

But she had just proven to me that music could never be demanded—at least not the musical harmony that stemmed from the soul. That was the kind I needed. Craved.

It was the type of music that had the power to make you forget. It had the ability to take the darkest memory and turn it into a distant dream. Watching her emotions cling to her expression while she played, the serenity that draped over her was like witnessing someone transport to a world of melodies and ballades and perfection, a world she created. But now, she was scared, and I needed to get a fucking hold of myself—calm the fuck down and gain control if I wanted to see this through.

I *had* to see it through.

God, I just needed her to play so I could think and slow down my racing thoughts. Music was the only thing that soothed me, which was why I had hundreds of orchestral compositions on my iPad, constantly playing it in my apartment, my car, everywhere it was possible. But even those had lost their appeal, not coming close to her solo acts when compared.

For years, I had tried to outrun the monster in my nightmares, attempted to escape the memories. But there was only one way for me to find reprieve from past laments that shackled me still. Blood. Death. The cries of a man seconds away from meeting the devil.

The fear of others. Their terror, it appeased me in ways nothing else could. If some psych-doctor had to analyze me, they'd probably declare me certifiably insane, lock me up, and throw away the key. All I cared about was spilling blood, killing those who deserved it, and make their screams blend with the bold, heavy, and mighty sound of the orchestra reaching the crescendo of a marvelous piece.

But fate had me cross paths with the raven-haired cellist whose dance with the majestic instrument silenced and tamed every sliver of darkness that consumed me since the night I changed from boy to beast. I had known of Charlotte and her mother for many years, but it was after her mother's death that her music started to reach out to me, as if it longed to touch my soul.

She was a job. A contract. Nothing more.

Those words became a fucking mantra to me the last few months—and I had to hold on to it now more than ever.

It was good to witness the fear in her eyes when she looked at me, reminding me of what I was and what I would always be. A sadist. A villain. A deviant. The terror burned as brightly as the sun in her blue-gray eyes, and to prove I was a bastard, it didn't bother me. Men like me, we thrived on fear. Fear was good. Fear made people cooperate. Made them complacent. I was not the type of man who had his emotions manipulated with tears, desperate pleas, or sad doe eyes. If it were so easy to distract me from the task at hand, I wouldn't have been in the business I was currently in.

Sympathy, empathy, mercy—those three things didn't exist in my world.

After that last night at the Alto when she refused my gift, I took time to change my focus and realign my thoughts to do what needed to be done. To do what I came here to do—the reason she had taken up so much space in my life during the last few years. Studying someone, watching them live their lives, day after day, it would be natural to eventually get tangled up in this substantial motherfucking mindfuck where lines blurred, and realities shifted. So, I took the time to get my shit together—which brought us here. Both of us.

I locked the door and held the key in my palm. Such a small and insignificant object, yet it had the power to cause immense trauma, pain, fear. To sit behind a locked door while harboring the crippling fear of being forgotten, it broke something in a person—especially a child.

My phone vibrated in my pocket, and I pulled it out, the name on the screen confirming it was the call I had been waiting for.

I answered as I moved to stand in front of the window. "Julio Bernardi. I was waiting for your call."

"Did you get my message last night?"

"I did."

"You didn't think it would be a good idea to respond?"

I straightened and stared out the window at the skyscraper rooftops. "You know I demand exclusivity, yet you approached two other contractors for this job."

The silence on his side confirmed it. "Things escalated. The administration thought it was in the family's best interest to make sure we have the incentive we need as soon as possible, and not put all our eggs into one basket."

"What escalated?"

Julio went silent. "Omertà?"

"You very well know I don't give a shit about your... Omertà." The vow of silence, punishable by death if not upheld. There was nothing as important, nothing that showed loyalty as much as a man's silence, protecting his own. "If you want me to handle this contract, I need full disclosure, and all those other *dilettante* contractors you hired pushed back. I work alone."

"This is a—"

"It's not negotiable, Julio."

More silence, and I imagined him red in the face with simmering anger knowing very well that if he wanted The Musician—me—on this job, he had to meet my every demand. Nothing was negotiable.

"Fine," he snapped. "You have two days."

"Five."

"The trial starts in less than two weeks."

"Six, then."

"Do not fuck with me, you son of a—"

"Julio," I interrupted, "if you want to give this job to one of your novices, do it. Do not waste my fucking time. Phone me when you're serious about getting this motherfucking job done." I hung up, an amused grin settling on my lips. It wasn't even two seconds before he phoned back. This time I let it ring for a while so the prick could stew a bit in the humble pie he was about to eat.

I slid my finger across the screen. "That didn't take you long."

"Fine. You have six days. But if you fuck up, so help me God, I will—"

"Payment will be split in four, each paid into four different bank accounts within the next hour. I'll send you the details."

"Yes, yes. I know. Listen," he paused, and I could hear him take a long drag from his cigar, "need I remind you how serious this matter is?"

Annoyance trickled along the back of my neck. "I don't need reminding of anything, Julio. I know exactly what's at stake for you."

"Do you? Do you really? Because I doubt a man who carries a reputation like yours knows anything about family."

My top lip curled into a snarl. "He won't talk."

"He better not. Two hundred mil is a lot of fucking money, and you better be good for it."

I placed my arm against the floor-to-ceiling window, leaning in. "Let's get one thing straight. I am very fucking selective when it comes to contracts. Why? Because I don't fucking need the money. Greed and money make you sloppy, reckless. It leaves too much room for error—which is why I am the best at what I do."

"If not for the money, then why do this kind of work?"

"It's simple. Because I can."

I hung up, my fingers tightening around the cellphone. I didn't like when clients assumed the pot of gold they paid me gave them the right to tell me how to do fucking anything. No one breathed down my fucking neck, including the motherfucking Bernadis. They thought because they owned half of New York fucking City they could piss on whoever the fuck they wanted. And the fucking nerve of this asshole hiring two other fuckers for the same job, trying to let us compete with each other? Fucker should have known The Musician did not compete. The Musician executed.

Nobody knew my true identity. I was a fucking ghost so many had attempted to find, yet failed time and time again. Even those old bastards who thought they ruled our society with an iron fist, who supposedly feared nothing and no one—they were the first to demand to know who this master was, the man who carved out the perfect treble clef on his victims' chests before killing them with a single shot to the head.

The Musician.

Me.

I slipped my phone into my pocket and turned to stare out the window once more, my thoughts bursting through my brain like a motherfucking aneurysm. Then I heard it, the smooth sound of a cello gently cracking through my thoughts.

She was playing, and it instantly swept through my

THE VILLAIN

insides, calming the storm that constantly raged within me. Slowly, effortlessly, her music settled the violent thrum in my blood, the melody giving me the high I had craved for weeks. God, it was like holy water showering over my soul.

I breathed, closed my eyes, and relished the moment of peace which I knew wouldn't linger for too long.

The song she played wasn't one I was familiar with, but it was beautiful, nonetheless. Sad, but beautiful.

While I stood there, swept away by the sound that now filled the hall of my apartment, spreading a warmth, comfort, peace—I was once again reminded of the Moore girl locked up in the room I had put her in.

God, her music was like salve on an open wound. A welcome reprieve from a torture that never ceased.

But she was no longer the cellist I observed, the soloist I watched perform in front of an empty theatre.

Things changed, and now my Requiem had become the target.

CHAPTER SIX

CHARLOTTE

The bow weighed a ton as I held it in my hand. I was scared. Cold. Even my thoughts were frozen. With the cello leaning against my chest, I stared out in front of me. It felt surreal being caught in this nightmare. It was something you'd only hear about on the news or read about in the papers. Girls being kidnapped. Girls who vanished, never to be seen or heard of again. Their families would plead with the public to come forward with any information about their disappearances. Mine wouldn't, though. I didn't have anyone who would search for me. No one would miss me or look for my face in a crowd. I would just stop existing.

I didn't know which was worse—being kidnapped, or having no one to search for me. No one to rescue me. It was such a hollow feeling, being without hope. So, I did the only thing I knew to fill the emptiness. I played.

I allowed my fear, my sadness, everything I felt inside to pour out of me and onto the strings as I effortlessly guided the bow. Whenever I played, my endless search for perfection replaced the terror I felt weighing heavily in every bone. Music had always been my escape. I allowed every note, every sound to infiltrate my thoughts and possess me. It transported me far away from everything. Far away from a life I hated ever since my mother died. Being here, kidnapped and held against my will, was no different than the life I lived out there in that shitty apartment with two jobs that required me to clean other people's messes. What was the worst that could happen to me here? What was the worst he could do?

Torture me?

Kill me?

I knew pain. I lived with it almost every single day. And death—if I were honest with myself—would be a welcome reprieve from a sad fucking existence. So, why fear him? Why fear a fate that had seemingly already been decided for me?

The low tenor slowly resounded. Angered and sad. Strong yet lost. The more I played, the more my dark thoughts subsided. This was why the world needed music. This was why God had created an angel dedicated solely to music in the heavens because He knew its importance. He knew music was food for the soul, a light when everything else felt dark.

As the final note resounded around the unfamiliar room, the music slowly fading—so did the peace that came with it. It took mere seconds for my resolve of not fearing the unknown to return with a vengeance, clawing at my insides and poisoning my blood.

I finally opened my eyes, only to find him standing in front of me, his gaze fixed on mine. But there was something different about him, his irises not as dark as they were before. He seemed...calm. Serene. Nothing like the wild beast who almost slammed my head into a concrete wall.

Although my heart pounded erratically inside my chest, I managed to lower my arm, holding the bow steadily in hand.

For the longest time, he didn't take his eyes off me, and I didn't dare speak. Somewhere in the distance I heard a clock, seconds ticking by—seconds that felt like hours while his presence filled the room little by little until it became increasingly difficult to breathe. But still, I refused to move. Refused to look away.

Not knowing whether I'd get the chance again, I observed every inch of him. If this weren't a case of kidnapping and abduction, I would have considered him a handsome man. He had the type of face that could stop you in your tracks to have another look. Dark, mysterious, beautiful. Curls of midnight hair touched his thick, dark eyebrows, and his strong jaw was perfectly accentuated with a well-manicured beard that was slightly longer than your average five-day stubble.

It was difficult to decide which color his irises were since they had been a dark chestnut earlier, yet now a more cognac gold. The lighter color made his stare more intense, as if it could reach out and caress my skin as he looked at me so brashly—as if he had every right now. As if I belonged to him.

The white dress shirt he wore was pulled taut as he held his arms crossed in front of his chest, the collar unbuttoned. The longer our gazes remained, the more difficult it became not to look away. He had an unyielding presence, the kind of self-assurance that made him difficult to ignore. The kind that held you captive, whether you wanted it to or not.

Unable to handle the intensity any longer, I looked down at my bare feet, the pin of the cello placed between them.

"When you—" My voice cracked, and I cleared my throat. "You said there's not much you don't know about me. What did you mean by that?"

My question was met with deafening silence, but I wanted him to talk. Earlier, his voice had sounded so familiar, and I simply had to place it. Place him. Figure out if I knew him.

I glanced up but couldn't look directly at him. "Am I supposed to know you?"

Still, he remained silent, and I diverted my gaze toward the window. At least I knew we were still in New York. I'd lived here long enough to recognize its majestic skyline.

The sound of his heavy footsteps filled the silence, and fear squeezed at my chest, forcing me to close my eyes so I could just focus on breathing.

God, I needed so much more air.

I didn't have to open my eyes to know he was close. I felt it—felt him as he leaned in, the warmth of his breath touching my cheek. My instinct to pull away was almost too strong to control, but my determination to not cower again proved more vital this time.

He gently brushed the hair back behind my ear, and my throat closed up, my skin ice-cold, yet I could feel perspiration bead at the back of my neck.

His hand lingered on the loose strands of my hair, and the fear he ignited had me clenching my fists, pushing my nails into the flesh of my palm.

"Charlotte," he whispered, and my heart stopped. It fucking stopped, the ground ripped from underneath me as his voice tore through the barrier of my memory, allowing me to remember.

My eyes shot open, and I looked at him, his face inches from mine. "It was you."

A threatening grin tugged at the corner of his lips.

"It was you, wasn't it? That night at the theatre."

He straightened and somehow made himself seem larger as he towered over me with a threatening stance. There was no need for him to answer or confirm. It was written on his face as he stared down at me, his expression stone.

"What is it that you want from me?" My voice quivered. How could it not? This man oozed malice and trouble with a capital T—all of it directed at me.

He reached out, and I flinched, but he merely brushed the back of his hand down the side of my neck—barely touching me. "These should heal easily enough."

I shuddered, thinking of his hands around my throat, squeezing.

He dropped his arm and took the cello from me. "You have a remarkable talent."

I pressed my lips together.

"Yet you're afraid to show it to the world." His eyes narrowed, as if he stared at a puzzle that needed solving, then stepped back, putting some welcomed distance between us. "It's quite ironic, don't you think?"

I stood, hoping that if I came closer to eye-level with him I'd be less intimidated. Turned out, I was wrong. It wasn't as much his size as it was the way he looked at me that unnerved me—as if I was nothing but prey, and he a predator who craved the hunt.

"I don't know what to think because I have no idea what's going on here."

"Why didn't you accept my gift?"

"What gift?"

He stretched his arm out, moving the cello to the side, answering my question without saying a word.

"Oh, you mean the cello you left on the stage for me that night? When no one was supposed to be there, yet this *gift* seemingly appeared from out of nowhere?"

He cocked a brow.

"That would be reckless of me, don't you think? Taking something that some stranger just randomly left for me."

He smirked. "I'm no stranger, Charlotte. If you think about it," his gaze settled on mine, "I'm the only person who knows who you really are."

Chills coursed through every bone, a trickle of warning traveling down my neck. "You don't know me."

"Oh, I think I do." His eyes darkened—focused. "One is only your true self when you have no other company but your own."

"What?" I frowned. "That doesn't even make sense. If I'm in no one else's company but my own, how could you—" I stopped mid-sentence, the penny dropping like a thousand-pound wrecking ball. Fear forced me to take a step back, needing space, needing air. "You...how..."

I couldn't get the words out because in my head it sounded so fucking absurd. Surreal, and just...sick.

My chest expanded as I forced myself to take a breath, sorting my thoughts. "You stalked me?"

The expression on his face remained stoic, and he placed the cello in the corner. "I *observed* you."

"This is insane. Who the hell are you, and what do you want from me?" I blinked back tears, my survival mode urging me not to show weakness. But I was passing the point of fear and nearing the part where I'd lose my mind because none of this made any sense. This man didn't make sense. Me being here didn't make sense. *God.*

I pulled my fingers through my tangled hair. "You know what, it doesn't matter. Just let me go."

"I'm afraid I can't do that."

"Yes, you can. You can open that door and let me walk out of here. Super easy."

"It's not that simple anymore."

I lifted my shoulders. "What do you mean it's not that simple *anymore?*"

He wiped his chin with his hand before crossing his arms. "Our situation changed."

"*Our* situation? I'm sorry, but there is no fucking *our.*"

"You have a foul mouth for a woman."

"I guess being kidnapped brings the worst out of a person."

His full lips pulled into a thin line, his dark brows slanted inward while he eased closer, his stare firmly focused. He didn't say a word, yet it felt like he was speaking volumes through his gaze alone—telling tales of darkness and sin, violence and menace.

"You shouldn't have invaded my privacy like that." It was one of those uncomfortable moments when words would just pop out of your mouth.

"There's a lot of things I shouldn't have done."

"You had no right."

He smirked. "Of course I didn't." Another step, and he came closer, sucking all the air out of the room as he closed the distance between us.

My back hit the wall, and I sucked in a breath, realizing I was trapped.

The heart of the prey beating rapidly under the predatory gaze of the hunter.

Brown irises gleamed with something primal as his gaze knotted with mine, and my insides coiled tight, my body rigid. The weight of his presence pinned me against the wall, and I couldn't fucking move. The moment, the way he stared at me, it was just too goddamn intense, like it held every muscle captive.

"I won't make this easy for you." I lifted my chin, determined to put on a convincing show of bravery, which could either work in my favor or potentially backfire by increasing the thrill of the hunt for this man.

A mischievous smirk curled at the corner of his lips, and I shuddered as he placed a palm against the wall, right above my shoulder. His pointed gaze drifted from my eyes to my lips, paused, and looked back up. There was something about staring into those cognac swirls, his irises giving me a glimpse of a silent devilry that lurked within. A certain magnetism that baited me, lured me in by seducing my fear and turning it into curiosity.

"Tell me," he urged, inching forward. "What do you think I'll demand?"

"I don't know." I rushed my answer. "But whatever it is, I'm sure you don't have my best interest at heart."

He licked his lips, amusement painted across his every

feature. For what felt like eons, we stood there in silence, our gazes locked as a silent war raged. My heart beat so fast, I was afraid he'd hear it, see the vein pulsing in my neck. But this was different than before. When he came in here the first time, I was overcome with fear, my mind was too scattered and drowning in adrenaline, rendering me incapable of thinking straight. Right now, though, there was this sliver of courage that peeked through the panic, allowing me to see past the fear.

The rich scent of musk blended with cardamom's earthy-sweet possessed the air. There was a sensual sway in the way he smelled, a hidden influence that strengthened his presence—a presence that was already hard to ignore.

His gaze dropped, but this time lower, staring at my throat as he brought his arm down, brushing a fingertip down the side of my neck.

"You almost killed me." I brought my hand up to my throat, reminded of what it felt like to have the air choked from my lungs.

His smile was sardonic. "If I wanted to kill you, you'd be dead by now."

"Is that a threat?"

"Just a fact."

"So, you don't plan on killing me, then?"

A half-hearted laugh left his lips, clearly the only answer he'd give to my question. He stepped back, pulling a hand through his midnight curls. "It's almost dinnertime. I would have offered you the option of eating with me at the dining table," he narrowed his eyes, "but I have a feeling you won't...*behave* appropriately."

"If by appropriately you mean not try to run and scream for help, then you're right."

He nodded. Still smiling. "I'll bring dinner to you, then." He turned, and I hastily stepped forward.

"What is your name?"

He stilled and glanced back.

"The least you can do is tell me your name."

"Let's get one thing straight." He turned to face me. "I don't owe you anything. There is no *'least'* I can do for you. You'd be smart to remember that." There were a thousand threats that laced his words, causing me to bite my tongue.

"I don't...I didn't—"

"Elijah."

His gaze was unsettling as it reached for me all the way across the room. "My name is Elijah."

I sucked on my bottom lip, shifting from one leg to the other. Such a beautiful name for a kidnapper. What a contradiction.

"Well, I wish I could say it's nice to meet you...Elijah."

"Yeah," he turned his back on me, "wish I could have said the same about you...Charlotte Leigh Moore."

CHAPTER SEVEN

ELIJAH

Roasted chicken with asiago polenta and truffled mushrooms. That was what I wanted to make for dinner, because ever since her mother died, Charlotte lived off cereal, simple fruit, and instant microwavable meals.

When was the last time she had a decent meal? A homemade meal that tasted like food and not cardboard? Apart from the life that I lived outside this apartment, cooking was my passion. To me, there was so much more to food than just filling your belly. It was about experiencing the bursting of flavors on your tongue, tasting the quality ingredients and savoring every bite.

Part of me knew my love for food probably stemmed from a childhood of going to bed on an empty stomach daily.

I was busy chopping thyme when I glanced at the skinned chicken breasts. Charlotte wasn't the type of woman to be impressed by fancy dining and elegant dinners. I was doing this more for myself than for her, thinking feeding her quality food would somehow be the first brick laid on my path to redemption.

Good God. Redemption for a man like me wasn't fucking possible, so I was just wasting my goddamn time, hence the reason I tossed it all in the garbage.

I waited by the foyer when the elevator opened, Josh appearing with a pizza box in hand.

"You ordered a pizza?" Disbelief clung to his arched ginger brow. Understandably.

Being the head of security, and the only fucking person I trusted in this city, Josh knew my opinion on pizza. And it was simple...

Pizza is not food.

At least, not the takeout kind.

I took the box from him. "It's not for me."

"Then who—"

"None of your goddamn business. Listen," I wiped at my chin, "did you do everything I asked you to?"

"Everything is arranged."

"Did you double security?"

"Yes, sir. And I have three unmarked black vehicles standing by and ready to leave at any moment."

"Good." I turned my back on him, a silent dismissal. In my profession, it would be reckless and stupid not to have the best security measures in place. Finding the cracks in any type of protection detail was easy for a man like me.

The smell of garlic and oregano filled my nostrils, the box still warm from the freshly made pizza. I never quite understood the love people had for what was nothing more than a sphere of dough with a fuckton of melted cheese. And all those different toppings? How were you supposed to taste anything when there were so many different flavors all mashed up together?

I unlocked the bedroom door and walked in, finding Charlotte standing by the window, staring out. Raven strands of braided hair cascaded down her back, but so many of her wild curls had already escaped, falling in disarray around her shoulders. All this was part of a well-thought-out plan which had been in the making for years, an inevitable contract—but I was still a man who knew when to appreciate an innocent beauty that wasn't forced or flaunted.

The black denims she wore were torn at the seams around her ankles, the faded color giving away its age. In all this time I'd watched her, it was clear that Charlotte chose comfort above fashion. That, or maybe it was just the fact that she couldn't afford anything other than a few pairs of jeans and hoodies. But my guess was, even if she could afford designer labels, she'd still opt for the comfort of the no-name brands.

"Dinner," I stated, and she glanced over her shoulder.

"You probably won't be surprised if I say I'm not hungry."

I placed the cardboard box down on the side table set next to the leather couch. "You have to eat."

"You know," she turned to face me with her arms crossed, "there's something about being kidnapped that kills one's appetite."

Her sarcastic tone earned an unamused glare from me. "Sarcasm is a cheap way to hide unintelligence."

"Kidnapping is a sure sign of mental instability."

"Then I guess we both have our...weaknesses. You know," I gestured toward the pizza, "the human body can only feed off adrenaline for so long. Sooner or later, your body will need more than mere determination and stubbornness to survive. And who knows," I sat down on the couch, "maybe I won't feel like feeding you then."

The way she bit her bottom lip, her silence stretching for miles, was a sure sign that she knew I had won this round. Before too long, she'd realize there was no negotiating, bargaining, or sparring with me.

"Besides," I lightened the conversation with half a grin, "I got your favorite. Pepperoni with extra garlic."

Her lips parted, and eyes widened. "Exactly how long have you been stalking me?"

"Observing."

"Stalking. Normal people who aren't psychopaths call it stalking."

I laced my fingers together, contemplating for a moment whether I wanted to go down this path and partake in the conversation she was pursuing. Would it be wise to humor her need for answers, her need to make sense of what was happening? Her entire life was about secrets, about hiding the truth. What would the risks be if I decided to lay it all out on the table right now, catapult her life into deadly chaos?

"How long?" She pressed for an answer, but this time there was a slight tremor in her voice.

"A while," I stated firmly, not entirely giving her the answer she wanted.

"You stalked me for...*a while?*"

"Eat, Charlotte."

She tightened her arms around herself, a blatant show of

defiance. But I had seen enough fear in my life to recognize it hiding behind pointed glares and brave faces.

I studied her as she looked down at her bare feet, placing one foot on top of the other. There was a certain allure in her vulnerability, a level of seduction in the way she unknowingly stirred to life this involuntary curiosity about her, to get to know her.

To own her.

I rubbed my fingers across my beard, studying her slender form, the gentle curve of her hips, the oversized T-shirt she wore hiding the swells of her breasts—and for a single fucking moment I imagined what her body would look like naked. Aroused. Entirely at my mercy.

My cock hardened, my skin set alight with anticipation. *Anticipation of what? Fucking the woman you kidnapped?*

I shifted in my seat. "Eat."

"No." Her fiery gaze met mine.

"Then at least take a fucking shower." There was no hiding the level of my annoyance, the frustration I felt over the hard-on I had developed for the cellist. After years of watching her, observing her, studying her, it was natural to assume I'd form some sort of familiarity toward her. God knew there was that unexplainable addiction toward her musical talent and that old fucking cello of hers, which was now broken, left to be forgotten.

"I don't have clean clothes." Her throat bobbed as she swallowed, the movement drawing my attention to the marks my cruel hands had left around her neck. It stirred a bitter taste on my tongue. I wasn't in the business of hurting women—except one, a long fucking time ago. But I had no choice, ignoring the one fucking moral I did have in life, and I hurt her. It could so easily have gone wrong. Just a few seconds longer, pressing down on her windpipe slightly harder, and she'd be dead.

That thought didn't sit well with me.

I stood and plucked the phone from my pocket, speed dialing Josh's number as I advanced toward her, her eyes regarding me like one would watch a starved animal. "I need you to phone La Boutique, ask for Marianne, and let her put together a few items of woman's clothing. Jeans, shirts, blouses." I stilled mere inches from her. "Five-foot-four. Just over a hundred pounds." I licked my lips as I looked at hers, her top lip adorned with a perfect goddamn cupid's bow. "Dresses too." My hand touched her waist, the sound of a gentle gasp leaving her lips making my dick swell. "And underwear. Lingerie."

Her cheeks instantly flushed, and my motherfucking cock liked that look on her.

The blue in her eyes glistened, and the predator in me allowed my fingertips to continue up her waist, dragging the shirt and exposing her belly, her ivory skin lacking the fake tan most women loved to flaunt. Beautiful, flawless and delicate—like white rose petals illuminated with innocence.

I watched her, kept her gaze captive, anticipating any kind of reaction from her. But she remained unmoved. Silent. I wasn't even sure she was breathing.

"Preferably white," I said into the receiver while I touched her side, the need to push boundaries pulsing in my veins. My finger drew leisurely circles across her naked flesh, the shirt bundled up and creased before my hand slid underneath.

Her eyes snapped shut, and my hand closed around her

breast, feeling its weight in my palm. "B-cup," I murmured, and those lush, rosy-pink lips of hers parted.

I squeezed, loving how her tit fit so fucking perfectly in my hand, my cock rock goddamn hard and twitching in response. How easy it would be for me to continue, to give my dick what it wanted. To cross the fucking line.

A single tear slipped down her cheek, her eyes still closed, lapping over a now trembling bottom lip.

"And, Josh, pay cash. Do not mention my name."

I hung up, and she finally opened her eyes—slowly, cautiously, as if she feared what she would see.

"Elijah," she whispered, and I could swear to God the sound of my name on her lips was the start of my fucking undoing. "I'm scared." Her shoulders shuddered. "You scare me. Please...don't do this." Tears made the blue in her eyes shimmer. Like diamonds. Crystals of unhappiness. Not even her fear, her sorrow, her pain could extinguish the desire that now burned like the motherfucking sun in my groin. A tear dripped from her chin, and I lifted my hand in time to catch it, my skin soaking up the wetness. There was something sensual about it—erotic, even—how I could catch her sorrow and let it soak through my skin.

I cupped her cheek, lowering my lips closer to hers. "Would you believe me if I said I'm not the one you should fear?"

"No," she answered with no hesitation, and I closed my eyes.

"Good." I touched her bottom lip with my thumb, almost able to taste her. "Because that would be pretty fucking stupid of you if you did."

My pulse raced, and lust simmered. The thought of how

easy it would be to pin her on that bed, tear off her cheap fucking clothes, and bury myself balls deep inside her fucked with my head. I wanted it. I wanted it to so fucking bad, the entire shitstorm that surrounded us seemed like goddamn smoke during a thunderstorm. In-fucking-significant.

But this wasn't a line I could cross with her because she was just too goddamn important—the most consequential element of a hefty debt I vowed to pay.

I took a step back. "Go shower, Charlotte. Your new clothes will be here within the hour. And then I suggest you try to get some sleep."

It was easy to see the relief on her beautiful face when I put more distance between us.

Her eyes locked with mine. "How am I supposed to sleep?"

"Sing yourself a motherfucking lullaby."

There was no way I could stay so close to her for one second longer without doing something that would hurt her —something I'd enjoy way too fucking much.

I stormed out, and the door slammed shut. It felt like I had the fury of hell hammering against my skull. So many fucking voices, racing thoughts pulling me in every goddamn direction. There was no margin for error here, no fucking time for blurred lines and shit that had the potential to complicate something that could not, and would not, be anything more than a job—a debt fulfillment.

Lusting after Charlotte Moore had the potential to fuck up everything I had been planning for the last few years. One wrong move, and I'd be utterly, completely, unequivocally...fucked.

CHAPTER EIGHT

CHARLOTTE

The water was hot, probably too hot. But I didn't care. I felt it burn my skin, but it didn't hurt. I was numb, my mind scattered and empty as water cascaded down my back. There was no telling how long I'd been in the shower. Time no longer mattered. It was ironic how time lost its hold on a person once you no longer had things to do or places to go.

I took the bar of soap, smelling the vanilla scent. A part of me didn't want to use it, didn't want its smell to linger on my skin, because *he* chose it.

Elijah.

Elijah who? Who was this man who claimed to know me better than anyone else? This man who managed to watch me for so long without me even knowing. God, that thought was terrifying, thinking of someone lurking in the corners, watching your every move. The magnitude of the invasion of privacy on that level was almost unfathomable, and it made my stomach turn. All the memories of my everyday life—was he a part of it? He made it clear he was there the days I worked at the Alto, but what about at the bar where I worked nights when the theatre was closed? Was he there? Was his face among the rest of the crowd? Had I served him, handed him a beer, poured him shots? Did he tip me, after which I'd politely thank him?

Jesus. Once you started going down, it was an endless rabbit hole, dissecting everything from something as mundane as going to the grocery store to something as personal and private like going on a date. Was Elijah always fucking there?

The soap slipped from my hand, and I didn't bother to pick it up. I didn't want to use his fucking vanilla-scented soap, anyway.

I stepped out of the shower, the entire bathroom steamed up. I wiped the mirror, forming a clear streak so I could see part of my reflection. How many times had he watched me undress? How many times had he seen me naked with the type of confidence that only came when you were alone?

There were just too many questions—questions for which the answers would just branch out to more questions.

When he touched me earlier, the way he moved his hand over the curve of my hip and up my side. It was like he already knew the way, like my body was a map he had already memorized. And when he cupped my breast, kneading, touching, something inside me broke. I was sure of it, because what I felt couldn't have been normal. My fear collided with fire, causing a hurricane of malignant desire I instantly despised. Surely, something, somewhere inside me had to be broken. No normal human being would find anything alluring about a kidnapper, an abductor who choked his victims and snatched them out of society in such a twisted, vicious way. Not even if he looked like Elijah, like God Himself had carved him from the night sky and adorned him with mysterious allure coated in goddamn perfection.

Maybe it didn't have anything to do with him at all, and it was just this twisted part of myself I never knew about.

Maybe he knew. The way he stared at me, waiting, watching—something he was so fucking good at—as if he wanted to witness when the realization set in that there was a part of myself I had never known. Why else would my body react with equal parts heat and disgust—liking and despising his touch at the same time?

But that didn't matter right now. What mattered was that this bone-deep fear I felt, this horrifying uncertainty that filled my insides, I had to fight it. If I wanted to survive whatever the fuck this was, I needed to get my head straight. My mom used to say that one should never fear the unknown, because nothing was more important than conquering the now.

The present.

Live it. Conquer it. Survive it.

Twice I had asked him, begged him to let me go, and he made it clear that it wasn't an option.

"I won't beg again," I whispered to myself as if the woman who stared back at me in the mirror was a complete stranger. Someone I hardly knew. "Not again." But I would fight him every step of the way, prove to him that I was more than just prey.

I wrapped one of the white towels around me and paused by the door, wondering if he would be in there. I hesitated, the idea of him seeing me in nothing but a towel sending a chill down my back. But then again, he had probably already seen much more of me while I was blissfully unaware.

Steam escaped the bathroom as I opened the door and stepped into the bedroom. My shoulders relaxed when I saw he wasn't there, yet the three La Boutique bags on the bed proved he had been.

The ceiling lights had been dimmed. The warm yet subtle lighting touched the gray, cool tones of the room, creating a calming atmosphere, especially with nothing covering the windows. The New York skyline was majestic, mesmerizing, creating the illusion of power for whoever stared out across it. The tall buildings, thousands of lights—if wealth had a picture, it would be this.

The bedroom was three times the size of my entire apartment. If this were under any other circumstance, I'd probably be ecstatic, sipping champagne while soaking in the giant spa-bathtub in the bathroom. It was just my fucking luck that the one time I got the chance to experience such luxury was by force and kidnapping.

Fuck you, Murphy.

I let out a sigh and took each bag, one by one, throwing the clothing in one big heap on the bed.

Jeans. Shirts. Blouses. It took me half a glance to know I hated all of it simply because he bought it. It would have been clothing made of gold and silver, I'd still fucking hate it.

I laced a finger through a silk strap, lifting the short, white nightdress. There was barely enough fabric to cover everything that needed to be, well...covered. And not just one. Three. Three goddamn nightgowns, all in white, but different styles.

I tossed all of it to the side and scoffed. He was sorely mistaken if he thought I'd wear those. This was a kidnapping, not a fucking honeymoon.

One powder-blue blouse seemed longer than the others, so I put it on and buttoned it up before slipping a pair of white panties up underneath.

"That color suits you."

"Jesus Christ!" I yelped and jumped to the other side of the bed, almost choking on a breath. "Elijah." He was standing in the farthest corner—the one part of the room the lights didn't touch. "How long have you been there?" My pulse raced.

"Long enough to see that the white nightgowns clearly don't appeal to you."

"You really are a fucking psychopath, you know that?"

He shrugged. "I won't argue that."

"What do you want?"

With a single step, he moved out of the shadow into the light, and for a moment I looked at a man. Not a kidnapper or a stalker. But a man soaked in magnetism, making it impossible to look away. This fleeting thought sneaked into my mind, making me wonder why a man like him would be interested in a woman like me. Being a coldhearted kidnapper aside, he was beautiful. Attractive. The epitome of perfection that allowed him the luxury of having his pick of women. Yet I was the woman he dedicated years of his life to.

Watching me. Studying me.

A borderline obsession.

Why me?

He stepped between me and the bed, and I glanced at

the clothes. Fuck. If I wanted to grab some pants, I'd have to get past him. Sly bastard.

He placed his hands in his black pants pockets. "I want you to play for me."

"What? The cello?"

"Yes."

"I can't play when someone's watching me."

He smirked. "Yet you've played with me watching you for years."

"I didn't know. Stalker, remember?"

"Observer," he countered, his gaze burning into mine. "What is it about playing in front of people that scares you?"

I bit my lip and looked down. "I don't know."

"Are you afraid people will judge you, criticize your talent?"

"That's part of it."

"What's the other part?"

"I'm not sure if this is an appropriate conversation to have with my kidnapper," I glanced down at my legs, "especially not when I'm half naked."

He arched a brow. "You're wearing a blouse."

"I consider that being half naked."

His eyes narrowed, and he rubbed the stubble beard on his chin—the action drawing my attention to his muscular, veiny hand. Judging by how perfect it was, flawless yet muscular, he wasn't in the profession that required any type of hard labor. I was momentarily reminded of how it felt to have his hand on my breast, igniting that unwelcome blend of fear and fire.

"I'll make you a deal." He tossed the heap of clothing around and pulled out a full-length nightgown, easing the silk fabric through his fingers—a simple movement, yet somehow he made it seem...sensual. "I'll give you this if you tell me the other part."

I cleared my throat, glaring at him, hoping he'd see in my eyes just how much of a bastard I thought he was. "Why do you want to know?"

"Tell me."

"First tell me why you want to know."

"Are you sure you're in a position to negotiate with your kidnapper?"

I squared my shoulders. "What do I have to lose?"

An amused grin curved at the corners of his mouth, and he took a single step toward me, instantly robbing me of air. "How about because you're half naked and I'm fucking dying to feel you up again?" His hot gaze dropped to my breasts and back up, his liquid cognac eyes swirling with a thousand immoral intentions, as if he hoped I'd give him a reason to do it. That I'd challenge him. What scared me the most was how it spoke to that dark part inside me, the part that stirred to life when he touched me.

I licked my lips. "It's personal."

"What is?" His voice dipped low with a sultry tenor.

"Playing." I swallowed. "It's personal to me."

"Why?"

"Jesus," I yelled. "It's the way it affects me, okay? How it allows me to escape. It's not something I want to share with anyone."

"Why not?" He shifted closer, taking up more air with his musky scent. "Why don't you want to share it?"

"Because when I play, I'm at my most vulnerable, and I don't want to share that part of myself with anyone."

"So, what you're saying is," he took one more step, and I had to crane my neck to look him in the eye as he stared down at me like a mountain of menace, "you shared your most vulnerable self with...me." The low, seductive thrum in his voice trickled across the naked flesh of my throat, and I swallowed hard, hyperaware of how he dominated the space around us.

"I didn't share it with you." I lifted my chin in a desperate attempt to show defiance. "You took it."

"I'm known to take what I want."

"So, you're not just a stalker and a psychopath, you're a thief too."

His top lip curled in a sinful smirk. "I'm sure during our time together you'll realize I'm a lot of other things as well."

There was no telling whether it was meant to be a threat or not. If I needed to fear those *other things*. It would probably be safer if I did—to expect the worst.

"Here." He handed me the nightgown. "I might be a lot of things, but I am a man of my word. A deal is a deal."

Hesitant, I took the silk garment from him, yet there was no haste to put it on. Somehow, I had forgotten about the fact that I was half-naked, too entranced by the presence of my captor.

He glanced at the cello, and I expected him to press the matter—to force me to play for him like he did after he brought me here. But he didn't. Instead, he turned and headed toward the door.

"Do you play?" The words slipped mindlessly out of my mouth, and I caught myself stepping closer.

He stilled, his shoulders broad, tips of his hair touching

the back of his collar. Without turning, he answered, "I don't. But I do share your appreciation for music."

Nervously, I twirled my fingers together. "Why me? Why spend all that time," I swallowed, "*observing* me?"

He glanced halfway over his shoulder, his jaw square and strong. For a second, I was sure he'd answer, but he merely let out a breath and walked out, his exit followed by the click of the lock. A cold, harrowing reminder that I was a prisoner...and nothing more.

CHAPTER NINE

ELIJAH

The ice clinked as I swirled the glass of whiskey. The half-empty bottle stood on the side table, close by for when I needed a top-up. Time pissed by as I stared at the flames flickering in the fireplace. One would think I lit it to ward off the early-autumn chill, but part of me wondered if it might be my subconscious trying to prepare me for an eternity in hell that awaited me.

What did it feel like to burn alive? To have flames engulf you, suffocate you while your skin melted off your bones? I could only imagine how terrifying it had to be to smell the stench of burning flesh, knowing it was yours—that soon you'd be nothing but ash.

Many religions taught us about hell. Hades. The underworld. That burning alive over and over again for eternity was what awaited you once you'd descended into the devil's realm. More than likely it was where I'd be heading to once my time comes. There was no redemption for a man who lived a life like I did...or for a child who did something so fucking unforgivable.

I swallowed the last mouthful of whiskey, relishing the sting as it went down and settled in my stomach.

I'd see her again in hell, the mother I thought I was rid of forever. But like every other fucking nightmare, she would come back someday, eventually. She was probably down there right now, tied up and getting fucked in the ass by the devil, thinking of the day I'd walk through those flaming gates and loving the thought. There was no escaping her. Even stuck in her grave, she haunted me, refusing to pull her toxic claws from my goddamn soul.

T*HE* *ENTIRE* *HOUSE* *smelled like cigarettes, piss, and the rotting meatloaf from last week. Occasionally, my mom would attempt to take on this daunting task called motherhood. But it wouldn't even last a night before she'd fall back into old habits.*

Alcohol.

Drugs.

Sex.

Ignoring us. Ellie and me.

Ellie, my little sister, would sneak into my room at night, get under my blanket, and snuggle up behind my back. It was the only comfort she had ever known, the comfort of sleeping next to her older brother. Mom never showed us any affection, cared for us when we were sick. Half the time she wouldn't even feed us, and we'd go to bed with nothing more than a slice of stale bread and half a glass of rancid milk. Eventually, we figured out dipping the bread in sugar water made it taste better and easier to swallow. Most nights, I'd end up sharing my piece with Ellie since her tummy would still be rumbling after she finished her slice. I was a bony little shit.

Some days, I'd wash the neighbors' cars, sweep their driveways—anything for a dollar or two. But I'd make sure my mom was passed out first so she couldn't see. If she knew I was hiding money to buy food for me and Ellie, she'd find it, steal it, use it.

Get high.

I had made peace with the fact that our mom would always be a drunk. An addict. I had been disappointed one too many times with her promises of sobering up. Ellie, on the other hand, she would fall for it every time, smiling and laughing the entire day after mom announced that changes would be made. That same night Ellie wouldn't sneak into my room to snuggle. She would go to Mom, snuggle with her, and fall asleep, only to be woken up by noises coming from downstairs.

I had made the mistake of going downstairs once to see what was going on. Never again. Walking in on your own mother bent over the kitchen table, panties around her ankles with some strange man leaning over her from behind, clutching her hair in his fist, was a sight no ten-year-old boy should see.

The strange men would leave, and I'd find Mom not long after that, naked on the kitchen floor, the needle still dangling from her arm.

It hurt every time. Seeing my mom so helpless, pathetic, and lost. It was like this ever since Dad died. Car crash. Ellie had just turned three, and I remembered how Mom wouldn't leave her room, forcing me to take care of my little sister. For *weeks, Ellie had to eat cereal every day, twice a day, because I didn't know how to make anything else.*

And then one day there was a knock on the door, both Ellie and I surprised and excited to see Mom coming down the stairs. Finally, she had come out of her room, tying her bathrobe around her waist.

But it was since she opened that door that our lives had changed. Inside that brown bag the man handed her was the thing that took her from us. Things were never the same after that day.

The men. The drugs. Our house was like a snake pit.

For too long, Ellie and I had to watch while Mom slipped down the path of destruction, putting everything else above her own children. The hatred soon smothered the love of a son for his mother. Soon she became nothing more than this toxic waste of space, and I hated every breath she took because she used air she didn't deserve. Ellie was the only reason I didn't leave. She never gave up on the hope that one day our mom would wake up and be the mom we deserved.

But that day never came, and escaping the hell our mother created was the only way for us to be free.

Unfortunately...Ellie never got the chance.

I REFILLED my empty glass and sipped more whiskey. The more I thought of the vile bitch, the more I needed something strong enough to numb the rage, the hatred. But by now I knew the only way to escape the demonic memory of her was with the thrill of taking another's life. To hear their screams, imagining that they felt the same kind of pain I did.

The same kind of pain Ellie did.

I glanced at the music box on the side table. The delicate floral design set in the burr walnut and palisander lid had faded over its lifetime, the wooden frame carrying its fair share of scrapes and scratches. Memories stirred as I picked it up, turning the windup key before easing it open, revealing the tiny ballerina in her torn tutu twirling to the tune of *Edelweiss*. I closed my eyes, allowing myself to go back there just for a moment, back to the house where all my demons died. The room where the few good memories I had were born. Memories with her. Ellie. The little sister I couldn't protect.

I slammed the music box shut and took a breath, steeling myself against the regret. But the voices were still there. It was always there. Apart from seeing blood run dry, there was one other thing that somehow silenced the voices.

The cellist.

But the reprieve I found from her music wouldn't be at my disposal for much longer.

My phone vibrated, and I swiped across the screen, checking all four payment confirmations into the selected accounts I had sent to Julio Bernardi. Fucker. Part of me hoped he'd slip up with the payment. It would have given me a reason to stop the entire goddamn operation. Call everything off and let Charlotte go. Question was, if the contract had to end today and there was no reason to keep her captive any longer, would I have let her go? Or would the sick fucker in me keep her, hoping she'd play that cello for me every goddamn day so I could lose myself in her and her music?

Blurred lines.

I stood and took the bottle of whiskey, strolling down the hall. There was too much adrenaline coursing through my system, too many racing thoughts for me even to attempt getting some sleep.

When I walked past the locked door that kept the cellist in, the key in my pocket suddenly felt heavier. I plucked it out and stared at it in my palm, easing my thumb along the curved ridges before I convinced myself it would be considered polite to check on my guest—make sure she was all settled in.

Of course, I didn't knock before I unlocked the door and stepped into the bedroom. This was my fucking apartment.

The dimmed lights were still on, and the blinds still open. But Charlotte had curled up on the bed, clutching a pillow, and seemingly fast asleep.

Purposely, I stepped lightly as I crossed the wooden floors toward the side of the bed. I took a large gulp of whiskey from the bottle, cringing as the alcohol burned down my throat.

How many nights had I watched her like this? Vulnerable, innocent, peaceful. How many times had I watched her cry herself to sleep? Alone. Heartbroken. Scared. One could say I had seen all the different sides to this woman. How her eyes changed color to a deeper, more vibrant shade of blue whenever she was happy. And how she would chew the inside of her mouth when she tried her hardest to hold back tears.

No matter how many times she had smiled, she couldn't hide her loneliness from me. She carried it on her shoulders since the day she said goodbye to her mother for the last time.

I shot back another mouthful of whiskey when Charlotte

stirred. "Pretending to be asleep with a stalker lurking in the room is really fucking hard."

I grinned. "Observer."

She sat up and leaned back against the headboard while holding the pillow in front of her chest. "Did you really think I'd be able to sleep?"

"Eventually, the adrenaline will wear off and your whole system will crash into exhaustion." From the corner of my eyes, I spotted the unopened pizza box. "You didn't eat."

"I'm not hungry, Elijah. I just want to go home."

"Home?" I lifted a brow. "You call that shithole apartment home?"

She toyed with the seam of the pillow. "That shithole is the closest thing I have to a home. Besides, right now I'd rather be anywhere else than here with you."

I swirled the amber liquid around in the bottle as I regarded her, her skin glowing under the pale light, her lips an enticing blush pink. The way her blouse fell along her chest exposed the swell of her breast, teasing the fuck out of me and my now hard cock. "Earlier, you said you were scared of me. Right now, you don't seem scared at all."

She glanced my way. "It's because I realized that being afraid of you won't stop you from doing whatever it is you plan on doing to me. Psychopaths like you feed on fear. I'd be stupid to cower."

"Or smart."

"Maybe. But if you kill me, I think I'd prefer to die knowing I fought."

"Remember that when you're staring down the barrel of a gun, or feel the cold steel of a knife against your throat.

Strength isn't defined by how you fight. Strength is being able to do what needs to be done in order to survive."

Those pretty doe eyes of hers looked up at me. "And what, exactly, do I need to do to survive you?"

And there it was again, the buzz of desire that vibrated through every bone in my fucking body, urging me to touch. Taste. Devour. The longer I stood there looking down at her, the more I imagined tearing through that silk blouse so I could wrap my lips around one of her pebbled nipples and suck it raw.

I reached out, brushing the back of my hand down the side of her face—her skin warm and smooth under my touch. She didn't flinch. She didn't shudder. She didn't even fucking move, and I weaved my fingers through her hair. A soft, tangled disarray of curls. "Fear, my sweet cellist, is the mind's best motivator when it comes to surviving."

I tightened my fist abruptly, gripping her hair tight and pulling her head back, exposing the beautiful, delicate arch of her throat, bobbing as she swallowed. My gaze held her captive, her pretty pink lips parted as I brought mine closer, hovering a mere inch away.

"It is our fear that fuels us," I eased my fingers along her jaw, "our fear of failure, of pain," I gripped her chin between my thumb and forefinger, "death. Those are the things that make it so fucking important for us to survive. Even if it means exploiting the fear of others by making their worst nightmares come true." I bit my bottom lip as I studied her, those blue orbs of crystal staring back at me with a burning determination to not. Show. Fear. And by God, I loved it.

"So, let me tell you what *not* to do in order to survive me." I tugged her hair in my fist, and she moaned, the sound burning its way to the tip of my cock. "Do not fight me if you want to survive me. All it does is make my dick hard and my control non-existent, and I doubt you're strong enough to handle that."

I let go of her hair, and I was sure she'd scramble to the other side of the bed like a scared little kitten with her tail between her legs. But instead, she sat up, not taking her eyes off mine for a second, her cheeks flushed, and upper lip curled with a snarl. Her face was the perfect picture of resistance and contempt. "You don't know what I can or cannot handle, Elijah. Just because you stood in the darkness and preyed on my life does not mean you fucking know me."

I wiped at my chin with the back of my hand, unable to stop myself from being amused by her. It was in her bones, in her blood—that primal need to fight.

"You know," I grabbed the bottle of whiskey, "you remind me of someone."

"Yeah, who?"

I smirked. "You'll find out soon, little cellist. Soon."

CHAPTER TEN

CHARLOTTE

I was wrapped up in a bundle of silk sheets when a loud slam of the door jerked me awake.

"Charlotte, get up."

A curtain of dark, disarrayed curls fell over my face, and I wiped it back with my arm. "What is—"

"Get the fuck up. Now."

The silk sheets swooshed as he pulled them off and grabbed my arm, hauling me off the bed so fast I tripped over my own feet. But he yanked me back up, giving me no time to find my goddamn footing.

"What is happening?" I tried to twist my arm free from his hold, but he only gripped tighter.

"We need to leave. Now."

"Why?"

We rushed out the door, and he pulled me down the hall so fast, my feet barely touched the wooden floors. It was still dark, maybe early morning hours since the windows revealed the black sky. Dim lights lit the way down the hall, and I tried my best to keep up without tripping over my own two feet.

"Where are we going?"

"It's no longer safe here. Shit."

"What do you mean? What is going on?" Pushing down my heel, I tried to stop and pull back. "Elijah, stop!"

He turned to face me, and my breath got lodged in my throat, his golden pupils all dark and dangerous. Wild and bewildered, he stepped right up to me, his shoes touching my naked toes. "Right now, I need you to trust me. Can you do that?"

"I...what...Elijah, what's—"

His grip on my elbow tightened, fingers clawing into my skin as he pulled me against him, leaning down as his stare burned into mine. "Tomorrow you can fight me all you want. Be defiant and act like I repulse you."

"Act? It's not—"

"Charlotte!" Like a sonic boom, his voice exploded down the hall. "Either you fucking listen and do exactly as I say and we both get out of this alive, or you continue to be fucking stubborn and you won't see another sunrise."

It was one of those intense moments when the sound of your racing heart drowned out the sound of your thoughts. When the rush of adrenaline stopped time, and you were frozen, unable to comprehend what was happening, what your options were, and what it was you were supposed to do.

"Mr. Mariano," a man came rushing down the hall, "all three cars are ready. They're waiting at the back exit. We need to leave now."

A loud crack blasted next to us, followed by the piercing sound of glass breaking. I crouched to the side and felt

Elijah's arms cover my shoulders. "Josh, switch off the lights. Now!"

Fear sliced my insides, and I looked up at the cracked window. "What was that?"

"Keep your head down." The lights went out, and Elijah kept his arm around me as we ran down the hall as fast as we could. Everything happened so quickly, it was just one giant blur. Wooden floors were replaced with the loud echo of tiles as we moved across it in almost total darkness. There was a glint of steel doors in front of us—an elevator, but Elijah pulled me to the right just as a door opened in the far corner.

"Come on, come on." Elijah's arm dropped, and he wrapped my hand in his as we started down two flights of stairs before we darted through another door. "Josh, keycard."

Josh swiped a keycard, and the elevator doors opened, my heart pounding in my ears as I struggled to catch my breath. Once inside, the doors slammed closed, and Josh pushed the last button on the panel.

For the first time, Elijah let go of me, pacing while holding a goddamn gun in his hand.

"Can someone please tell me what the hell is going on?" I demanded between rapid breaths, my hands clinging to the support rail behind me.

Elijah completely ignored me. "Is the plane ready?"

"Yes, sir."

Elijah nodded, still pacing. I wanted to press for an answer, raise my voice and make myself heard so I could find out what the hell was happening. But the ping of the elevator door signaled, and it opened, two men and a woman waiting on the other side.

"Charlotte and I will go in the last car."

"Sir," Josh paused, "he'll expect that. I suggest you take the first car."

Elijah shook his head. "They'll expect me to think that taking the last car would be the obvious choice, therefore opting for the middle one. Here, put this on." Elijah handed me a black hoodie and glasses, the exact same as the other woman was wearing.

I opened my mouth, but his pointed stare warned me to keep it shut. "Do as you're told." Then turned to the woman in the hoodie. "Vivian, you go in the middle car. They won't know which one to follow."

She nodded, and Elijah grabbed my hand, all of us scattering in different directions toward the black SUVs.

"Is she supposed to be me?"

"Just to throw them off our trail."

"And by them, you mean...?"

"Not now, Charlotte."

We reached the car, the cold air stinging my cheeks, and Elijah opened the door.

"Oh, by the way, Josh?"

"Yes, sir?"

Elijah lifted his arm, the metal glint of the gun a harrowing warning before a sharp strike sliced through the air, followed by a blunt crack. My reality got severed as I watched Josh fall to the ground with a blood-oozing hole in his forehead. Everything went mute. All I heard was my erratic heartbeat echoing between my ears, my skin numb and ice cold.

"Oh, my God." My voice quivered, and I couldn't stop

shaking my head, refusing to believe this was really fucking happening.

"Come on." Elijah grabbed my arm, but this time I managed to twist out of his grip.

"You killed him."

"Thank you for stating the obvious. Now get in the motherfucking car."

"Why?" My legs grew weak, and I fell back against the car. "Why did you kill—"

"The man was a fucking traitor, Charlotte."

An ache spread through my chest, the bitter taste of bile leaking on my tongue. "What...what...Jesus." I couldn't even think straight, teetering at the edge of hysteria while my brain threatened to shut down. "You killed him."

"Just get in the motherfucking car." He grabbed me behind my neck, fingers biting into my skin. I tried to fight, to kick and grab at his arm, but I was no match for him as he shoved me into the back seat, getting in behind me and shutting the door.

"Drive," he ordered, and I got knocked back in the seat as the car pulled away, screeching tires hurting my ears.

The two SUVs in front of us each split up in different directions, and we drove straight. I tried to catch my breath, my hand gripping the doorhandle tight. "What the fuck just happened? Why...why did you kill—"

"He fucking talked, and now they found you. Fucker!" Elijah pulled out his phone, threw it on the floor, and crushed it with his heel. He scavenged the pieces and found the tiny SIM card, pulling a pocketknife from his jacket and stabbing the card straight through, tearing the leather seat, before tossing it out the window.

"What do you mean, they found me? Who are they?"

"Un-fucking-believable." He slammed his fist into the back of the font seat, the leather creaking under his anger. "Fuck! Henry," he said to the driver, "give me your phone."

The driver didn't hesitate, handing his phone over to Elijah. Sweat dripped down my spine, my palms wet, and breathing rapidly as I watched Elijah's fingers fly across the touchscreen, making a call.

"It's me. Plan A has been compromised. We're moving on with plan B...Yes, we're headed there right now. Okay."

He hung up and tossed Henry's phone to the floor and crushed it the same way he did his, stabbing the SIM and throwing it out the window.

"Is that really necessary? That's not even your fucking phone." I was stunned.

"You don't mind, now, do you Henry?"

"No, sir."

Elijah shot me an arrogant glare, annoyance rippling from his rigid shoulders. There was so much rage, panic, fear, I had my body pushed up against the door. "What is going on right now?" I didn't even realize I was crying until I tasted the saltiness of my tears on my lips.

He dragged his hand through his hair, then straightened his collar as if he tried to slip that cool façade back. Meanwhile, I was busy hyperventilating while my brain splintered inside my skull, trying to make fucking sense of what just happened.

There was this heavy silence around us, and not even the bustling New York crowds and traffic could penetrate it. The grueling sense of foreboding filled my lungs, and I sat back, waiting for him to say something. Anything.

He glanced in my direction. "Not yet."

"What?" I glowered at him. "What the fuck do you mean, not yet?"

"I mean not yet!" he snapped. The tension that rolled off him was frightening, his dark gaze holding a secret he struggled to share. "Things are not as they seem, Charlotte."

"No shit. First you kidnap me, and now you shot a guy?" I tugged at my hair as I weaved my fingers through the curls. "I can't even fucking think straight right now."

He rubbed his palm across his beard, the scratchy sound scraping against my last goddamn nerve.

"I can tell you more when we get to our destination."

I balked. "Our destination? Where are we going?"

Elijah eyed the driver, the look of distrust flashing across his face. "You'll know when we get there."

Something inside me snapped—my sanity, maybe. But every muscle in my body reacted as if there was something inside me that needed to get out. To escape.

God, *I* needed to escape.

"I can't. No. No. I can't do this. I can't be here." With panicked breaths and adrenaline gushing through my veins, I grabbed the doorhandle, desperate to get out. I didn't care if I died while jumping out of a fucking moving car, I just wanted to get away from all of this. From him.

"Jesus, Charlotte. Stop." Hands grabbed my shoulder, and I pulled my knee up, kicking at him, screaming for him to leave me the fuck alone.

"Let me go." The door wouldn't open, and my throat started to close up, panic wrapping its poisonous tentacles around my lungs. "Let me out!"

"No, stop!"

He pulled me back, slamming me into his chest as he wrapped an arm around me, pinning me so I couldn't move.

There was a sharp stab in the top of my arm, a needle, and I felt the liquid burn as it spread through my veins. "Why are you doing this to me?" I cried. My pathetic attempt at staying strong didn't even last a fucking day. "Why?"

"Shhhh, little cellist. Soon."

"No, no, no." My words got lost and my body went numb, my thoughts vanishing, until it was all...black.

CHAPTER ELEVEN
CHARLOTTE

I could hear it, the rich, stately sound of a cello playing far away in the distance. It reached for me, wanting to envelop my soul and create a hunger in me to play, touch the strings and allow its music to carry me away.

It reminded me of her—of how she'd play for me every night before bedtime. It was the most beautiful music I had ever heard, not because of the instrument, but because of her—how her love for playing echoed in every sound.

My mother had been my tutor from the day my arms were long enough to hug the cello. The first lesson she taught me was that the cello could not be mastered, it could only be danced with while its music effortlessly guided you to where it wanted to go. Not to where you wanted to take it.

I opened my eyes and stared at an unfamiliar dressing table of bold mahogany wood. My fingers were stiff, my joints flaming hot like a coal had been lit inside them. I eased my hand into a fist and gently opened it again, slowly warming the muscles so the pain would subside. Rheumatoid arthritis—the irony in a cellist player's life.

I pushed myself up, my head pounding and mouth dry. My insides turned, and nausea curdled in my stomach as bits and pieces of my memory trickled back, until it all gushed toward a reality I'd much rather have forgotten.

Elijah.
Josh.
Blood.
Needle.

I grabbed my arm, remembering the way it burned, how Elijah held me against him so I couldn't move.

"Jesus." I breathed and placed a palm on my forehead and glanced down, the unfamiliar navy-blue sheets jumping out at me.

Where am I?

I launched out of bed, the white nightgown fanning around my legs. This wasn't the bedroom Elijah had me in the first time I woke up trapped in this goddamn nightmare. The walls consisted of mahogany wood panels, two single plush chairs placed on either side of the bed. The carpet beneath my feet was soft, warm, and under-bed lighting illuminating the floor area.

"You're awake."

His voice forced a cold chill down my neck, and I turned to see him standing by the door, leaning against the frame, the epitome of sophistication and poise. One would never think he was a cruel kidnapper who suffocated his victims and shot men without blinking.

"You drugged me."

He shrugged, nonchalant, as if drugging and abducting women was part of his fucking daily routine.

I glanced around. "Where are we?"

He straightened the sleeves of his black dress shirt and strolled into the bedroom, his increasing proximity forcing me to step back, watching him like he could turn into a poisonous viper at any moment.

"Italy."

I balked. "Italy? You're kidding, right?" Jesus, the last time I remembered, we were in New York, and now he was saying we were in Italy?

He nodded. "Well, we're somewhere off the coast of Rome, to be exact." He spread his arms out wide. "A very good friend of mine was kind enough to let us borrow his yacht."

"A yacht?" I breathed. "Rome?"

He arched a brow. "Would you like a moment to process that?" Sarcasm dripped from his words, and I wanted to smack that amused grin off his face.

"Care to tell me why we're in Italy, and on a yacht?"

"So," he feigned a look of thought, clearly enjoying the theatrics, "imagine you're trying to get away from some really bad men, and the—"

"Oh, you mean men like you?"

"Hush, woman. Has your father never taught you not to interrupt a man when he's speaking?" He held up his hand. "Oh, that's right. You never had a father."

It stung more than I'd care to admit, the way he used the truth to take a stab at me, and also to remind me just how much he fucking knew about me and my life.

"Now, as I was saying—if you wanted to get away from

some bad people, where do you think is the safest place for you to hide? Someplace they couldn't easily find you?"

It clicked, sliding in like a puzzle piece. "The ocean."

"The ocean," he reiterated. "Hence why we're currently on my friend's very expensive, and if you ask me, far too extravagant yacht."

What I wouldn't do to find answers without engaging in more conversation with him. It seemed he loved treating me like a child, talking to me with sarcasm, patronizing me. But right now, my mind was spinning in a thousand different directions, and I had to somehow figure out what the hell was going on before my thoughts would drive me mad.

"So, I'm assuming we're hiding from someone." My voice was soft, my head still pounding along with the racing beats of my heart. "And that this has something to do with someone shooting at you back in New York. And you shooting Josh."

"Wow," he smirked, "that is one loaded assumption."

"What the hell is going on, Elijah?"

"Firstly," he held up a finger, his shirt pulled taut across his broad shoulders, "that someone wasn't shooting at me. That someone was shooting at you."

Ice exploded in my spine.

"Secondly, I shot and killed Josh because the man was a fucking snitch. He sold me out, and that's how they found you."

"Who are *they*?"

"The Bernardi family."

"You say that like the name is supposed to mean something to me."

He slipped his hands in his pants pockets and stilled on

the other side of the bed, his gaze as intense as ever. "Does the name Gianni Guerra sound familiar to you?"

"No."

He shrugged. "That's understandable, the fact that you don't know of him."

"How so?"

His eyes met mine. "He's your grandfather, from your father's side."

My skin went cold. "Excuse me?"

"Your grandfather." A grin tugged at his lips as if my shock amused him. As if dropping a bomb like this on me gave him sort of fucking kick, mindfucking me. "Gianni Guerra is your grandfather."

My legs felt weak, and I needed to sit down, but I wanted to look the devil in the eye, to not show him how he had just pulled the rug from right under me. "How do you know?"

He scratched his temple and shot me a cocky grin. "Really? You're going to ask me how I know who your grandfather is? Your father? Charlotte," he took a step closer, "I know what you had for dinner last Tuesday. I know what flavor cupcake you bought yourself on your birthday last year."

I frowned.

"Red velvet," he stated to prove his point, then twirled his fingers, "but with the meringue topping, not the cream cheese. You're not a big fan of cream—"

"This is all a game to you, isn't it? A sick, twisted hunt where you can play God and fuck with people's lives."

His expression hardened, and his jaw clenched. "I can assure you this is no fucking game."

"Then tell me what is going on." My skull prickled with a curiosity that had a thousand questions bombard my thoughts, but at the same time, my instincts sounded with alarm. "How do you know my grandfather," I breathed out, a sharp pang slicing through my chest, "my father?"

There were so many nights I lay awake wondering where my father was, *who* my father was. My mom never spoke about him, never made any reference of him. He might as well have been a phantom, a ghost, someone who didn't exist. I used to watch other dads with their kids—dropping them off at school, playing with them in the park, laughing and smiling. And one day after school, I asked my mom about him, and why he wasn't with us. I never made that mistake again. The hurt, the pain, the complete heartbreak I saw in her eyes was too much for a little girl to take. She never answered me that day. She simply hugged me and said good night. But I heard her cry that night, and I hated that I was the cause of her tears.

I never asked again after that.

For the longest time, Elijah just stood there, easing his fingers along the silk sheets on the bed, looking down as if he too tried to sort through his thoughts. Maybe trying to choose his words wisely.

"Elijah, what—"

"Do you know what I am?"

"A psychopath?"

His gaze shot up to mine. "You want answers, then I strongly advise you not to fuck with me right now, Charlotte."

I bit my lip, feeling like a goddamn schoolgirl who just got scolded, my cheeks burning and my chest tight.

Cognac irises kept me captive as he approached me with slow, calculated steps. There was something unsettling in the way he looked at me, something sinister and dark—his expression guarded.

I crossed my arms, rubbing a shoulder with my palm. Maybe it was a way to protect myself from what was to come. As if I knew that whatever he was about to tell me would rock the very foundation of the life I'd lived until now.

One more step, and he stilled in front of me. His scent enveloped me while his lustrous amber eyes dared me to ask the question he was burning to answer.

"Do you know. What. I. Am?"

I licked my lips, my mouth suddenly dry. "No," I whispered, hating that I sounded so scared. Vulnerable. Weak. But I bet he fucking loved it.

"I'm a master." He inched forward, and I moved back, hating that his heavy presence penetrated my space, taking control.

Dominating.

My back hit the wall, and I shut my eyes—trapped between the devil and the gates of hell. Air swooshed from my lungs as he placed his hands above my shoulders at either side of my head, cocooning me in, leaving me trapped with him entirely in control of whatever move I made.

He leaned closer, his scent wrapped around me, the coarse hair of his stubble beard grazing against my jaw, sending a wave of shivers down my back. The sensation drowned out the threat and replaced it with an impulse to want to be closer, my skin ignited with a toxic fusion of fear and seduction. I had no idea how this was possible, how a man could instill terror and ignite a sensual attraction at the same damn time.

I sucked in a breath and closed my eyes when I felt his lips brush against the side of my ear, my body lit with a dangerous desire to submit.

"Master of what?" I whispered, and I heard him take a breath.

"Killing people. They call me...The Musician."

Fear slammed into my chest, breaking shards of ice in my veins, my lips parting as I whimpered. Every muscle in my body went rigid, and I couldn't move. I couldn't breathe, and I couldn't think.

"Judging by how you just paled, I'm guessing you've heard of me."

The Musician. The man I'd heard Chase and the other guys whisper about. The man who carved out a treble clef on the chests of his victims. The man everyone knew about, yet no one had ever seen. A ghost. A phantom.

Not anymore. Not to me.

"Tell me, my little cellist," he dragged a finger down the side of my face, "are you afraid of me?"

I swallowed before choking out a shaky, "No."

"Liar." He gripped my jaw and forced me to look the other way, pressing his nose against the skin below my ear as he inhaled. "I can smell your fear, how it radiates off your flesh. It's fear that feeds men like me. Do you know the kind of high it gives you, the rush of power seeing a grown man piss himself while looking you in the eye?"

"You're a sick son of a bitch."

"You say that like I have the ability to give a fuck." His

grip tightened on my jaw, my body growing weaker beneath his cruel touch. "I kill people for money. I live off the death of others, eat food and drink whiskey bought from blood money. And yet you think to insult me will make me give a damn."

I bit the inside of my cheek, desperately trying to hold on to whatever strength I had left. "Did you kill my father? My grandfather? Is that what this is all about? And now you want to kill me too?"

"Again," he lifted a finger, "if I wanted to kill you, you'd be dead."

"Did you kill them?"

"I did not."

I swallowed, my throat dry and mouth feeling like I had eaten sand. "Then what does all of this have to do with them? With me?"

"Shhh," he cooed. "We'll get to that part soon enough."

"What do you want from me?"

He jerked my face, forcing me to look him in the eye. "See, the answer to that would have been simple, had you asked me three years ago. But now," his tongue darted from his mouth, licking his lips, coating them with a shimmer of wetness, "now it doesn't seem so simple anymore."

The sting of unshed tears threatened to break down my resolve, and I tried my hardest to bite it back. "I guess this is the part where I ask you what changed."

"That's another tricky question to answer."

I didn't even realize he had dropped his other arm to my side until he gripped the silk of my nightgown between his fingers, touching my waist through the smooth fabric.

I desperately tried to ignore how his touch burned like a

simmering coal that had the potential to ignite a fire that would destroy everything in its path.

"So, what...I'm a job?"

"Indeed, you are. A unique and extremely complicated one."

"What does that even mean?"

His fingertips touched my naked flesh as he held the fabric hostage, and it was impossible to ignore the tainted desire that infected me. This must have been that twisted part in me, that part he woke when he cupped my breast, making me aware of the dark warning of something perilous flickering inside me like a stalking threat.

"It means"—his hand slid down the side of my leg, only to return up across the inside of my thigh—"that you are a job that has the potential to ruin me." With leisurely circles, I felt him move his fingers up...up...until a single digit brushed against my sex. The involuntary moan that slipped from my lips left a bitter taste on my tongue. I was supposed to hate his touch, to fight and scream and beg him to stop. To feel violated and repulsed by him. Yet my body felt bewitched by the dark seduction that emanated from him, wrapping its tendrils of twisted temptation around my body. I was desperate to keep my expression cold and hard, unaffected by his sick, twisted fucking game. But the longer his touch lingered, the weaker I became, and I couldn't stop my eyes closing as that flicker turned into a flame, his finger continuing its delicate caress against my panties, my body building with a strong rebellion to betray me.

He brushed his lips up the side of my face, my skin now hyperaware of every touch, every breath, every sound. "I have killed enough people to earn me an eternity in hell.

And even though I can kill just about anyone I fucking want without the slightest of hesitation, you, my dear cellist, are the one person in this entire goddamn world I *can't* kill."

I sucked in a breath, not knowing whether it was relief or disbelief that caused me to shudder. "Why?" I swallowed thickly and licked my lips. "Why can't you kill me?"

"Because you're special, Charlotte Leigh Moore." My name rolled off his tongue like a prayer and a curse combined, as if I were his saving grace and the sin that would cause his descent from the heavens. It was equal parts terrifying and enticing, causing every muscle to tremble while my thighs clenched.

His finger prodded at the hem of my panties, my body humming with anticipation, yet my mind was screaming, yelling at me to stop him. To fight. To not let him tip my body over the edge, because if he did, I'd never be able to come back from it. But I was caught in his web of seduction, my fight tangling me tighter until there was no way out, and I could only watch as my demise approached.

I squeezed myself against the wall. "What makes me so damn special?" My voice echoed the staccato of broken resolve that possessed me while his touch burned.

"You were just a means to pay a debt owed." His lips grazed all along my jaw. "You were a promise, nothing more. But after all this time, watching you, studying you, infiltrating your life—your music...Jesus, your music," he breathed out, the hot air that left his lungs easing along my flesh, igniting a flame in my core, "it became my drug, my escape from this wretched fucking world. And then I found myself being around you, close to you not because I had to," he looked at me, a maze of secrets and confessions, "but because I wanted to. Because I was drawn to you and this emotion your music stirred inside me." His voice trailed off, and I found myself swept away by his every word—entranced, captivated by everything he had just said, and I allowed myself to forget the events that brought us to this moment. The fear, the panic, the lies, it evaporated, replaced by this burning need to know more. To know everything about this man and whatever the hell this was that pulsed and beat between us.

"So, you see? You became something more than just a debt, or a job," he continued as his fingers lingered against the side of my face.

"What? What have I become?" There was no rhyme or reason for me wanting an answer, for even pursuing this conversation. But there was a burning need to know what it was that earned me the attention of a man like Elijah. A man who bathed in darkness and basked in sin. A man who did whatever he wanted, took whatever he wanted.

His gaze dropped to my lips the moment he managed to get past the barrier of the thin piece of fabric between my legs, slipping a finger through my heat. I craned my neck, leaning against the wall as evil desire gripped me, twisted me, and tied me up in the barbed wire of his vicious and ruthless seduction.

"You, my dear little cellist, became an addiction I willingly surrendered and drowned in night after night. And now," he slipped a finger inside me, and I gasped, my body climbing from the unwelcome intrusion. "Now you're an obsession."

CHAPTER TWELVE
ELIJAH

Perspiration beaded all along her hairline, the vein in her neck throbbing impossibly fast. Her warm breath caressed my skin, and I wanted to feel more of it. I wanted her rapid breaths to kiss my neck while I fucked her, hear her gentle moans as I rocked her body toward a release, and watch her come apart beneath me.

"You're going to do something for me."

Her eyes glanced back at me in question.

I slipped my hand from between her legs and placed my finger on her mouth as I hungrily stared down while I coated her bottom lip with her glistening arousal. "Ask me."

Her lips parted.

"Ask me what you're going to do for me."

She swallowed, her throat bobbing. There was a war raging inside her. It was there, in the way she looked at me with equal parts hate and desire. Even for her it was undeniable, this fucking connection we shared long before she laid eyes on me.

She cleared her throat, brushing a curl from her face. "What am I going to do for you?"

I shot her a smug grin. "So glad you asked." I stepped back and strolled to the closet without taking my eyes off her while she kept still with her back against the wall. Either she was too scared to move, or too intrigued to look away.

Her eyes widened when I revealed the cello—and I wondered whether it was surprise or excitement that swirled in her eyes when she gazed at the instrument.

"You are going to play for me."

Her gaze snapped up to mine. "You know I can't."

"You can. And you will."

"Elijah—"

"Sit."

She frowned, snapping her mouth shut in a clear display of defiance.

I moved the navy-blue velvet ottoman with my foot and gestured toward it. "Sit down."

"I can't—"

"Sit the fuck down, Charlotte."

Her chest rose as she took a deep breath, her eyes uncertain as she stepped closer, one hesitant step at a time. It took every ounce of my self-control not to grab her, kiss her, consume her. The nightgown she wore fanned around her legs, the white silk accentuating her innocence and classic beauty. To me, Charlotte was the personification of classical music—an entire fucking orchestra on her own, able to make me feel things a man like me never should.

As she settled on the ottoman, I held out the cello, and she took it from me with an unsteady hand, staring at it as if she feared it. Like she feared whatever was about to happen next.

I pulled a scarf from one of the drawers, lacing it through my fingers while she watched me intently, too afraid to look away.

"Just do exactly as I say. Understand?"

"I can't—"

"Understand?" I raised my voice. Demanding.

She nodded in submission, but her eyes burned with an inner fight that tempted the fuck out of me. My life consisted of power, dominance, breaking people's souls. And with her, the thought of taking her fight, her strength, and owning it made my blood hum with excitement.

I placed the scarf over her eyes, tying it at the back before dragging my fingers down her curls. Soft, smooth, a fucking vision clutched in my fist.

"What are you doing?"

"I'm giving you what you need to play for me." I dragged my thumb along the arch of her top lip. "Darkness."

Guiding her hand, I let her take the bow, and then I moved in behind her, snaking my arm around her waist, pulling her close—her back against my chest. I leaned in over her shoulder and placed a hand on each of her thighs, winding the fabric up with my fingers until my palm met the warmth of her flesh—skin on skin. "Some of us need the darkness to flourish. The freedom that comes with the night allows us to be who we truly are, away from society's judgmental glares. Now," I brought my lips to her ear, "play for me."

She trembled, and I felt every shiver that wracked through her, radiating toward mine. All I wanted to do was drink her in, her scent, her body, the way it felt against mine. The softness of her long curls, the sight of her flawless skin—ivory fused with the simplicity of seduction. A lethal blend for a man like me. A man with a great appreciation for the classic and timeless pieces that brought light to a life that had only known the harsh reality of a never-ending eclipse.

I wanted to relish it all while she stilled the chaos in my soul with the beautiful music I knew she had within her.

"Now, imagine you're at the Alto," I whispered against her ear. "There's no one there...but me. *Only* me." My hand eased up her thigh, her skin warm and my touch hot. "Focus on the music in you. Let it out. Set it free."

Her body straightened, her posture firm and feet flat on the ground as she lifted the bow, her other hand touching the neck of the cello which rested against her heart. Even with an assumed threat like myself, sitting behind her, holding her captive in more ways than one—she still felt the music. She hadn't even played a single note, and already my soul was quiet, at peace.

I closed my eyes, waiting, foreknowing the bliss of the escape her music gifted me—the sound of her pursuit of perfection.

The moment her bow touched the strings, that first note awakening a need for more, I closed my eyes and allowed the silky, eloquent tenor to possess me. Nothing thawed the ice in my veins as the instrument's warm, sensuous tone that inspired so many great performers and composers.

"Hmmm," I moaned in appreciation. "*Camille Saint-Saëns', The Swan.*" A beautiful composition she had perfected with a talent that rivaled all others.

"Why music?" She kept the rhythm low, slow, and gentle.

I opened my eyes, her head leaning in the direction of where her fingers glided up and down the cello's neck. "Because nothing has the power to manipulate emotions the way music does," I whispered as not to hinder the music that filled the room, wall to wall, and floor-to-ceiling. "Music can make you feel whatever it wants you to. It can fuel happiness just as much as it can intensify a heartbreak."

"Why classical music? Orchestra?"

I smiled. "Who needs words when you have music?"

She started to sway, compelled to dance with the instrument. "Have we ever met, spoken before?"

"Shhh," I slipped my palm down toward the inside of her thigh, her skin like velvet against mine. "Play."

"Please," she begged me with a whisper, and I licked my lips.

"The night at the Alto when I left you the cello was the first and only means of contact I made with you."

"Why then?'

"I was foolish." A simple answer to such a complicated question. I didn't know why, I just felt compelled to do it. To give her the kind of masterpiece instrument her talent deserved to play.

I shifted closer, our bodies flush against one another as I allowed my touch to travel up her thigh.

"How many times have you watched me play?"

"Not nearly enough." My fingers touched her panties, and I felt her suck in a breath. "Whatever you do, do not stop playing."

"How can I play when you're—"

"Focus on the music, the sound," I traced a finger along her slit through her panties, "Let your emotions carry you."

It took a mere flick of my wrist to tear through the thin fabric of the hindrance that kept me from exploring her body in ways which my sins demanded. My finger brushed against her clit, and she whimpered, a sound that shot down my spine, crashing against the tip of my dick.

"Do you know how many nights I watched you play your cello? Witnessing how your body moves as the music carries you, the way your face shows every sound, every vibrato penetrating your soul?"

"Elijah, what are you doing?"

"The music, Charlotte. Don't stop playing."

I slipped my hand deeper between her thighs, her arousal coating my fingers. Fuck, I wanted to taste her. I wanted to bury my fucking face between her legs, lap and lick her cunt until she came on my tongue. *Not yet.*

"Elijah," she whimpered, and the pitch of the cello slipped as she lost her focus.

"Concentrate," I scolded, gripping her tighter against me.

"Don't."

"Don't what?" I murmured against the skin of her neck, allowing my lips to caress the sensitive flesh as I got high on her scent. "Should I not do this?" I grazed my thumb against the tiny bundle of nerves, and she stiffened against me, her arousal soaking my palm.

I leaned my head to the side so I could watch her beautiful face, her cheeks a sensual pink against the black scarf. "Or how about this?" I found her entrance and slid a single finger inside her. The most beautiful whimper left her lips, and she lost control of the bow, its snares causing high harmonics to scratch and cut the tempo of what was a perfect composition so far.

"Start again."

"I can't. Not with you touching me." Her voice was a mere whisper, and she rolled her head back, settling it on my shoulder, her raven hair brushing against my cheek. It smelled of orange blossom and coconut. Fresh, delicious...erotic.

I eased my finger out of her wet cunt and slipped it back in. This time harder, deeper. "I said. Start. Again."

"Jesus," she breathed, and her bow touched the strings, starting the piece from the beginning.

The music, her talent, her scent, her fucking arousal that pooled between her legs had my cock aching to find release inside her slick cunt. I wanted to feel her pussy wrap around me—stretching, throbbing, aching to come. My hips rocked behind her as I searched for friction to alleviate some of the pressure of my throbbing dick, my finger spreading her wetness to her clit—circling, teasing. Her legs trembled and thighs clenched, but this time she kept the music flowing without a hitch, without losing her focus. I massaged that tight bundle of nerves harder, faster with this cruel need to mindfuck her—tear her in two as I forced her to play that fucking cello while I played with her body.

"Elijah," she started, "please..."

"Please what?" I glanced at her parted lips, plump and pretty, begging to be kissed. "Tell me what you want."

Her hips rocked, demanding to be filled as I traced back to her entrance, allowing my fingertip to linger, my senses utterly consumed by her, hyperaware of her every breath and subtlest movement. "If you want to come, all you have to do is ask."

She snapped her lips shut, leaning her head more to the side, eyes closed—a beautiful display of defiance. A silent refusal to speak.

God, I loved this game.

"Your body is on the verge of snapping in half...isn't it? Your warm cunt is throbbing. It's aching for a release. I can give it to you. You just have to ask me."

A moan vibrated against her closed lips, her mind still fighting against her body's need to submit to the man who played the part of the monster.

I eased my finger into her completely, the smell of sex and arousal wrapping around us, pushing us closer to the edge with every breath. "If you don't ask me, I swear to Christ I won't let you come."

Finally, her lips parted, and I waited for her to say the words, to submit and hand me the victory. Because God knew, I loved the hunt. I loved the game. I thrived on it. It was like looking at my next victim through the scope of my M2010—waiting, breathing, relishing the power of deciding which moment would be their last.

Charlotte groaned, but her lips snapped shut, once again defying me, robbing me of the satisfaction of breaking her. Owning her.

God, I wanted to bend her over, fuck her until she screamed, taking her to the edge with my cock over and over again without allowing her to tip over. Torture her with the absence of a release until she fucking wept.

If she were any other woman, I'd do exactly that. But she

wasn't. She was the one person I couldn't hurt—at least, not without permission.

"You think you've won," I bit out between clenched teeth. "You haven't." I pulled my finger from her wet cunt, surprised when she grabbed my hand, wrapping her fingers around my wrists and keeping it there.

Both of us stilled, the silence deafening with the sudden absence of the cello's sound. My heart raced, and her chest heaved, the air between us buzzing with a wicked desire that had the potential to either crumble or explode.

Without saying a word, she guided my hand, silently searching for the feel of my fingers against her sensitive folds.

The bastard in me wanted to deny her, pull my hand back and walk away. But I couldn't. So, I watched her from the side without fucking blinking, my cock painfully hard, twitching as her heat wrapped around my finger once more.

There were no words, just feelings. Emotions. Like when she played the cello. Words weren't needed to know what she felt. It was inconsequential. Unnecessary noise in a world like ours, a world where music sang to our blood and spoke more truths than any words ever could.

I just prayed she'd be strong enough to survive what lay ahead, and that I would be able to protect her.

CHAPTER THIRTEEN
CHARLOTTE

It was insane. I knew this. There was no plausible reason for me to feel the way I did. Why my body burned for this man's touch. A man who snatched me from my world and thrust me into his, and I still had no clue why.

He hurt me. Kidnapped me. Killed a man, and confessed to many more. Yet here I was, seduced and submitted, craving a release my body had no right to demand. But there was something about him. Something familiar. Call me crazy, but was it possible that I knew about him lurking somewhere around me? That I knew he was watching me?

Maybe I did. Perhaps on some subconscious level I had always been aware of him silently watching me from the shadows. Could that have been possible? Or had I officially gone mad?

While his hand cupped my sex—stroking, touching, brushing—I felt something other than fear and hatred and cold terror. But in between the sensual longing and burning desire, there were many questions stacked in chaotic rows inside my head.

My father.
My grandfather.
Me.
Elijah.
My body craving his touch as if it had always known him.

Was this what insanity felt like? The voices tearing you apart, ripping you in two—your body and mind at war with each other?

His touch was hot, his presence heavy, and the longer I lingered within this high, the harder I would fall once I came down.

The blunt intrusion of his finger forced a whimper to slip from my lips, my hips rocking, rubbing myself against his palm.

So close. I was so fucking close I could feel it build all the way from my toes, growing stronger, demanding more.

He rubbed his cheek against mine as he leaned over my shoulder, one hand between my legs, the other gripping my hip. "If you come, I'll take it as an invitation to fuck you."

I leaned back, sinking into him, eyes closed and body willing as I kept control of his wrist, steadying his hand, while my hips rocked and swayed.

"You're close, aren't you? I can feel it. Your body is ready to fucking snap in half."

God. All I wanted was to tip over that ledge, to fall and drown in an endless abyss of depravity. Because that was what this was. Fucking depravity. A sordid kind of madness. An erotic game of power.

His hand traveled from my waist, his palm easing across

the soft white silk and covering my breast, kneading while the tension built, taking control of every muscle and every thought.

"Listen to me, Charlotte." His voice dipped low, husky, laced with a sensual allure that kissed every inch of my skin. "If you come around my finger, you better be prepared to come with my cock inside your cunt."

It was foul and vile, something a woman like me should have found insulting and disgusting. But instead, it was like oxygen around an open fire, spurring it on to burn brighter, fiercer.

I spread my legs wider, needing more, needing it fast and hard.

"Is that what you want, my little cellist? To be fucked by me, your stalker?" I whimpered as he pressed his lips against my ear. "Your psychopath?"

"Jesus." I launched up, the nightgown falling down my legs. My cheeks burned hot with embarrassment. "I'm sick of your goddamn games."

"Yet you rode my finger as if you loved playing."

"What the hell is this?"

He placed a palm on his crotch, the same palm he had between my legs a second ago, and adjusted himself before straightening. "This is a real fucked up situation with the potential to get so goddamn complicated we'll both drown in it. But here's the thing," he stalked closer while I stood my ground, "as long as you play for me with that cello settled between your legs, the entire world can burn down around me." He lifted his hand, cupped my cheek, and I could smell myself on his fingers. "I will have you, Charlotte. They won't take you from me. They'd have to kill me first."

"There you go again, talking about *they*. You keep going around in circles, giving me nothing."

He bit his lip, and like a goddamn veil, the mask of secrecy fell over his expression. "The less you know, the better."

"Bullshit. People always say that when, in fact, the more you know the better you can prepare yourself." My heart raced, and my mind was on the verge of fucking crashing. "First you mention my grandfather, my father—a man I have never seen before. God, my mom never even spoke about him. And now...now you're bringing him up like he's the fucking topic of a casual conversation."

He dragged his fingers through his hair, and the veins in his hand bulged. His silence was excruciating, and I had to fight the urge to wrap my hands around his neck and force the truth out of him.

"Tell me what the hell is going on, or I swear to God I will jump off this motherfucking yacht the second you're not looking." I was desperate and at the point where I'd threaten the goddamn Pope if I had to.

He sucked air through his teeth, the black fabric of his dress shirt adding more mystery to a man who already bathed in it.

Okay," he conceded, "I'll tell you everything you want to know."

Relief eased over my shoulders.

"Over dinner."

"Dinner?"

"You have to eat, Charlotte." He brushed past me toward the door. "I'll go prepare dinner, and then we can talk."

I arched a brow. "You cook?"

"There's so much more to me than just killing people." He glanced over his shoulder. "Maybe you'll be able to see that someday."

"And maybe you'll start to realize that there's more to me than just a cello."

He scoffed. "Do not fool yourself. That instrument is the largest part of who you are. The cello is in your blood."

The sound of his heavy footsteps resounded as he walked out, and all I could do was stare at the open door after he left. He didn't lock me in this time. No slam of the door or click of a lock. What did this mean? Could I trust it?

God, I'd be a fool if I did.

The weight of everything that had happened weakened me and forced me down as I fell on the bed, my back hitting the mattress.

I wasn't sure what fucked with my head more—the fact that he brought me two breaths away from an orgasm, or the fact that I liked it. That I didn't want him to stop. Every inch of my skin was sensitive, my sense of smell and touch heightened all because of him—my kidnapper. A confessed contract killer. What the hell did that make me? A masochist. An idiot. A profoundly stupid human being.

I counted the ceiling lights, twirling a curl around my finger. Eight lights cast the room under a blanket of cool white. To think that I had never traveled outside of the US, and here I was in Rome, yet I hadn't seen a sliver of it. Kidnapped, drugged, transported. All these years, I suspected the universe had some personal vendetta against me.

A talent for music threatened by an immune disorder.

The most beautiful man I had ever seen stained with the blood of his victims.

A trip to the world's most romantic city ruined by abduction.

All of this was just a giant vortex of one ultimate mindfuck, and my mind was teetering at the edge of breaking. The worst part? I was starting to wonder if he had to offer me my freedom, would I have left? Would I have left knowing this man knew my father, my grandfather—had the answers to so many questions—all for the sake of freedom?

At least, my version of freedom.

Would I have run if I had the chance? If I were totally honest with myself, I'd admit the answer would most likely have been no.

A defeated sigh brushed past my lips, and I forced myself to get up and get dressed.

There were two double-door closets filled with designer labeled clothing. Ralph Lauren, Donna Karan, Vera Wang. Ranging from dresses to skirts to blouses, rompers and stylish jumpsuits. The shoes and handbags alone made the closet look like a Louis Vuitton boutique. Who the hell was this person Elijah referred to as his friend?

An all-black, long-sleeve jumpsuit was the nearest thing I could find that remotely looked like something I would wear. The low-cut neckline revealed far more skin than I had hoped, so I wore my hair loose, hoping the curls would drape over my shoulders and down my chest to hide most of it.

"Miss Moore?"

My heart slammed against my chest as I turned, frightened by the unfamiliar voice.

A man dressed in a black suit, white shirt, and black tie

stood by the door like a goddamn powerhouse of pure muscle and brut. "Mr. Mariano said to escort you to the deck when you're ready."

"Who are you?"

"My name is James, Mr. Russo's head of security."

"Mr. Russo?"

He nodded. "The man who owns The Empress."

I scowled.

"This yacht," he clarified. "May I suggest a jacket or scarf? Autumn nights at sea could get quite chilly."

At sea. Italy. It still felt surreal.

I shook my head lightly. "Okay...um, give me a minute."

"Of course. I'll be right outside the door."

I smiled, trying my best not to show how damn awkward I felt. This wasn't my world, adorned with wealth, yachts, designer clothing, and heads of security prowling around in Armani suits.

Please, God, let there be alcohol at dinner.

I searched through what seemed like two hundred pairs of shoes and decided on a pair of black and silver closed-toe heel pumps about half a size too big for my feet, but it just had to do.

From the corner of my eye, I spotted the black scarf Elijah had blindfolded me with. The memory stirred the ache between my legs, my body still hellbent on proving desire was stronger than common sense.

I grabbed the scarf and wrapped it around my shoulders, hoping it was enough to ward off the autumn chill. Just as I was about to walk out, I glanced in the direction of the bed, sheets all ruffled and unmade. The perfectionist in me cringed as I bit my thumbnail, trying to suppress the need to smooth out the creases.

"Goddammit," I muttered to myself, succumbing to my pedantic tendencies, lifting the sheet and draping it over the bed, easing my palm across the silk until every crease was gone.

Plumping up the pillow, I glanced down at the bedside table and saw the bottle of perfume placed next to the crystal lamp.

Could it be…my perfume?

From the moment I woke, I was caught up in this whirlwind of madness, not noticing it before now.

I picked it up, my fingertips gently brushing against the blush pink glass bottle. A pang of grief snuck up on me as I turned it to look at the bottom, the tiny red heart doodled on the label sticker. It wasn't a new bottle, or a coincidence. This was *my* perfume, the bottle I bought for myself a few weeks ago.

"I've always wanted to know about that."

I didn't turn to face him.

"You worked two jobs, lived in a crummy apartment, and scraped by each day. Yet you managed to afford such an expensive brand of perfume."

My skin flushed as I listened to his footsteps approach and still right behind me.

"Why?"

I traced a fingertip along the little heart. "I would think that since you know me so well, you'd know why."

"Some things can't be learned by observance alone." He was so close, I could feel him breathe over my shoulder as his authority wrapped around me like I was already his. As if he had claimed me a long time ago.

"It was a gift from my mother on my sixteenth birthday," I started, my heart already hurting. "She said that perfume is the keeper of memories. That a scent can breathe life and color into a faded memory, and make it seem like yesterday." Tears prickled my eyes, and I took a deep breath before placing the bottle down on the table. "I've been buying myself this exact brand of perfume ever since, drawing that little heart on each one." I turned to face him, surprisingly unintimidated by how close he was. "How did you know to take this? To bring it here?"

"I knew it meant something to you, I just didn't know why." He reached up and brushed the back of his hand down my cheek. "You loved your mother."

"She was all I had." The truth in those words made my insides bleed. Not a day went by that I didn't think of her, miss her, long to hear her voice one last time.

I glanced down, making a steeple with my fingers. "She wasn't just my mom, Elijah. She was my best friend too." I couldn't fight the grief any longer. My heart, my soul, my body—all of me was just too fractured to pretend I could talk about her without breaking down.

A tear escaped, and I was back there in that dark hole. A place where I was alone, where I had nothing or no one to help ease the grief and the pain of losing not just my mother but a part of myself as well. I was completely and utterly alone. My tears were my own. My loneliness and heartache were my own.

It was a moment of profound weakness, the moment I crumbled beneath the overwhelming need for comfort, warmth, anything that could lessen the pain. And he was so close, so damn close, I couldn't fight it. I couldn't stop myself from leaning into him, pressing my cheek against his chest, weeping as if I had only lost her yesterday.

Perfume.
Memories.
Yesterday.

Little did I know that I had never truly broken down before. I had never allowed myself the freedom to cry and mourn and hurt without limitations. Thoughts of how I had to stay strong, how I had to keep moving on and live a life that stood still for no one, kept me from emptying my soul of the grief that had crippled me ever since.

But here, now, with him, I broke. I shattered. And I fell.

Into the arms of my captor.

The Musician.

CHAPTER FOURTEEN

ELIJAH

It wasn't the first time my mom took in a stray—a man who came packing with the promise of money to feed her drug addiction. Many had come and gone over the years, but Roland stayed, and even put a ring on Mom's finger. My guess was the others had half a brain to realize that fucking my mother wasn't worth the shit they had to put up with. Roland, on the other hand, was too much of an idiot to see it.

I sat at the top of the stairs watching him scratching his belly while laughing at some shit show or other on the television. My mom was in her room, covering up the bruises and getting high. Ellie was busy rummaging through the kitchen cupboards in search of something to eat. But I already knew there was nothing. The fat pig ate it all, stuffing his face like a savage, not caring that there were other hungry stomachs in the house as well.

"Ellie," I called, and she peeked out of the kitchen. "Come on. Let's go play cards in my room." It was code for 'I have food.' If I didn't keep my stash a secret, Roland would take it all and stuff his face, leaving nothing for us.

Ellie's blonde ponytail bobbed as she rushed up the stairs, her eyes gleaming with excitement. I stood, and she stilled next to me, glancing up. "Oh, no. What happened to your face?"

I touched my cheek, my skin still burning. "I fell over a log in the Johnsons' garden. That's all." There was no way I could tell her the bruise on my cheek was because Roland caught me taking money from his jacket pocket. I didn't see him come from behind. I just felt the blow against the side of my face, his large hand sending my bony ass skidding across the wooden floors, hitting my head against the wall.

I wasn't in the habit of stealing. But Ellie's birthday was in three days, and I just needed five more dollars so I could buy her the ballerina music box she wanted. Every time we passed the gift shop, she'd stop and lean against the window, her tiny palms flat against the glass, staring at the wooden music box. Sometimes, the shop attendant would turn the windup key and open it so Ellie could watch the ballerina turn to the most annoying music. Part of me hated that attendant for making my little sister want that damn box even more, yet Ellie loved every second of watching the ballerina twirl.

Luckily, Roland only saw the ten-dollar bill I had swiped from his pocket, and not the other dollar bills I had shoved inside my underpants two minutes before he caught me.

I was able to go to the gift store and buy the music box which played the most annoying tune, and it was safely hidden away in my room, wrapped with a pretty little pink bow.

I glanced down at the living room one more time before closing my bedroom door, latching the handle with the old wooden chair so no one could come in.

Ellie jumped on my bed, the spring coils squeaking. "Please tell me you have chocolate."

"Chocolate isn't food, Ellie." I opened my closet and fell to my knees, reaching all the way to the back and grabbing one of the old shoe boxes.

"You have a choice between canned chicken or beef jerky."

Ellie's face beamed. "Oh, that's easy."

"Beef jerky," we both said at the same time, and I tossed her the packet, along with a granola bar.

"Don't gobble it all down at once," I said as she tore it open, shoving the beef jerky into her mouth. "Ellie!"

"I can't help it," she mumbled with a full mouth. "I'm just so hungry."

A sharp pang ripped my chest. She was getting bigger, hungrier. Skinnier.

I glanced at the Twinkie still left in the box. I planned on giving it to her on her birthday, the closest thing she'd get to a birthday cake. But seeing her so damn hungry left me no choice but to give it to her.

"Here." I placed it in front of her on the bed.

"A Twinkie?" Her eyes lit up, the tiny freckles moving as she wiggled her nose. "You got me a Twinkie?"

"Yeah."

"Where's yours?" She glanced at the now empty box and back at me.

"I ate mine earlier," I lied. If she knew I didn't have one, she'd want to share hers.

"You dummy." She slapped me on my shoulder. "You should have kept it so we could eat it together."

I smiled. "Would you have been able to wait that long if you knew there was a Twinkie for you?"

She took a large bite. "Probably not. Do you think Mom will remember my birthday this year?"

I settled down next to her, knowing the bitter answer. "Maybe," I lied again. But I didn't have the heart to disappoint her yet. She had three more days to hope.

A sudden bang on the door had both of us on our feet.

"Where are you, you little mutts?" Roland yelled. "Get your bony fucking asses out here." He tried opening the door, the handle rattling against the chair. "Open this motherfucking door."

I stepped in front of Ellie, shielding her. My heart hammered, and I prayed the chair would hold.

"Elijah, you little fucking thief. I know you took money from me."

"Did you?" Ellie whispered over my shoulder, but I shooshed her.

"I had two hundred-dollar bills in my pocket. Where is it?" This time he hammered against the door, pieces of wood cracking next to the hinges. "Elijah, I swear to God if you don't give me my money back, I will beat your bony ass to a pulp."

"Elijah," Ellie whispered, "I'm scared."

"No. It's okay."

"Did you take his money?"

"Of course not." This time I was innocent. I didn't take the fat pig's money. Besides, I wasn't that stupid to steal two hundred dollars. The times I did steal from him, I made sure I didn't take too much, so he wouldn't notice there was money missing.

"Open this goddamn door, boy."

My heart was beating in my throat as I struggled to push down the fear.

"Elijah." Ellie grabbed my arms and pressed her body flush against my back. "I'm scared."

"Get under the bed." I grabbed her wrist and forced her to the ground. "Stay there. Do not come out. Understand?"

She nodded frantically as tears welled up in her eyes, her face pale with fear. God, I hated it, seeing her so damn scared.

I shot to my feet as a loud crack sounded, the door breaking in half as it hit the floor.

Roland rushed in, his face red and eyes wild, glaring at me from across the room. "You better give me my money back, boy."

"I didn't take your money." I inched back.

"Liar. I had two hundred dollars in my pocket this morning, and now it's gone."

"I didn't take it!"

"You little shit." He launched at me, but I ducked out of the way, and he slammed into my desk, my lamp falling and shattering on the floor.

"I swear, it wasn't me," I yelled at him and glanced down to make sure Ellie was still hidden.

"What is going on here?" My mom walked in, looking worse than shit with one eye swollen shut, her skin blotched and hair a mess.

"Your piece of shit son stole from me, that's what's going on."

Mom glared at me, yet she could hardly stand. "Is that true?"

"No! I didn't steal anything."

"You fucking liar!" Roland grabbed the stapler that stood on the desk and threw it in my direction. I ducked, and it hit the closet door. "I caught him with his hand in my pockets this morning. That's what earned him that fucking bruised face. But seems like I didn't beat you hard enough."

It was an impulse, an instinct when I glanced at my mom, hoping she'd say something now that she knew her boyfriend beat me. But she remained unmoved, an empty vessel of festering flesh.

Roland looked down toward the bed, and my heart stopped. Ellie.

"Well, well, well. What do we have here?"

I darted toward him when he crouched, pulling Ellie from under the bed by her ankle. "Leave her alone!"

He reached out and grabbed me by my throat while jerking Ellie to her feet. "If you didn't steal from me, then it has to be this little shit."

"It wasn't me," she cried while trying to get away from him. But he grabbed her by her ponytail and yanked her back, causing her to cry out in pain.

My insides exploded, rage swallowing my fear. "Let her go!" I yelled, kicking while his fingers tightened around my throat. But I cared more about getting Ellie away from him than I did about my next breath.

"Aww," Roland mocked, his fat face that of pure evil. "Look at you, all protective over little sis. What the fuck do you think you can do with that bony ass of yours? You couldn't even protect a goddamn fly if you tried."

"Mom!" I called. "Please, stop him."

I scratched at his hand, clawing at his skin. But he didn't even flinch, and Mom didn't move. She just stood there, a miserable void.

Ellie's cries pierced my ears, and I watched helplessly as Roland pulled her tiny body up by her ponytail and threw her against the wall like she was nothing but a ragdoll.

"Ellie!"

She didn't move.

"Ellie!" I cried. "Ellie, get up."

Nothing.

"Ellie! Mom, help her! Help her, please!"

Mom merely glanced from me to where Ellie lay eerily still. Something was wrong. Everything was wrong.

The empty beef jerky packet slipped from the bed and onto the floor, right in front of Roland's feet.

"You little shits were stealing food as well?" He lifted me, my feet dangling from the floor while his hold tightened, my lungs crying out for air. "You're nothing bust wasted fucking space. You better hope your sister is dead, because if she isn't... I have a friend who would love to take her off my hands." He cackled like a maniac, and my thoughts went quiet and body numb. "And believe me, she'll be better off dead."

"Please," I whispered, the edges of my sight dimming, growing darker. "Don't...hurt..."

It went black.

"So, why the bodyguard?" Charlotte gestured toward James, who sat by the bar, back turned toward us and out of ears' reach.

"Precaution."

"Why?"

"James is the head of security of one of the most powerful men in Italy."

"This friend you mentioned?"

I nodded. "Marcello Saint Russo. He has eyes and ears everywhere, which is exactly what we want right now."

I glanced in James' direction, specifically at the cellphone placed on the marble countertop next to his hand. If that phone had to ring, it would be to signal that shit was about to hit the fan, and our plan B would be compromised... and we'd be fucked.

Charlotte glanced around, her gaze soaking up the pristine interior surroundings of a yacht with a fifteen-million-euro price tag.

"If you think this is impressive," I waved around, "wait until you see the outside."

She bit her lip and dropped her gaze, staring down at her fingers in her lap. So innocent. Naïve. Unsullied by the tainted riches this world offered in return for your fucking soul.

I watched Charlotte from across the table, something I was fucking good at. She could be stubborn, act strong, appear resilient, but her face reflected her genuine emotion. It was there in the way she'd suck on her bottom lip when she felt insecure. The way her eyes would change from sky-blue to sapphires when she got excited, and how her cheeks would glow a resplendent pink when she was shy...or aroused.

Behind her defiance, her fight was a delicate soul and a fragile heart. So easily breakable. For the coldhearted bastard side in my dark soul, who liked to break things, her fragile existence was a temptation that plagued me. I wanted to know how far she'd bend before she broke, how strong her mind could be before it shattered. But there was a different part in me I had long forgotten, a sliver of my humanity her beauty and innocence had reminded me of—a part which grew stronger the more I lingered around her.

When she cried into my chest earlier, breaking in my arms, it felt foreign having someone search for comfort from me. The last time anyone needed any type of solace by being close to me was the night Ellie had snuck into my room and snuggled up behind my back for the last time. I remembered how annoyed I was with her over waking me after I had cleaned two of the neighbors' yards that day. Little did I know that would be the last night my little sister slept beside me.

I OPENED *my eyes and immediately knew it wasn't my room when I looked up at the ceiling. This one didn't have clots of dried paper stuck to it, paper I'd chew and shoot through a straw whenever I was bored.*

The bed squeaked as I pushed myself up on my elbows, glancing around. It was Ellie's room, the dirty pink curtains torn at the seams and hanging off half the curtain rod. The only two dolls she had were placed on the old bedside table, the paint peeling off the sides. Next to it stood the music box, the one I bought Ellie for her birthday, but never got the chance to give it to her. What was it doing here? Did they find it?

Oh, no. Ellie. Where was she? Why was I in her room?

The memories of Roland, and Ellie, and my mom exploded into my head, and I leapt off the bed. "Ellie! Ellie, where are you?"

I tripped over the dirty carpet which was once a pretty purple, but now mucky gray.

"Ellie!" I tried to open the door, but it was locked. "Ellie!" I kept screaming, slamming my fists against the door. "Where is Ellie?"

All I remembered was Roland throwing her, her tiny body hitting the wall, making the most sickening sound. Or maybe it was my heart that broke. Either way, she didn't get up. She didn't move.

"Let me out! Ellie!"

The click of the lock made me step back, my heart racing at a million beats per second. Roland appeared, his large frame, broad shoulders, and fat belly blocking almost the entire entryway.

"Where is my sister?"

"Who?" He slanted a brow, his dirty green eyes glaring in my direction.

"Ellie. Where is Ellie?"

"I'm sorry, Elijah. But I don't know who you're talking about."

My skin went cold, chills slithering around my body. "My sister. Ellie." My nostrils flared. "Where is she?"

Mom stepped in behind Roland, glancing around him. "What is going on?"

"Your son is acting fucking crazy again."

"No. What?" I frowned. "I'm not crazy."

Roland pointed at me, his lips curled as he leaned closer to my mom. "Do you know an Ellie?"

Her eyes met mine, a moment of recognition flashing between us. It was a single second of unspoken truth, until she opened her mouth and spat out the lies.

"We don't know an Ellie, Elijah."

"No." I shook my head. "You're lying. Where is she?"

"We're not lying, son." She stepped in, watching me with caution. "There's no Ellie here."

"This is her room!" I shouted. "This is her bed, her toys. Her clothes." I pointed at the broken laundry basket in the corner.

My mom picked up one of the dolls. "Elijah, this is Harley's room. Roland's daughter. You remember her?"

I shook my head vigorously, my hands trembling.

"She visits us every second weekend. She was here two days ago."

God, I was so confused. My mind was like a maze of things that made no sense.

"I'm not crazy," I bit out between clenched teeth. I was so scared and so angry, I want to run and throw up at the same time. But I knew I wasn't crazy. Ellie's face and the memories were just too real to be a lie. "You killed her...didn't you?"

Something dark flashed in Roland's eyes, every crease and crinkle of his face drenched in evil.

"You hurt her. You killed her." I sucked in a breath. "Didn't you!" I screamed so loud, I was sure the neighbors heard, but I still didn't care. I hoped they heard. I hoped they'd send help so I could find Ellie.

"Listen, boy." Roland walked past my mom, shoving her to the side. "I won't tolerate your lies. I don't care how crazy you are."

He reached inside his jacket pocket and pulled a needle out. "Now, you need to calm down, son."

"Don't call me son," I seethed. I wanted to spit in his face like a poisonous viper. "Stay away from me." I inched back, regarding the threat in front of me, glancing at the needle in his hand. "What is that?"

"It's just your medicine, Elijah," my mom chimed in, her face more pale than usual. "It will help you relax."

"No." I pursed my lips, my back hitting the windowsill. "Don't come near me."

It took Roland no more than three steps to close the distance between us, but I dodged him, ducked underneath his arm, and ran toward the door. But someone grabbed my elbow and pulled me back.

My mom.

My own mother.

"Please, Elijah," she urged as she grabbed my other arm. "We just want to help you."

Tears slipped down my face, yet all I felt was hate as I looked at her. For the first time in my life, since this nightmare with her started, I hated her. I wanted her dead. I wanted to watch her die and pray to God that he wouldn't have mercy on her soul.

I sucked air through my teeth and leaned closer. "You know her. You know Ellie. Your daughter."

"No, son." Her eyes softened with something that mirrored compassion. But it couldn't be. My mom was incapable of feeling anything but a rush and a high. "I don't know who Ellie is."

"That's a lie," I bit out, and then felt the prick of the

needle into my arm. "I hate you," I whispered. "I hope you rot in hell."

CHARLOTTE PLACED her fork down and took a sip of her white wine, her plate of seabass fillet and zucchini hardly touched.

I lifted a brow. "Something wrong with your food?"

"No. It's perfect. I'm just...feeling a bit out of sorts." She placed her glass down. "You made this?"

I nodded.

"You're a good cook."

"I'm good at a lot of things."

She looked at me from under her long, thick lashes, pulling her lips in a straight line, knowing exactly what I was insinuating.

"So, this yacht," her blue-gray eyes glanced around, "it's quite something."

"Saint has a taste for the ridiculously expensive." I took a bite of the seabass, its taste mild, delicate, buttery —perfection.

"How exactly do you know this Saint person?"

"A mutual friend."

"How about an answer that's slightly less vague?"

I shrugged, taking another bite of my food, making no attempt to further the conversation. It didn't sit well with me to discuss matters that included work, acquaintances, or anything about my life. A man like me built his entire professional foundation on discretion and confidentiality. We didn't fucking talk.

"You said you were going to tell me everything."

"I was hoping we could get through dinner first before we discussed other matters."

She leaned back in her seat, the night sky casting beautiful shadows across her face. "I'd rather we get all the secrets out in the air first."

"Will you eat once I've told you everything?"

"That depends on what you're going tell me."

"I'm serious, Charlotte. You have to eat. Bribing and force-feeding are not beyond me."

"And neither is killing people." She crossed her arms.

"You know," I wiped my mouth with the napkin and placed it on the table, "you seem to have this need to remind me of my...*profession* every chance you get. As if you think it's something I can forget."

"Oh, no, you have it wrong. It's me I have to keep reminding." She reached for the bottle of wine, filling her third glass for the evening. I understood her need to numb the chaos with alcohol. God knew, I had done the same more times than I cared to remember.

She took a sip, her luscious lips kissing the brim of the crystal glass. My cock stirred as I watched her swallow, her delicate throat practically begging me to trace my tongue along its arch.

"Let's start with my father. How do you know him?"

"I don't." I eased back in my seat. "I know *of* him."

"Great. That makes two of us," she sneered, sampling her wine.

"I know your grandfather. Gianni Guerra." I studied her closely. "He used to work for the Cosa Nostra."

She frowned. "The Cosa who?"

"Cosa Nostra, also known as the Italian mafia."

Her eyes widened. "Mafia? Are you serious?"

"Very." I shot her a stern look, showing her exactly how fucking serious I was. "Gianni Guerra used to work for the Bernardi family."

"As what?"

"A contractor."

"That's like code for hitman, right?"

I nodded.

"Jesus." She took a sip of her wine, followed by a larger gulp, closing her eyes as she swallowed. "Okay," her shoulders lifted as she inhaled deeply, "where do you fit in? How do you know my grandfather? No, wait," she held up her hand, "where do I fit into all this? Why am I here?"

"You—"

"Wait. Wait." She closed her eyes. "Who is the Bernardi family?"

"They—"

"No, wait." She scrunched her nose as if thinking caused her physical pain. "Jesus, wait. Hold on." The ice clinked against her glass as she swallowed last of it, cringing. "I literally do not know where to start."

I sat up, placing my hands on the table. "Then how about you just keep quiet and listen?"

Her plump lips pursed, and she crossed her arms, conceding with a silent huff.

"Your grandfather was a member of the Italian mafia, a soldier for the Bernardi family. For years, he carried out various...assignments for them."

"Killing people?"

"Among other things. But yes, silencing those who betrayed the family, owed them, and those who planned on talking against them was your grandfather's main area of expertise."

She scoffed. "I love how you talk about mafia and killing people as if it's this normal thing in the world."

"It is in mine."

Our gazes fused, neither of us blinking—her defiance versus my dominion. Soon she'd realize that going against me was just a waste of fucking time.

"Your grandfather," I started again, "knowing the life of a mafioso, the dangers, the threats, he never married."

"But how—"

I silenced her with a glare. "This would go much faster if you'd just shut up and listen."

"Sorry." She bit her lip, and I had to fight the urge to leap across the goddamn table so I could be the one to bite that enticing as fuck bottom lip of hers.

"Gianni fell for a girl, but he knew loving her would send her to an early grave. So, he did the noble thing and left without knowing she was pregnant."

She glanced down, and I could see in the look on her face ten new fucking questions just popped into her head.

I poured her more wine, knowing she needed it, then filled my own glass. "Gianni eventually found out about his son—"

"My father," she breathed.

"But knowing he had a son made him more determined to keep his distance."

Charlotte tightened her crossed arms, resentment swirling in the blue hues of her eyes. "What kind of man does that? Deliberately staying away from his own flesh and blood?"

"The kind of man who puts their safety above his own need to know his son. The kind of man who spends every day of his life missing the memories he never had of a son he didn't know. A son who ended up being nothing more than a drunk. A man who abandoned his wife while she was pregnant." I leaned my head to the side, watching her face, her expression. "A man who got stabbed in a drunken brawl and died on the pavement outside a whorehouse."

Charlotte's throat bobbed as she swallowed, her jaw clenched and eyes shimmering with tears she was determined to bite back. There were so many other ways for me to tell this part, to lighten the blow of her father's death. But the truth was, no matter how you tried to ease your way around the cold, hard reality, it still fucking hurt. It was best just to rip the Band-Aid off and let it bleed.

She looked away, staring out the closed stacking doors which shielded us from the cold night air. I wanted us to have dinner out on the deck tonight, but the weather proved to be a dick.

I remained silent for a while, giving her some time to digest the fact the father she had never known was dead, and all hope of ever meeting him was gone.

"I'm an orphan," she said softly before taking a deep breath, appearing to steel herself. "Lucky for me, you can't mourn something you never had. He might as well never have existed."

I settled back. "That doesn't make him any less real, Charlotte."

IT HAD BEEN WEEKS. *Maybe days. Maybe years.*

I didn't know.

I didn't care.

They had locked me in my room, pretended I was crazy while I rocked myself in the corner staring at the wall Roland had thrown Ellie against.

At least, the wall I thought he had thrown Ellie against. That was if Ellie even existed.

According to them, I was crazy. I didn't have a sister named Ellie, only a stepsister. Harley.

Every day, Roland would come in here with a tray of food, suddenly caring enough to feed me. He'd be dressed up real nice, pretended to be concerned about my well-being, reminding me how broken my mind was.

Every day, he'd say the same thing, like a rhyme, over and over again. 'You're different, Elijah. Your mind works differently than a normal person's would. It's unique, but broken. And this Ellie person you say is your sister, she's not real."

Oh, but she was. Her face was as real to me as the bullshit that oozed out of his mouth. I didn't tell him that, though. I soon learned that fighting him, screaming Ellie's name, earned me another prick in the arm, and then...darkness.

I hadn't seen my mom since the day she betrayed me by taking Roland's side, both of them pretending and insisting I was crazy. She shattered something in me that day, and the part in me that felt, the part that hurt so damn much I could hardly breathe...I shut it off. I compartmentalized and shoved it back in my mind, making sure it would never surface again.

Knowing her, she was probably high, drunk, or passed out.

It was a Sunday morning, and the only reason I knew that was because of the church bells that rang and chimed for what seemed like hours. But apparently, my mind was too broken even to be annoyed by it.

Keys rattled, and the doorknob turned, but I didn't even bother to turn and look, knowing it was Roland bringing me my first and only meal of the day.

The hinges squeaked as the door creaked open. "Elijah, I have someone here who would like to see you."

No matter how gentle his voice sounded, how compassionate he pretended to be, it still grated at my bones.

I stopped rocking, glancing halfway over my shoulder. All I saw was this tiny figure and the striking light, honey-blonde hair. My heart, stomach, and lungs all coiled together, and I fell over my own two feet as I stumbled to get up, my legs weak and arms numb.

"Ellie?" God, it had been so long. Days, weeks, an infinity of time spent thinking of her, imagining her sweet face and gentle voice. There were times Roland was so convincing I found myself doubting my own sanity more than once.

"Ellie!" I exclaimed, putting one foot in front of the other, wanting to run to her, wanting to hug her and thank God she was okay.

"Elijah, stop!" Roland stepped in front of me, blocking Ellie off. "Calm down, son."

"I am not your son," I hissed, glaring up at his giant frame.

"Listen." He placed his hands on my shoulders, but I shrugged out of his hold, growling at him like I would tear him apart at any moment. I wanted to. I wanted to pop his eyes from his skull and cut his damn tongue out. I dreamed about peeling the skin off his bones with the blunt potato peeler down in the kitchen drawer.

"Listen, boy." He held out his hands and urged Ellie to step in next to him while wrapping an arm around her shoulder. "This isn't Ellie."

"What? No." I looked at her, those familiar green-brown irises staring at me. "That's Ellie. I told you I wasn't crazy. Ellie, come here." I held out my arms, wanting to get away from the monster, but she wrapped her hands around his leg and leaned into him.

My skin turned cold and clammy. "Ellie. It's me. Elijah."

She placed her little, round cheek against his knee. "My name isn't, Ellie," she said softly. "I'm Harley."

CHAPTER FIFTEEN

CHARLOTTE

It was hard to put into words what I was feeling. There was no reason for me to feel gutted by the knowledge that my father was dead. I didn't know him at all. I had never even seen a picture of him. But there was this dull ache in my chest. Disappointment, maybe. Perhaps, somewhere deep inside, I had always hoped my father would one day just knock on the door, suddenly wanting to be a part of my life.

I cleared my throat, the wine already stirring a buzz in my veins. "Okay, so my father is dead. Where's my grandfather? Gianni?"

Elijah dragged a hand through his hair, placing his wine glass down, rubbing his thumb and forefinger around the thin stem. "He's in prison—a special prison for mafia informers in Northern Italy."

"Oh, my God." It was almost comical, the amount of irony I had been slapped with. An absent father who turned out to be dead, and a grandfather I never even thought about being stuck in prison. "You know what, I'm not even going to be upset over any of this." I threw my hands in the air. "Just cut to the part where you tell me how all this affects me. Why you went from hitman, to stalker, to kidnapper."

His dark brows drew together clearly, unamused, but I was one glass of white wine past giving a rat's ass.

Elijah stood from his seat and removed his gray jacket, placing it over the chair, and started to roll up his dress shirt sleeves. Of course, all my attention had to drift to his arms—strong arms I had felt around me, the taut muscles and bulging veins covered with flawlessly tanned skin.

"James, would you mind throwing me a glass of whiskey? And bring the bottle too."

James nodded, and Elijah sat back down waiting for his drink. The ice clinked against the crystal as he took a large sip and placed it back down.

I crossed my legs under the white oak dining table. "What is it?"

"What?"

"Whatever you're about to tell me." I gestured toward his whiskey. "Clearly, it's one hell of a bomb you're about to drop on me since you need liquid support to do it. Just tell me."

For the longest time, his gaze lingered on mine. It was like a sea of secrets and mysteries, a vortex of all the darkest parts he tried to hide.

"A year before you mother died, Gianni turned himself in."

"Why would he do that?"

Elijah weaved his fingers together on his lap. "He turned himself in, hoping he could strike a deal."

"What kind of deal?"

"A deal that would protect...you."

"Me?" Confusion dropped like dead weight around my shoulders, my thoughts suddenly eerily quiet. "Why would he want to protect me? He doesn't even know me."

"The day your grandfather found out about your mother's cancer, plans had been put in motion."

"What plans?"

"Plans to ensure that you wouldn't be alone."

"Why now? After all these years, he suddenly cares about me now?"

"Everything he's done, he did to protect you."

I shot to my feet. "You expect me to believe a man who has never worried about me or my mother in the past now suddenly made this huge fucking sacrifice to protect me?" My heart was beating so damn fast, I was sure James could hear it from across the room.

"Sit down, Charlotte."

"No. I won't sit down."

He darted up, and slammed his hands on the table, cutlery and glasses shaking and rattling like his anger had just become an earthquake. "Sit. The fuck. Down."

He tilted his head, eyes filled with warning. All it took was a simple glare, a brief scowl, and I cowered under his silent authority, slowly easing back into my seat. I hated that he had this kind of power over me, as if he owned me. Like I was his fucking lapdog who would obey his every command.

Elijah's expression remained hard and unreadable as he slowly sat back down. "Are you ready to listen, or are you planning on throwing another temper tantrum?"

"I'm not a child."

"Then stop acting like one and fucking listen."

"I am listening. It's not my fault nothing you say makes any sense."

He scoffed and diverted his gaze across the room. "I knew you'd be hard to tame."

I crossed my arms. "I'm not a goddamn animal who needs taming, Elijah. And frankly, I don't even know if I need to hear all of this. I spent my whole life surviving without a father or a grandfather, and I'm still alive and breathing. So, my guess is I don't need this mysterious grandfather who just decided to pop up out of fucking nowhere."

He scoffed, the vein in his neck throbbing. "He was always there, Charlotte. You just never saw him. How the fuck do you think your mom was able to pay the bills? Do you think her half-decent wage from being in an orchestra was enough to put you through school, pay for a roof over your heads, and have food on your goddamn table every day?"

"I'm well aware that her job didn't pay well," I spat out, "but we received monthly payments from my—"

"—grandmother's life insurance?"

My heart turned inside out, pounding against my throat. I could feel all the blood in my body drain to my cheeks.

"Your mother came from a low-income family, Charlotte. Do you really think they could afford life insurance?"

My entire world spun off its axis, like I got sucked through a giant vortex of lies and deceit. As if I had lived a life that was never really mine.

"It was him," I murmured.

"He sent the money pretending it was coming from some

bullshit life insurance company so there was no trace back to him."

I fell back in my seat, dropping my gaze to the barely eaten seabass on my plate. The sight and smell of food suddenly made me sick to my stomach while I struggled to digest everything Elijah was throwing at me.

"Now, may I continue, or can I expect more rude interruptions from you?" His condescending tone pissed me off, but I was big enough to admit when I was cornered, and nodded reluctantly.

"Good." He leveled me with his stare. "Gianni turned himself in to protect you, hoping the deal he struck would grant him a new identity, and then he'd be able to"—he pressed his lips in a thin line, clearly searching for the right words—"be a part of your life without having to constantly look over his shoulder."

I narrowed my eyes, my head about to snap in fucking half as I struggled to grasp the magnitude of what Elijah was telling me. "So, surrendering, this deal he made was because he wanted to be in my life?" Disbelief dripped from my every word. "My grandfather is stuck in a prison somewhere because of me?"

Elijah shook his head. "Not because of you...*for* you. He didn't want to repeat the same mistake he made with your father. He wants to know you, Charlotte. He wants to be there for you in ways he can't if he's still Gianni Guerra. His past sins won't allow it."

"Jesus." I pulled my palms down my face, not knowing whether I wanted to cry or scream. Maybe a little bit of both, but my insides crawled, as if I would jump out of my skin at any moment. "Which prison?" I asked without looking at him.

"A prison that protects mafia informers. He was hoping he'd be out by now, but unfortunately, it seems there's a lot of shit happening behind the scenes, and it delayed the process."

"What things?"

"I can't be sure." Elijah's expression darkened as a heaviness descended around us, the air almost too thick to breathe. "But Gianni has enough information to lock away a lot of bad people for ten fucking lifetimes."

And like a fucking mudslide of fifty-ton boulders, it hit me. It struck me right in the gut, leaving me breathless and ice fucking cold. "And that's why I need protection," I whispered, my every muscle numb. "Back in New York, someone was trying to...kill me?"

Elijah didn't move. He didn't even blink, giving me nothing to confirm what I was saying was right. But he didn't need to. I knew I was right. Pieces of the puzzle were starting to slip into place, and yet, the more I placed together, the more distorted the picture became.

Elijah shot back the rest of his whiskey, cringing as he slammed the glass down on the table, still not giving me an answer. God, he could hardly look at me.

"So, this means all these bad people, they know about me, that I'm Gianni's granddaughter?"

His shoulders rose as he inhaled deeply. "Yeah."

"And now they want me dead, to what? Keep my grandfather from talking?"

"Oh, no. They know if they kill you, Gianni will sing like a motherfucking bird to every goddamn press and journalist who will listen. No," he shook his head, "they don't want to kill you, Charlotte. They want to use you as collateral. As long as they have you, they know Gianni won't talk."

Ice pierced my chest. "So, my grandfather is the informer, and I'm the surety these *people* need to keep him quiet."

Elijah nodded, his eyes reflecting a sliver of sympathy.

"And you?" I toyed with my thumb cuticles on my lap. "Who are you supposed to be in this war?"

With his nostrils flaring, jaw clenched, and every ounce of air sucked out of the room, Elijah placed a hand on the table, tapping his finger. "I'm the man who owes your grandfather a debt. And kidnapping you, bringing you here...is me paying that debt."

CHAPTER SIXTEEN

ELIJAH

Every day I recited the same sentence over and over.
I'm not crazy.

I'm not crazy.

I'm not crazy.

I wasn't crazy. Harley was Ellie. Ellie was my little sister. But Roland kept telling me otherwise. I expected these kinds of lies from a bastard like him, but what I didn't understand was how they got Ellie to lie. How he brainwashed Ellie into playing along, pretending she was Harley. My stepsister. That monster's flesh and blood.

Maybe it wasn't Ellie. The girl Roland brought in here the other day sure looked a lot like her, but he didn't allow me to get close to her. Maybe it was a trick of the mind, my subconscious so damn desperate for Ellie to be alive I only saw what I wanted to see. I had to get Roland to let me see that little girl again so I could make sure.

What would have been worse?

Ellie pretending to be Harley, proving that Roland had brainwashed my little sister somehow?

Or Harley not being Ellie at all, proving that Roland killed her exactly the way I remembered it—throwing her body against a wall as if she were a puppet?

My stomach curdled at the thought, and I had to get up and move. Pace. Walk up and down from one wall to the other, trying to forget about the memories that crawled across my skin like insects, trying to find a way in so they could infect me. Turn me into rotten flesh like my mom.

I stood in front of the window and stared out on the street. The neighbors' gardens and driveways needed cleaning. But I no longer had a reason to get blisters on my fingers from working for money so I could feed Ellie.

A man walked up to the stop sign across the road carrying what looked like a guitar case. I sat down on the windowsill and watched him as he adjusted his classic striped beret hat, wiping snow from the shoulders of his gray coat. He was probably one of those street performers, about to play his guitar, hoping someone would stop and drop him their change.

"Elijah?"

I looked up at the sound of my mom's voice. It was the first time I had seen her since the day she refused to help me save Ellie, playing along with Roland's scheme to cover up the truth.

Her hair was a mess, her eyes framed with dark circles and lines a thirty-eight-year-old woman shouldn't have. There was almost nothing left of her—just a sack of pathetic bones and broken dreams.

She walked in and picked up the bucket I used to pee in.

THE VILLAIN

"Is Roland tired of cleaning my piss?" I glowered at her. "Now he's sending you to do it?"

"He'll be here soon. Go take a shower."

"I don't want to."

"Go take a fucking shower, Elijah. You stink. This fucking room stinks."

"I don't care if I stink. I'm crazy, remember?" I crossed my arms and leaned against the wall. "You've been smelling like vomit and piss for as long as I can remember. Maybe we are the same."

Her tired eyes flashed, and she walked up to me, nostrils flaring, lips curled and exposing her decayed teeth. "You little bastard."

She hit me, her palm leaving a red-hot sting on my cheek. "Ungrateful little shit."

"Ungrateful?" I didn't cower away. At the age of ten, I was already taller than she was. "Tell me, Mom. What should I be grateful for, exactly?" I stepped up to her, and she inched back. "The fact that you haven't been a mother to Ellie and me since Dad died?"

"Elijah."

"The fact that you chose drugs over us? Getting high rather than feeding your own children?"

"Shut up," she warned with a hiss, yet continued to slither back as I stalked closer.

"Or should I be thankful that you allowed your psycho husband to kill Ellie, and pretend like I'm the crazy one?"

Her bottom lip trembled, her eyes wide and shimmering with unshed tears. Usually when Ellie's eyes saddened, tears slipping down her cheeks, I'd feel this immense need inside me to comfort her. To do whatever I could to make whatever was hurting her okay again. But with my mom, staring at her sorrow-filled irises...I felt. Nothing.

There wasn't a glint of sympathy or compassion that shimmered inside me for a mother who was nothing more than wasted space. My heart was as black as her soul, and as dead as the love she hadn't shown either Ellie or me.

Her back hit the wall, and she dropped the bucket of piss on the wooden floors. The stench was horrid, but not as vile as this woman's face in front of me. It felt good to see how intimidated she was with me standing an inch from her, glaring at her like she was the spawn of satan. But I wasn't stupid. I knew half of her paranoia was thanks to the poison she injected into her veins. Ellie and I and endured countless nights of her crying and screaming, thinking there were people after her—monsters trying to cut her ankles off. It was terrifying to witness it, but now I loved the memory of seeing her like that.

Scared.

Panicked.

Sick.

"I know what you and Roland are trying to do, trying to convince me that I'm crazy so you can cover up whatever it was you did to Ellie." I watched her, studied her, hating every contour of her face. "At least being crazy has its perks. I can kill you and blame it on the voices inside my head."

"What did you just say?"

Roland towered in the doorway, the red T-shirt he wore barely covering his belly, his faded jeans torn at the seams.

"Did I hear you correctly? Did you just threaten your mother?"

I inched back, narrowing my eyes as I regarded him with

caution. It was one thing to be able to intimidate a woman as weak and timid as my mother, but Roland was a completely different threat. I'd been on the receiving end of his big hands and hard fists before. The man was a mountain of malice, and he could easily kill me...as I suspected he did Ellie.

Roland's eyes glowed like a predator's in the night, and a low growl tore from his throat as he launched forward, grabbing me around my neck. It was just like that night, the night he took Ellie from me. His fingers bit into my skin, pressing down on my throat, causing me to choke and gasp for air.

"I've had enough of you, boy. I have tried everything I possibly can to help you, but clearly you do not want to be helped." His grip tightened, and my feet lifted off the ground. "I can tolerate your insane accusations of murder, killing someone who doesn't even exist—"

"Ellie is real!" I clawed at his arm.

"I can deal with just about anything you throw our way, boy, but I will not stand by and allow you to threaten your mother."

"Screw you," I spat out. "Kill me. Do to me what you did to Ellie. I don't care, you hear me? I don't care anymore."

I wanted to die.

For the first time ever, even after all the hell Mom had put us through, I finally stepped on that ledge wanting to tip over. Fall. And just...vanish. If I couldn't be where Ellie was, I didn't want to be anywhere at all.

Roland slammed me onto the bed, air rushing from my lungs as his arm pressed down on my chest so hard, I was sure my bones would crack at any moment.

"I've had it with you, you crazy piece of shit."

I kicked and clawed, fighting him with every ounce of

strength I had. Not because I wanted to survive, but because I wanted to hurt him. I wanted to tear his flesh off and watch him bleed, witness the life drain from his eyes.

He snaked his thick fingers around my throat. "You should have died, too. You should have died with him. At least then your mother would have been rid of you, you fucking psycho bastard."

"What are you talking about?" I choked out, my hands wrapped around his wrist, trying to pull his hold from my neck.

He leaned down, spit spraying from his dry, chapped lips. "Fuck knows why God decided you had to survive that car wreck. You should have gone to hell with your father that night, along with that fucking demon inside you who helps conjure up these damn lies."

"What?" I snapped, trying to turn so I could see my mom, who simply stood to the side and watched as Roland choked me. "Mom, what is he talking about?"

Roland's fingers tightened, and my lips parted as I struggled for air.

"Mom...what..."

Darkness flickered across my vision, my lungs burning to take a breath. It started at my toes, the cold spreading up my legs, turning every muscle in to ice. My mind screamed at me to move and to breathe. I could feel the adrenaline pulsing in my veins, but my body was numb. Uncooperative. Slipping away.

Dying.

I could still hear Roland spitting fire with his anger, but I kept looking at my mother, wanting her face to be the last thing I saw before I died. No amount of flames or torture throughout infinity would have been able to wipe her face from my mind. I wanted to make sure I remembered what she looked like right here, right at this very moment as she watched me die. One day I'd see her again in hell, and I would watch the devil skin her, witness her eternal suffering while thinking of this exact moment.

The moment she didn't save me.

The cold reached my chest, and my arms went numb, falling down beside me. I closed my eyes and saw Ellie's beautiful, innocent little face. I knew I wouldn't be joining her in Heaven. No child whose mind was filled with so many murderous cruel thoughts could ever walk past the Pearly Gates. But I would never forget her, and I would never forgive myself for not being able to save her.

"I'm sorry, Ellie," I whispered with my last breath, finally surrendering to the dark.

A scream tore through the silence of my thoughts—a soul-crushing, horrifying shriek. The pressure on my chest was gone, the cold melting away as my lungs expanded. I gasped and sucked in a breath, my hands touching my throat as the oxygen burned its way down.

The darkness dissipated, and I could see the terror that paled my mom's face. A thud sounded, and I shot up as Roland's body hit the floor, blood oozing from the back of his head. Thick, dark, crimson liquid spread through the wooden floor's crevices, his hair and shirt soaked in blood. My heart pounded, but it wasn't fear. It wasn't panic.

It was...exhilarating. Seeing Roland's corpse, knowing he was no longer here to make my life a living hell, but instead he was now burning in it, made me feel more alive than I ever had. I could feel it on my skin, the way my insides fluttered with adrenaline, my mind processing the scene in front of me with a rush.

"Please don't hurt me." My mom's desperate pleas grated at my spine like fingernails on a chalkboard.

I jumped off the bed, and in the doorway stood the man with the classic striped beret and gray coat, holding a gun in his hand. It was the man I saw on the corner earlier, the man who carried the guitar case.

His unfamiliar presence filled the room as if he owned it, his large frame built to intimidate.

"Who are you?" I stepped over Roland's dead body without blinking.

The man placed his finger over his lips, touching his mustache, gray-blue eyes peering from underneath his beret. Maybe I was a fool, but I didn't fear him. I was drawn to him and the power he bathed in. The mystery that radiated off him. How he just walked in here, killing Roland without blinking, as if he had the authority and the right to take a life. Everything about this very scene captivated me, as if something inside my head had slid into place, and I found myself. Knew who I wanted to be.

I wanted to be...him.

My mom cried, and I looked her way as she slid down the wall like the pathetic mess she was. Her eyes were wild, glazed, her left arm raw, scabbed and bruised from her constant drug abuse. I would have pitied her if I weren't on the receiving end of her destruction.

The man held out his hand, revealing a syringe in his palm. I knew what it was. I had lived with a junkie long enough to know what heroin looked like. I also knew what the silent man was saying, what I needed to do.

THE VILLAIN

He knew.

He didn't know me, but he knew.

She had to pay. My mother. She had to atone for what she did to me. To Ellie. It was the only way; I could feel it in my blood. The need to try and right all the wrongs this miserable human being had caused.

I took the syringe and turned before crouching in front of her, my eyes level with hers. There was no life, no soul, just an empty vessel of broken dreams and shitty choices.

"Please," she begged, tears and snot dangling from her chin. It was clear as daylight that she was high, her mind no longer present. But she felt the fear. She felt the panic. The terror. "Don't let him hurt me."

Music started playing, coming from my mother's room. It was an orchestral tune I didn't recognize, but I instantly loved it. I couldn't explain it, but the music sounded as if it was composed for this moment, meant to be played while I looked into my mom's bloodshot eyes, her lips parted as violent sobs poured from her miserable existence.

The syringe was almost weightless inside my palm, but carried so much weight, and I knew the only way to be rid of it —to be rid of the load—was to do this one thing.

I eased forward, gently taking her arm in my hand. My mom whimpered, but her tears seemed to have subsided.

"Where is Ellie, Mom?" I stroked her skin along the inside of her elbow. "Where is my little sister?"

"Ellie? No. No. No, Ellie." Her words came out with panicked breaths. "Elijah."

"Where is Ellie?" I yanked her arm, my patience wearing thin.

"No, no, no. Ellie. It's not real."

"You're lying!" I snapped, and she closed her eyes, rolling her head from side to side against the wall. "You bitch!"

My anger fueled my actions, and I pulled her closer, placing the tip of the needle against the vein in her bruised arm. Some of the wounds oozed from infected flesh, but I felt nothing.

No compassion.

No sympathy.

No heart.

"This is for me," I said, piercing her skin as I slid the needle under her skin. Her eyes met mine, and there was this moment of profound truth. Surrender. There was no doubt that she could have easily overpowered me. She could have stopped me...if she wanted to, but her addiction had robbed her of all her strength, her fight, her will to live. A part of me wondered if she always knew this would be how it all ended.

As I looked into her glazed eyes, I applied pressure to the syringe. "This...this is for Ellie."

The world paused, and time stood still. It was as if the universe knew this moment would be a memory I'd keep returning to every day of my life.

"Elijah," she whispered. "I'm...sorry."

My heart clenched, the orchestra playing in the background reaching its peak. "It's a little too late, Mom."

She closed her eyes, and her head lolled to the side. Her chest was still moving, but soon her shallow breathing would stop...for good.

I felt nothing. No pain. No tears. Nothing. Within the span of minutes, I had gone from a twelve-year-old boy who wanted nothing more than to find his sister, to a coldhearted killer who didn't feel the faintest amount of regret while watching my mother die.

I straightened, the strange man appearing in the doorway once again. His scrutinizing gaze dropped to my mother, his face darkened with hard lines. It seemed like he hated her almost as much as I did, and I liked it. That alone convinced me that I could trust him.

"Can I come with you?"

His expression remained unchanged, and for a second I feared he'd say no. What would I do then? Where would I go? What would happen to me?

He looked at my mother, unconscious or dead—it was all the same to me—then back at me. All it took was one nod, and my entire life changed. One simple act, and my future got altered.

The only thing I took with me that night was Ellie's music box. The one thing that reminded me that I wasn't crazy. That Ellie was real.

One day...I'd prove it.

CHAPTER SEVENTEEN

CHARLOTTE

"My God, Elijah."

I had no words after what he had just told me. The entire time I sat there listening to him, watching his expression go from angered to sad and heartbroken, was painful to witness. There was no way I could have imagined what it had to be like for him as a boy. Apart from never knowing my father, my childhood was good. Great, even. My mom and I didn't have a lot of money, but we had each other. We had love. There wasn't a day in my life when I felt neglected or unloved. I never went to bed with an empty stomach or a broken heart.

Elijah swallowed his last mouthful of whiskey, the ice clinking against the glass. His gaze drifted everywhere but at me, actively avoiding eye contact. It was the first glimpse of vulnerability I had seen in him. The first time he was something other than a hardened man, but rather a man who felt. Who hurt. Who carried around a past heavy enough to cripple even the strongest. I cleared my throat. "Did you ever find her? Figured out what happened to Ellie?"

His gaze was fixed on the empty glass, swirling the ice around and around. "No," he answered abruptly and poured himself another drink. "I never found her."

My chest constricted. "Do you think Roland really—"

"I don't know. And I don't know which is worse—not knowing whether she's alive, or knowing that she's dead." There was a faraway look in his cognac eyes, as if his thoughts drifted back to the past, to a memory of the little sister he lost yet wasn't sure how.

"You know," his finger played along the rim of his glass, "after listening to my story, your first question was about something that affected me rather than searching for an answer that affected you."

"What do you mean?"

"You didn't ask me who that man was. The man in the beret. The man who gave me the means to kill my own mother."

Unsettled, I shifted in my seat. "I think your suffering as a child trumps my need for answers as an adult."

"I don't need your pity." His words were laced with poison. "I didn't tell you the pathetic story of my past so you can pity me."

"I'm not—"

"I merely told you so you could understand what kind of debt I owe your grandfather. I owe him my fucking life. Everything I am today is because of him. And you know what? He never pitied me." He tapped a finger on the table. "Not once. We walked out of that fucking hell-house that night and never spoke about it again."

"So, my suspicions are correct. The man who helped you is my grandfather."

He leaned forward, leveling me with his intense stare, dark eyebrows furrowed, not saying a word.

"And now you're repaying that debt by what? Kidnapping me?"

"By keeping you safe."

"And that's why you stalked me."

He raised a brow. "Observed."

"Whatever you want to call it." I leaned forward, placing my elbows on the table, silver cutlery glinting under the dim light.

"I had to make sure you were protected."

My insides tightened, the thought of him protecting me lighting a flicker of a flame inside my belly. "So, you're a hitman turned babysitter, then?"

He snickered. "If that's the way you choose to see it. No one knows my connection with your grandfather, which makes it easy for me to play both fields. To everyone else, I am The Musician—a faceless hitman with a hefty price tag and a one-hundred-percent success rate."

"A one-hundred-percent success rate?" I slanted a brow. "What does that even mean?"

"It means I've never missed a target. Ever."

Sweat beaded down my back even though the air was far from warm. My thoughts raced with images of him playing his role as The Musician, killing people without blinking. It scared me, reminded me of how easy it was for him to plant a bullet in Josh's skull. But it also made this unexplainable attraction I felt toward him more...distorted. What kind of woman was I for being attracted to a killer? Why would I imagine having his hands all over my body when I knew those hands carried the blood of so many?

I cleared my throat, shifting uncomfortably. "Okay. So, we're out here hiding on a yacht because the fucking mafia is after me?"

His lips pursed, his eyes searching my face. "In a nutshell, yes. Until recently, your grandfather's identity was managed to be kept secret."

"Until recently," I muttered in a mocking tone. "Jesus." I closed my eyes, rolling my head from side to side, practically feeling my muscles getting knotted by the second. "God, it feels like I'm trapped in some Al Capone movie, and I have no idea why I'm a part of all this. It sounds so..." I struggled to find the words, "so...not like me. Like it doesn't fit into my mundane life. Can I have more wine?" I held up the empty bottle. "James. Big, scary-looking bodyguard guy." I glanced around, James nowhere in sight. "Where is he? I need a whole crate of these bottles right about now."

"I think you've had enough, Charlotte."

"Oh, no." I waved my finger in front of his face. "You do not get to kidnap me, drug me, drop all these fucking bombs on me, *and* tell me when I've had enough wine." I stood. "No way, Master Musician kidnapper hitman stalker and whatever else you fucking are. Not today."

My heeled pumps clicked across the floor as I walked to the bar which was stocked with every kind of alcohol you could think of. Shots, wine, beer, ciders, champagne—you name it, and this yacht stocked it. For a second, I felt overwhelmed with the endless possibilities of how I could drown this fog of confusion currently occupying my brain.

I spotted the tequila bottle and had one of those "ah-ha"

moments, realizing that nothing helped a person forget about their problems quite like tequila did.

"Charlotte." I heard Elijah come up behind me, but it didn't stop me from reaching for a shot glass.

"I can promise you, your problems aren't going to look any better tomorrow."

"But it can make it look better *now*, which kinda is my short-term goal here."

"Charlotte." He wrapped his long fingers around my elbow, but I yanked free.

"Don't touch me." I opened the bottle, but just as I was about to pour tequila, he grabbed my elbow and twisted me around, causing me to drop the tequila.

Cold liquid splashed around my feet, glass pieces shattered with the pungent scent of alcohol instantly burning my nostrils. But neither the strong smell or the need to get drunk compared to the tension that instantly exploded around us, his eyes burning, his gaze hot and hungry.

His fingers tightened, his tongue darting out to lick his lips, leaving a tempting shimmer. I found myself wanting to taste it, wanting to feel it against my own lips which now ached with the need to be kissed. Devoured.

God. I had to fight it. I had to stop myself from giving in to the erotic pull that swirled inside me while staring into his eyes, feeling his fingers burn my flesh.

He stepped closer, glass cracking and breaking beneath his shoes. Would I end up being that glass? Broken and ruined beneath his feet? Surely, what I was feeling right now would only end in chaos.

The air around us turned static as he leaned down, my insides coiled with anticipation as he held me hostage with the power that radiated off him. Trapped. Caught and imprisoned.

I lifted my chin. "Earlier, when you said I became an obsession," I breathed, "what did you mean?"

His fingers traced up my arm, setting my skin aflame, torturing me with such a simple touch. "I spent years watching you live your life...only to realize that I wanted to be in it." His fingers cupped my chin. "Even if it meant spending the rest of my days in the shadows."

He dragged his hand from my wrist, snaking it around my waist, abruptly pulling me against him. A breath escaped me with a huff, and my body powered up with a need to be filled.

He slipped a finger underneath the fabric on my shoulder, gently easing it down my arm. Logic demanded that I fight, that I object—but the primal instinct that burned throughout my body made it impossible.

"Tell me something," he started, his gaze fixed on my naked shoulder. "There's one thing I never could figure out about you."

Intrigued, I held my tongue and focused on my labored breaths, trying hard to keep hold of a sliver of control.

He kissed my shoulder, the feel of his lips against my hot flesh causing me to whimper. "In all the years I've watched you, I haven't seen you with a man once. Why?"

"Maybe I was. Maybe you weren't looking."

He brought his hand to my chest, his palms brushing against my nipple—now hard and needy. His fingers spread along my throat. "That's impossible."

"How so?"

His hold clamped down around my neck. "Because if I

had seen you with a man," he kissed along my jaw and stilled a breath away from my parted lips, "he'd be dead."

It was a split-second of absolute madness, the moment he crashed his lips against mine, kissing me so hard the edge of the counter bit into my back. A growl tore from his throat, like an addict finally finding the fix he had craved.

I kissed him back, allowing him in to explore and ravish. He tasted of whiskey and sin, a lethal combination that threatened to incinerate me from the inside out. Our fevered kisses turned into a duel, a fight to devour each other—intoxicated and frenzied.

It didn't make sense. Nothing about us made any sense. But with the buzz of alcohol in my veins and the crackle of electricity around us, it made it impossible to make a single rational decision.

Elijah reached between us, clutching the fabric of my pantsuit between his fingers before tearing it straight down the front, shoving it back, my breasts open and aching to be touched. There wasn't a part of my body that didn't hum with a need stemming from deep inside my core—ready to be consumed. My skin burned with a need to be touched by him, every muscle aching for more.

He straightened, watching me as he palmed both my breasts. I moaned, and he squeezed harder. "Tell me, Charlotte. Have you been with a man before?"

"I don't see why that matters," I panted.

"It matters because that will be the deciding factor here."

"Deciding factor for what?"

Our gazes latched, his eyes hooded with dark intent. "Whether I'm going to fuck you or not."

My sex throbbed, my body wound up tight with a band

of desire that demanded release. He affected me so easily, without even fucking trying. It was like my body already knew him, wanting him no matter what.

He stepped closer, slipping his hard thigh between my legs, pressing it against my highly sensitive flesh, and I had to stop myself from moving my hips with the overwhelming need to ride his thigh until my body snapped in half with the pleasure it craved.

"Elijah."

He wrapped both arms around me, winding us tightly together, pushing his hard body against mine, forcing his thigh deeper between my leg, providing the friction I needed.

"Well, have you?" He demanded an answer, and I craned my neck, leaning my head back, moving my hips lightly in an attempt to find the tiniest bit of relief from the pressure.

"I'm not a virgin, if that's what you're asking."

I trembled as his lips brushed down my naked throat. "That leads me to my next question, then." His hands slid down to my ass, cupping and pulling as if close just wasn't close enough. "Who do I have to kill?"

He thrust against me, and I moaned with parted lips. There was so much heat, so many unwanted desires that swirled inside me like a whirlpool about to suck me in and drown me.

"The thought of another man being inside you drives me to the edge of madness. I can't let him live, allow him to walk this Earth after he's tasted what's mine."

"I wasn't yours then," I countered.

"Don't fool yourself, Charlotte. You've always been

mine, even when you didn't know it yourself." He yanked me up and forced my legs around his waist, carrying me down the hall. With every step, desire grew more potent, and I couldn't stop myself from latching on to him, kissing him, my tongue dueling with his as we greedily tried to ravish one another.

My feet hit the floor as he slammed the bedroom door shut behind us, but his mouth never once left mine—our lips refusing to part, drugged with a taste of ecstasy.

It was foolishness. Reckless. And my rational side begged me to be strong enough to fight it. To fight him. But his touch, his kiss, how his presence owned me every time he came close—it had me hypnotized and bound, unable to stop falling into the darkness with him.

He inched back, tearing his lips from mine, leaving me panting as he wrapped an arm around my waist, twisting me around before yanking me closer, my back flush against his chest. He rolled his hips, allowing me to feel his hard cock against the hollow of my back. "I'm a lot of things, Charlotte. Gentle isn't one of them."

I brought a hand up to my neck, reminded of what it felt like to have his fingers tighten around my throat. "Will you hurt me again?"

His lips brushed along my naked shoulder, his fingers sliding the torn pantsuit down until it pooled around my feet in a tattered mess. "If by hurt you mean fucked raw until my name is engraved on every bone in your body, then yes." His hands trickled down my naked arms, my body trembling against his. "You have no idea what kind of torture it was for me watching you from the shadows, desiring you, wondering if you'd still smell like delicate jasmine the morning after I came inside that sweet cunt of yours." He nipped at my earlobe, earning a soft moan from my lips. "But I wasn't allowed to touch, to taste, to sample you...my beautiful little cellist." His hand dipped down, slipping between my thighs. "Every day was a constant war, knowing what needed to be done but wanting to do something different."

"What did you want to do?" I whispered, sounding out of breath as I panted.

"This." He dragged a finger through my slit, and I moaned, my eyes closing. "And this." He dipped low, slipping a finger inside me so easily as my body welcomed the intrusion. "I want to hear your moan when you feel my cock inside you for the first time, see how your lips form the perfect fucking O when your pleasure crests around my dick, your walls milking me for every last ounce of pleasure."

His lips brushed along the naked skin of my shoulder, peppering kisses across my flesh until he reached my ear. "Get on the bed, Charlotte. On your back, and spread those legs for me."

"We can't do this, Elijah." A sliver of inhibition cracked through the haze.

"Do you want to do this?" His other hand snaked around my side, palm cupping my breast as he rolled my nipples between his expert fingers, sending a shockwave down my body—his touch electrifying me. I relished his touch, yet hated how my thighs clenched—hated how easily I succumbed.

"I asked you a question. And do not play games with me right now. If you do not answer me, I will take it as a yes and be inside you before you have a chance to stop me."

"I wouldn't be able to stop you even if I tried."

I felt him smile against the skin at the nape of my neck. "You're a fast learner."

"Apparently, I'm also a masochist."

"Why?" His finger slipped from inside me, tracing along my wet folds. "Simply because you desire to be fucked by me? Used?" Abruptly, his finger and hands were gone as he turned me around, inching forward while forcing me back, unbuttoning his shirt. "Because you want my name to be a prayer on your lips while you come with my face between your legs?"

He pulled off his shirt, and even if I wanted to I wouldn't have been able to tear my gaze away from his naked chest. Hard, defined, his muscles roped across his abdomen. But it wasn't the ripped features of his bare chest that had me intrigued. It was the tattoo just above the waistline of his pants that caught my attention. An image of an opium poppy flower, blood dripping from its petals. After hearing his story, I knew what it symbolized, and it was beautiful in its sadness.

I touched his skin over the flower, my gaze following the movement of my finger as I traced upward along the several intricate music notes that stretched from the poppy petals all the way up his side. "There's so many of them."

He grabbed my hand, and I glanced up at him, his irises dark. "Each note represents a target."

My heart stopped. "You mean...this," I looked down, "these are how many people you've killed?" I started to count but decided against it, diverting my eyes up to him, finding my answer right there in the way he stared at me. There was no compassion. No regret. No humanity. It was clear that not one of his victims was anything more than a job, a contract. They were nothing to him. What was I? I didn't dare ask, afraid the answer might shatter the glass that kept the world out while we got drunk on one another in this moment.

Maybe I was sick. Insane. Why else would I care more about the desire that currently rippled in waves between us, than the fact that the man in front of me was a coldhearted killer? A man who had the blood of others on his hands?

He touched my chin, forcing me to look up at him. "Are you afraid of me now?"

This time there was no doubt in my mind what my answer was. I started with his belt, my fingers easing across the leather as I unbuckled it. "No," I answered simply, unzipping his pants.

Tomorrow I could hate myself for what I was about to do. There would be more than enough time for me to regret this moment and wallow in a pit of humiliation because of my actions, and the choices I was making right now.

But tonight, I wanted to be free of all inhibitions. I wanted to taste sin on my lips, feel depravity coat my skin while wickedness exploded inside my core.

I wanted Elijah.

I wanted...The Musician.

CHAPTER EIGHTEEN

CHARLOTTE

I would burn in hell for wanting the devil. But I was too intoxicated to care—drunk on his earthy-sweet scent and high on the taste of him on my tongue.

Elijah hungrily stared at where he touched my bottom lip with his thumb. "Since you don't respond well to questions, how about I just tell you what my intentions are, what I plan on doing to you? Then you can just nod that pretty little head of yours." He stepped up close, his naked body a breath away from mine, the tip of his thick length brushing against my stomach. Every move he made dominated my senses, his presence filling every bone in my body that was primed to be taken and used. To be swept away by ecstasy.

He wrapped his palm around his swollen cock, and I looked down, his thumb wiping at a drop of pre-cum before pumping with slow, leisurely strokes. My thighs clenched, my sex throbbing with need, wanting him inside me.

"I'm going to take you, fuck you, make you come so hard it's going to feel like your body is about to break. And once your first orgasm tears through you, I'm going to fuck you again, feel you from the inside while your slippery heat coats my cock until I cream that sweet cunt of yours, marking you, staking my claim. Now nod."

I swallowed hard, my body so fucking needy from his words alone, I was sure just a single stroke of his finger would push me over the edge.

He stepped up, my hard nipples brushing against his dark dusting of chest hair, my oversensitive flesh hyperaware of even the slightest touch. "I said nod," he ordered, his gaze boring into mine.

I nodded, refusing to deny myself the sordid pleasure I sought from this man.

"Get on the bed."

I inched back, feeling the silk sheets against the back of my knees when he grabbed my wrist.

"Turn around, and get on the bed. On your hands and knees." It wasn't a request. It was a demand, an order.

"Why?" My voice was nothing but a whisper.

He let go of his cock and cupped my cheek, gentle, like a lover, and I could smell him, his sex, his dominance. His arousal.

"This is the only reason I won't be killing the man who had you first."

I whimpered as he leaned down, his lips brushing gently against mine.

"Because now there's no need for me to be gentle. I can do what I want to." He kissed me—no tongue, no open mouth, just a tender kiss. "And right now, I want to fuck you, my sweet, beautiful cellist. Now, be a good girl and turn around. Get on your hands and knees."

There was a fleeting moment of weakness that passed through me, a moment of hesitation when I doubted myself.

Am I good enough for him?

Am I beautiful enough for him?

Will I be enough for a man like Elijah?

Powerful. Dominant. The kind of man who would have women flocking his way. Yet here he was, a sheen of sweat covering his chest, his eyes hooded and dick hard...for me. A poor girl who had nothing but a broken cello.

"I said get on the bed." He grabbed my shoulders, spun me around, and forced me onto the bed with cruel, cold hands.

"Elijah—"

"You agreed, Charlotte. I told you, there's no going back now."

I swallowed, my heart pounding in my throat, yet my body yearning for him to do whatever it was he wanted. For him to make my body his playground. I had never been so at war with myself—how my mind fought my body, wanting to deny that which it desired most.

The silks sheets were soft against my palms and knees as I steadied myself, staring straight in front of me at the blue velvet headboard.

"Jesus, Charlotte. If only you could see yourself through my eyes right now. You're glistening."

The thought of him staring at me from behind ignited more flames that raged through my core. I had never been so exposed, and I could feel my arousal coat my thighs.

"So fucking beautiful," he murmured, and I groaned when he dragged a single finger through my slit—slowly, gently, yet the shockwaves it caused were powerful enough to make me arch my back, pushing out my hips, wanting more.

"Look at that." Again, he slipped a finger through my wetness. "You're a greedy little cellist, aren't you?"

The mattress dipped as he got on behind me, dragging the head of his cock down my thigh, earning a desperate moan from my lips.

"Does it ache? Wanting a release so badly?" He placed a kiss on the soft skin of my ass. "Is your pussy throbbing, clenching with a need to be filled and stretched? Used?"

Jesus. God.

"Elijah. Please." My eyes rolled closed, and I buried my face in the silk sheets, pushing my hips up and out in search of him, of anything that could give me the friction and touch I needed for a release.

"Please what? What is it you need, Charlotte?"

"You. I need you." I was past the point of pretending, of fighting. "I need you inside me." I had never been this aroused with lust that threatened to drive me mad.

"I'll be inside you soon enough." His voice was a low rumble, like thunder, lightning, a threatening storm that would capsize me, drown me, ruin me. "But first, I want to taste you." His palms flattened on my ass as he stretched me open, cold air brushing against my sensitive folds before his tongue lapped against my slit, his hands spreading my pussy wider, his tongue dragging all the way from my entrance to my clit, my body trembling so hard I could no longer hold myself up with my arms, surrendering.

His tongue felt exquisite against my cunt, licking, lapping, dipping inside me. Euphoria slithered up my spine as he enclosed my clit with his lips, sucking hard, only to replace it with a few gentle flicks of his tongue, then sucking again. It was a rhythm, a beat, the way he played my pussy like a filthy, erotic melody.

It wasn't a lie when I said I had been with a man before, but it wasn't anything like this. God, this was a lethal mix of desire and ecstasy, and I was sure insanity would claim me if he didn't let me tip over the edge.

"Elijah...Jesus, please." My body writhed, my hips pumping back and forth, wanting to fuck his mouth, needing more as I felt the pleasure start at my toes, flowing through my body, up my spine. I was lost in the massacre of wills and inhibitions while my body hummed with the wicked desire my stalker stirred to life—as if the depravity of it all was the vice that made it possible for me to surrender willfully.

"Do you want to come?" He slipped a finger inside me, his tongue licking around it, leaving no part of my sex un-kissed and un-licked.

"Yes. Please. I have to come."

"How?" I shuddered when he lightly blew against my wet sex, his breath warm as it caressed my skin. "How do you want to come? Like this, with my mouth, my finger? Or do you want to come with my cock inside you?"

"I just..." I clawed at the silk sheets, convinced my body was about to snap in half. "It doesn't matter."

"Pick, Charlotte." As if he wanted to make it more difficult for me, more torturous, he straightened behind me, slowly stroking the head of his cock through my pussy, coating himself with my arousal, nudging at my entrance. "Should I fuck you now? Or keep licking your cunt?" His lips were down there again, sucking my pussy as if he was starved for my taste.

"Anything, Elijah. Just...do whatever you want." I reared back, rocking my hips, forcing my sex harder against his mouth.

He groaned, and it sent a wave of vibrations against my clit, forcing a whimper from my lips. A cry. A moan of pure torture.

His mouth was gone, and my legs pulled tight when I felt his cock at my entrance again. "I think this body of yours deserves to come with me inside you. Don't you agree?"

"Yes, please. Please. God." I panted, whimpered, my nails clawing into my palms, my toes and knees pulled taut. My hips moved on their own accord, pushing back just as he thrust forward, impaling me with his thick length, causing me to cry out, tears prickling the corners of my eyes.

He grunted, slamming into me completely, filling me to the brim, stretching me to a point where it hurt. But it felt so fucking good, his cock so incredibly hard inside me, forcing a pleasurable pain that rolled in waves to every corner of my body.

"Fuck," he groaned behind me. "Your cunt is so tight. Warm. Jesus." He placed his palm on the small of my back, steadying himself as he reared back only to delve back into me—harder this time.

My cheek was firmly planted on the sheet, my lips parted as he drove his cock in and out of me with relentless thrusts.

"Ask me if you can come," he demanded, but my mind was lost in the haze of lust and primal instincts. I was too busy getting high on the feel of him inside me, but he pulled out abruptly, his palm slapping my ass hard. I gasped as the searing pain spread along my flesh.

"I said ask me if you can come, or I swear to fucking God I will pump my seed on your back and leave you here panting like a little slut, desperate for cock."

"Okay!" I cried out, unable to take the torture anymore. I no longer felt the sting of his palm against my ass; all I felt was the ache that throbbed, consumed, possessed. "Please. Please let me come."

Like a wild fucking animal, he growled and plunged into me so fucking hard I had to clamp down with my hands to stop myself from falling forward.

We were both lost. Willingly ravished. And I screamed as my climax tore through me, leaving nothing but shattered fragments of pleasure in its wake.

My knees trembled, my back arched, my goddamn mind scattered. It was everywhere—in my skin, my bones, my head—everywhere, the pleasure he fucked into me. And there was nothing else I could do but lie there and take it, letting him take possession of my mind, body, and soul.

"Fuck!" he roared, and then I felt it, the way his cock jerked, spilling his cum inside me—the ultimate act of possession. And I loved it. I wanted it. I relished the thought of his seed spilling into me. Filling me. Tainting me as his.

That was the moment I realized we were both thoroughly and utterly fucked. There was no going back from this. I was claimed and ruined by the man who dragged me into this hell with him. And there was no escape. No way out. But even if there were...I knew I wouldn't want to.

CHAPTER NINETEEN

ELIJAH

Buried to the hilt inside her cunt was better than I imagined. Not only did it feel good, having her wrapped around my cock, but it felt fucking right. As if her body had been made for me. I chose to believe that, convinced that Charlotte was mine.

The Musician wanted to hunt and slice the throat of the fucker who tore through her virtue, claiming her first. But a part of me loved that I could fuck her the way I wanted to without being gentle, without worrying about hurting her. The only way I wanted to hurt her was having her body ache for me, her pussy soaked and swollen for my cock.

I pulled out of her and winced, my entire body alive with sensation, and I felt this primal sense of ownership staring at her swollen pussy creamed with my cum. God, it was the most erotic thing I had ever seen in my life, and I couldn't fucking wait to be inside her again.

Charlotte collapsed onto her stomach, my red handprint still blooming on her ivory skin. It was fucking beautiful.

I lay down on top of her, her ass spooning against my cock. I brushed her hair, sweeping it to the side so I could kiss her shoulder. "You okay?"

She nodded, her eyes closed and lips parted, still panting.

I continued to pepper kisses along her naked back, caressing her skin with a single fingertip. She shivered, and I bit my lip. "You have five minutes to catch your breath and ready yourself for me again."

Her eyes shot open, glancing at me over her shoulder. "Are you trying to kill me?"

"Death by orgasm. Sounds like a good way to go."

She writhed beneath me, trying to turn, and I lifted myself before lying down beside her, watching as she settled on her back. She pulled the sheet to cover herself, but I grabbed her wrist. "Don't."

Her gaze locked with mine, her cheeks flushed. "I'm shy."

"Don't be. Not around me."

"Especially around you."

I leaned in and kissed her, my cock twitching at the thought of her tasting herself on my lips. "You don't ever have to hide yourself from me. Your perfection is breathtaking."

I loosened her grip on the sheet, letting it fall beside her before weaving my fingers with hers. "Does it hurt?"

Her chest rose as she breathed. "Not today."

I glanced in awe at her delicate fingers, knowing the beauty it could create. But, by God, I cursed the irony of having such enormous talent tainted with blight.

"Some days I'm able to forget about it completely." She

twirled her fingers alongside mine. "Other days I can barely hold the bow."

I remembered the day she found out, the day her doctor informed her what was causing the pain in her fingers and hands. It was raining as if the weather were a precursor of the bad news she'd receive. But even through the storm and the rain, I could see her tears, feel her pain, and I almost slit her doctor's throat that day. After she left his office, I stormed in and demanded to know what was wrong with her. It took a violent threat and a sharp blade to get her doctor to talk, but that was something I knew how to do.

Make people talk.

Her diagnosis gutted me as if it were my own. As if it was *my* love for making music that hung in the balance. That night at the Alto Theatre, I waited for her, sitting on the edge of my seat in the back row, shrouded with the familiar darkness. I wasn't sure she'd come, and when she did, I felt the kind of relief that could mend a man's soul. Only, she didn't play that night. Instead, she just sat there on the stage with the cello between her legs. Not once did she lift the bow or caress the strings with her fingers. She remained still, eyes closed, and the neck of the cello resting against her heart. It was as if she created music inside her mind, feeling it in her soul without making a single sound.

It was one of the most powerful moments I had ever been a part of without her consent. We were worlds apart even though I was right there with her, feeling her, wanting to comfort her. But it pained me just as much as it did her because her music had become my heroin. My drug. My addiction.

Silence settled between us as we both stared at our

joined hands. I silently vowed to get the world's best doctors, spend every cent I had in the quest to cure this disease that slowly caused the beauty of my cellist to wither away.

"I'm sorry," I whispered, still staring at her fingers—hating that her talent was slowly becoming her worst enemy.

"I don't need your pity." She unlinked her hand from mine, and I smirked.

"Yet you expected me to accept your pity earlier at the dinner table."

"That was different."

"How so?"

"You were just a child. Both you…and Ellie."

A sharp pain shot across my chest hearing her say my little sister's name.

"It's different when it comes to children who can't defend themselves," she continued. "I'm a grown woman, strong enough to carry my own cross." She gazed up at the ceiling as she folded an arm across her breasts.

"I told you," I took her arm and eased it down her side, "do not hide yourself from me."

She huffed, blowing a stray curl from her face, and I leaned in, smoothing my lips against hers, beckoning for her to open for me. Our tongues danced, slow and sensual, allowing me to savor her taste, committing it to memory. My fingers stroked up her arm, leisurely making their way over the swell of her breast, drawing lazy circles around her pebbled nipple. "Play for me."

Her eyes studied me as she bit her bottom lip, the silver-blue of her irises reminding me of a cloudy sky in May. I half expected her to counter my request, knowing she found it hard to play while someone watched. But instead, she nodded, and my body hummed with the anticipation of hearing her play.

I sat up on my elbow, palming her breast before taking her rosebud nipple in my mouth, gently sucking while teasing with the tip of my tongue. My cock stirred to life, and by the way her back arched, pushing her tit deeper into my mouth, I knew she was ready for me again. The sheets smelled like sex and cum, fused with the scent of her skin.

I wanted to take her again. Claim her. Fuck her until my name was carved on her bones and inscribed on her fucking soul. There had to be no doubt about who she belonged to, who owned her. And I wanted her to be reminded of that every goddamn day, living a life where not a single day passed without me being inside her at least once.

But right now, I needed her to play for me. I let go of her nipple with a pop, and a moan brushed past her lips. "Soon," I promised as she stared at me with disappointment swirling in her eyes. "But first, you're going to play for me."

"Why?" she whimpered, clenching her thighs, fighting the lust.

Wanting to tease her some more, I reached down and dragged a finger through her soaking slit. "Because I need to be that man again." I touched her clit. "The man who watches you play, a witness to your most vulnerable moments."

CHAPTER TWENTY

CHARLOTTE

Elijah had left to get the cello in my room, and I scooted up, finally able to drape the sheets around my body. I wasn't one of those confident women who could walk around naked, wearing their skin like it was a Vera Wang outfit. I had always been aware of my shortcomings, my lack of curves in all the right places, my pale white skin that lacked the kiss of the sun. All my life I had been the girl who never got noticed. The face that got lost in a crowd. And there was some part in me that fancied the idea of being the kind of obsession that would force a man to watch me. Stalk me. Observe me. Even if it had only started as a contract, a payment to a person he owed such a heavy debt. And now, knowing he had spent years protecting me, keeping me safe —it made the attraction I felt toward him even stronger.

I placed my palm on my forehead. God, I was losing my mind. Elijah had fucked me into a swirl of madness. "Jesus, Charlotte," I muttered to myself and leaned my head to the side.

On the bedside table stood what looked like an old, vintage jewelry box with a beautiful floral design set in the wooden lid. I traced a finger over a scratch that stretched across the side, then picked it up. It was light, small, and intriguingly delicate.

I opened it, and inside it was a ballerina twirling as the music started playing.

Edelweiss.

"What are you doing?"

I slammed the lid closed and glanced at Elijah standing in the doorway with the cello. "I'm sorry. I was just looking at...um," I hastily placed it down. "It's a beautiful music box," I managed to say without stuttering like a blabbering idiot.

He placed the cello down on the end of the bed, and I studied him as he walked over, the pair of joggers he pulled on a sexy change from the suit pants I was used to seeing him in. The tempting V that disappeared below the waistline of his pants had my fingertips aching to trace along it...down... down...until it reached the part of him that had me screaming earlier.

He picked up the music box, staring at it as if it held a thousand memories. "It was Ellie's."

My heart hiccupped.

"I bought it for her as a birthday gift, but never got the chance to give it to her." His brown eyes settled on mine. "This is the first song I heard you play on the cello. *Edelweiss.*"

I smiled. "It's one of my favorites."

"Play it for me." He placed the music box down and

reached for my hand, helping me up as I clutched the sheet. "I want to hear you play it."

I swallowed, nervously brushing my fingers through my hair, now a knotted mess of raven curls.

"Elijah, I don't know if I can play that song now that I know what it means to you."

"You can." He kissed me, his broad shoulders enveloping me. "And you will play it...naked."

"What?" My cheeks burned, and he eased the sheet from my body, letting it drape around my feet.

"Naked."

"Elijah, I can't—"

His strong fingers circled around my neck, his palm pressing against the hollow below my throat. "Do not force me to retract my request and replace it with a demand."

There was no mistaking the threat laced within his words, his darkened gaze holding promises of bad intent. I knew fear was the rational thing for me to feel while he had his hand around my throat, but instead I felt this twisted hunger, an intense thirst for him to dominate and demand. It was there, between my clenched thighs—pulsing, throbbing, begging to provoke. How was this even possible? Never before had I been made aware that this darker side of me existed. That I wanted to be dominated.

Maybe it was because of him—the man who had awakened the wicked part of my soul.

I squared my shoulders, scraping together every ounce of confidence I had, and sashayed past him, picking up the cello. My sex ached as I settled on the plush white couch, the fabric brushing against my naked pussy.

Elijah's eyes were locked on me as he sat down on the edge of the bed, scrutinizing me with his hungered gaze.

Never in a million years did I ever think I'd be on a yacht, playing the cello...naked, for a man like Elijah. But I'd be lying if I said I didn't love it, embracing the erotic aspect of it all.

I spread my legs, Elijah's gaze dropping and staring between my thighs. There was a dark flash in his eyes, and his cock hardened beneath the fabric of his black jogger pants.

Purposely, I took my time settling the cello between my legs, teasing him, tempting him, wondering how far he'd allow me to push.

With this bow in my hand, the cello's neck resting against my shoulder, I closed my eyes and breathed, turning my focus from Elijah to the instrument. From the instrument to my heartbeat. And from my heartbeat to silence.

Silence.

It was a precious sound. A sound so many took for granted. A sound no writer or poet could put into words. It could only be experienced. Appreciated. Longed for.

People claimed to know what silence sounded like. But to most, silence was merely the absence of noise. To others, it was that time when you were finally able to hear your thoughts.

To me...it was this. This moment. This point in time when there was nothing, not even the sound of a single breath. The few seconds of peace when my mind was free of every thought. Free of the troubles that stirred the disquiet in my soul.

Free of the pain.

I settled my feet flat on the ground, my body relaxed yet posture firm. For thirteen years, every muscle was trained to release the tension so nothing hindered my pursuit of perfection. And no matter the chaos that surrounded me, or the pain that crippled me, there was nothing more important than that.

Perfection.

I held the bow between my fingers, leaned my head a little to the left as I focused on the smooth touch of the wood and the scent of rosin. That pine smell alone had the power to calm a thousand storms that raged in my veins. So familiar. Comforting.

During these moments, I never thought about what would come next. The road ahead was always dark, unknowing, and uncertain. But that was the part I loved the most. The mystery, the excitement of wondering what perfection would look like this time. It was never the same. Constantly bending and shaping differently than it did before.

I let out a breath and slowly moved the bow across the strings, the first note causing chills to flow down my back as the anticipation started to build. The deep yet soft sound reached inside my chest, allowing me to feel it—to feel the music that escaped my heart only to echo off the strings and create the most beautiful melody that had the power to make souls weep. Even the cruelest and wickedest couldn't resist the seduction of music.

With every move of my fingers along the neck of the cello, the sound, the vibrato swept me away—out of this room, out of this world, far away from the pain.

Far away from...him.

Soon the music entranced me, the cello and I moving as

one. Note after note, I laid my every fear, my every dream out on the ground beneath my feet, because there was no place for anything but the resonating tenor of the instrument that rested against my heart.

With my eyes closed, I moved the bow flawlessly across the strings, the music filling the room, touching the walls as it built—louder, stronger, more powerful. I would solely exist to help it find its way toward the crescendo it deserved. And once it did, it would explode into fragments of unsurmountable splendor.

This was my life. This was what defined me.

Music.

As the final note played, I lifted the bow away from the strings and exhaled. Silence slowly smothered the sound until there was nothing left of the music I had just played.

My chest rose and fell, my skin electrified and sweat beading at my temples. I opened my eyes and stared out in front of me, straight at him.

The man who demanded I play for him.

The man who took me.

CHAPTER TWENTY-ONE

CHARLOTTE

It had been days since I woke up on this yacht. The Empress.

Now that I had the chance to see it in all its luxurious splendor, I knew what Elijah meant when he said his friend had a taste for overly extravagant things. I could only imagine the parties and social events hosted on the large deck area, champagne flowing, women sunbathing on the open flybridge. It even boasted its own helicopter pad, and a fleet of Jet Skis.

On my way out, I caught a glimpse of Elijah in the study, talking on his phone. When he saw me standing there, he approached, his liquid gaze drifting down my body, causing my pulse to beat like a drum. But he merely stopped by the door, leveling me with his cognac eyes before closing the door—placing a barrier between us.

I made my way up the spiral stairs to the upper level. It was the first morning since we arrived that it wasn't too cold to be outside for longer than five minutes. It was early morning hours, and I had merely draped a blanket over my shoulders and nightgown. I was desperate for some fresh air and the faintest glimpse of Rome. Elijah made it clear that we would not return to land unless he was thoroughly convinced it was safe to do so. But I so desperately wanted to see Italy, Rome, one of the most romantic places in the world.

I reached the top level and tightened the blanket around me as I leaned against the barrier, glancing out over the sea. It was misty, sunrays bursting through crevices in the gray clouds.

It was beautiful, and I could only imagine how exquisite the scenery would be in summer when the world shined at its brightest.

"There you are."

My heart fluttered when I heard his smooth, baritone voice. I glanced over my shoulder at Elijah standing a few feet away, looking as majestic and powerful as always in his black pants and black dress shirt, sleeves rolled down to ward off the chill in the air. He might be a confessed killer, but in a short period of time he had become my fierce protector—and the man my body desired every minute of every day.

"Did you conclude your business?" I couldn't hide the feint snark.

"My business will only be concluded once I know you are safe and out of harm's reach." He walked up to me from behind, slipping the blanket off my shoulders and pressing his chest against my back, placing his hands on the rail on either side of me.

Cocooned against him, the cold dissolved as his heat swept over me.

"Julio Bernardi knows you're with an Elijah Mariano. Lucky for us, he only knows me as The Musician, which puts us in an advantageous position."

"How so?"

He placed a kiss against my temple, and his cock hardened against the hollow of my back. "He divulges every last piece of information he has on your whereabouts with me, thinking it will help me find you. Little does he know, I already have you. Lift your skirt."

Heat spread from my chest, radiating up to my cheeks. Like his good little cellist, I obeyed and wound up the skirt of my nightgown.

"Drop your panties."

"Elijah, someone will see."

"Drop. Your panties."

Already I felt arousal pool between my legs, the deep tenor of his voice adding weight to his demand.

I shimmied out of the tiny lace garment Elijah had insisted I wear this morning when we woke up—now realizing why.

I gripped the rail as he reached between us, the sound of his pants zipper creating an inferno of anticipation in my belly.

"On your toes."

I lifted myself as far as I could, panting as I felt his hard length against my naked thigh as he bent his knees, slipping his cock in between my legs.

"Tell me, Charlotte." He guided himself to my entrance,

prodding, nudging, teasing me while my body became pure sensation, waves of jaded lust crashing against my bones. "When you think of me watching you, does it turn you on?"

"Maybe."

He slipped the head of his cock inside me, earning a whimper from my lips before pulling out. "I'd like a better answer than that."

"You like torturing me...don't you?" I tried to rear down on him, but he simply flexed back, denying me the pressure I needed between my legs.

"My dear, beautiful little cellist. You know nothing of torture." His other hand snaked up my front, pulling the silk nightgown down, exposing my breast. The cold air caressed my nipple, the sting of the autumn air touching my skin. It was such a sensual contradiction—having his warmth overwhelm me while the cold air assaulted me. "Torture is watching a woman day after day, drinking her in, infiltrating her life while falling into the trap of wanting to be more than just a shadow."

His fingers pinched my nipples, and I wanted to curse, the morning breeze growing stronger, its icy tentacles wrapping around my naked thighs as if it too wanted to feel the electricity that crackled between Elijah and me—our bodies in tune with one another. Feeling. Wanting. Craving.

"Once this is all over," he rolled his hips, slipping his cock inside me without fully thrusting in deep, "I'm going to make you my wife, Charlotte."

My blood ran cold, my heart no longer racing, but pounding as if it wanted to break free.

"I'm going to make you mine in every way fucking possible." He plunged into me, hard, my feet lifting off the ground, wiping my thoughts of anything but my own search for pleasure. Wrapping his fist in my hair, he pulled my head back, causing my body to arch as I lifted my hips. I tried to spread my legs as wide as I could without losing the height he needed to penetrate me, to thrust as deeply as possible. "And once you're my wife," his hand slipped from my breast, his palm flat on my stomach, "I'm going to plant my seed inside you. Create a life inside your belly."

"Jesus Christ," I whimpered, out of breath, his primal words causing the flames to erupt, threatening to burn me to fucking ash right there.

I gripped the rail tight, pushing my hips out, wanting—no, needing to be fucked by him. His fingers bit into my waist, and his growl echoed through the morning breeze as he pistoned in and out of me, one relentless, hurried thrust at a time.

It was surreal. Unexplainable. The way we unleashed our most primal desires whenever we were together like this —as if society's bounds no longer had a hold on us as we delved deeper and deeper into the darkness. I no longer cared if I lost myself—lost my way. All I cared about was this, us, how we so effortlessly succumbed to one another, bathing in the sin that had the power to drown us both.

"Touch yourself," he rasped behind me, out of breath and consumed with lust.

Without thinking twice, I reached between my legs, my arousal gushing down my thighs, coating my fingers as I touched my clit.

My breaths morphed into whimpers, until I panted with

my lips parted, my fingers stroking through my sensitive folds. Elijah pumped his cock into me—harder, faster, the sound of skin slapping against skin—it was utter madness, chaos, sweet anarchy as both of us chased the release we needed to come down from the high that threatened to suffocate us.

Pleasure exploded, and I came violently, my screams rippling across the open waters. Elijah followed, his cock throbbing inside me as he came, his growls and labored breaths carrying my orgasm until I could no longer stand.

My legs buckled beneath me, and both of us collapsed into a giant puddle of spent lust and lingering ecstasy.

Elijah wrapped his arms around me and scooted me against his chest, and we sat there for the longest time, nothing but the waves and seagulls disturbing the serene silence around us.

I knew I was lost since the first night he claimed me. I knew there was no way back for me, not after I had tasted the bittersweetness of sin with this man. Not after he had awakened this side of me that craved the erotic depravity only he could offer me. The Bernardi family no longer mattered. The whole story surrounding my grandfather and how my life was in danger no longer mattered. All that mattered to me was him. Being with him. Belonging to him. God, when did everything become so distorted? Fractured? As if the life I had lived until now was nothing but a glass cage waiting to be shattered.

But I didn't know or understand the extent of how deep I had fallen down this rabbit hole with Elijah. Not until he scooted up against the barrier, winding an arm around my waist and placing his palm against my belly, saying the words that slammed ice against my chest. "Who knows, my little cellist, maybe my seed has already started to bloom inside you."

And that was the moment the Earth gave way beneath my feet.

CHAPTER TWENTY-TWO

CHARLOTTE

I poked at the eggs benedict on my plate, my appetite nonexistent. How could I have been so stupid? There was no need for me to be on the pill since I wasn't sexually active. That one guy—*just one*, happened years ago, and it was a one-night wonder that ended in disaster with me being punched in the face with reality. The reality being that your first was not even close to what they portrayed it to be in sloppy love stories. There were no floating lanterns by the ocean, no romance drifting in the perfect summer breeze. There sure as hell were no butterflies and rainbows popping up in the air while you got deflowered with Barry White singing in the background. It was unromantic. Awkward. Painful. And the Earth sure as fuck did not move for me with a guy named John settled between my legs, making it feel like he was tearing me apart from the inside out.

It was terrible. Something I never wanted to experience again—hence the reason I never had the need for birth control...until now.

"I'm starting to think I'm going to have to tie you up and force-feed you." Elijah slanted a brow.

"Sorry." Why did I just apologize? "I'm distracted, that's all." Distracted by the fact that we were two very irresponsible adults caught up in one giant vortex of the world's most fucked up situation ever.

I sliced my knife through the poached egg, the soft yolk popping over the English muffin, smearing the plate. Elijah sure was an excellent cook. Everything he made was perfect.

"So, how long do we need to stay here, on the yacht?"

"We'll stay here until things change."

"What things?"

He picked up his cup of coffee, settling his lips on the brim as he took a sip. "I know you don't agree, Charlotte. But I promise you, the less you know, the better. The last thing I want is for you to worry over things you can't control."

I frowned. "Things I can't control?"

He placed his cup down, settling his hand on the table. "I told you, it's my job to protect you, and I plan to do just that. There is nothing, and I mean nothing I wouldn't do to keep you safe."

I believed him.

It was there in the color of his eyes, the determination, the truth, the resolve to protect his own—and after the last few days, us sharing the same bed, spending our nights getting high on sensual, erotic, mind-shattering fuckery, I had no choice but to admit that I was his. His to use. His to claim. His to protect.

In a bid to ease Elijah's need for me to eat, I placed a bite of the egg in my mouth. The hollandaise sauce was perfectly buttery and delicious, the hint of lemon giving it a burst of freshness. "I know I've said this before, but you are an excellent cook."

"I have a great appreciation for food."

"That's understandable after...well, what you've been through."

An uncomfortable silence settled between us, but even through the awkward moments there was a constant buzz of energy that had us hyperaware of one another. Even from a distance, a simple glance could set my skin alight, as if his gaze caressed my flesh.

I shifted in my seat, needing to change my train of thought before I became a panting mess at the breakfast table. "Is there any way I could get into contact with my grandfather?"

"Not now. It's too risky."

Of course. What was I thinking?

Elijah tapped a finger on the table, pinning me with his stare. "Once all this is over and it's safe, I'll take you to him."

I smiled warmly at the thought of seeing the grandfather I never knew, finding family again after spending years alone. "Thank you."

"Don't thank me yet, Charlotte."

A distant pulsating thump-thump-thump disrupted the calm. Both Elijah and I looked up and out over the ocean at a helicopter approaching from a distance.

"Is that helicopter coming here?"

"I believe so." Elijah stood and immediately turned to face James, who positioned himself a few feet behind us. "Is it him?"

James merely nodded without saying a word and disappeared off deck, making his way to the back of the yacht to the helipad.

"A little warning would have been appreciated," Elijah muttered more to himself since James was no longer there. He rolled his shoulders and cocked his head from side to side.

The black helicopter slowed down to a hover, the noise of the rotor blades impossibly loud. We weren't even near the helipad, and the gust of wind had my hair blowing into my face, and I tried brushing it out of my eyes, clutching the turtleneck jersey tighter to ward off the chilly air. "Who is that?"

Elijah pulled his lips in a thin line before dragging a hand through his now disheveled hair. "A friend."

"A friend?"

The helicopter landed, and Elijah took my hand as he led me inside, past the bar and down a long hall before we entered a large entertainment area. I hadn't been on this side of the yacht before, not even aware there was this vast open space that held a twelve-seat dining set, a white corner couch, and a billiard table placed close to a second bar area. It was impossible not to gawk at the lavish surroundings that could easily become the envy of any person not accustomed to this kind of lifestyle.

We reached a black door, and Elijah stilled, turning to face me. "Do not say a word, do you understand me?" His somber expression made my stomach tighten, warning prickling the back of my neck.

"Who is this person? What's going on?"

"Do you. Understand me?"

His dark gaze burrowed into mine, determination

rippling off his shoulders. It scared me, as if a dark storm of foreboding was approaching, threatening to break all around us.

"I understand." I bit the corner of my mouth, struggling not to bombard him with anxious questions and demanding answers.

He opened the door, the sliver of sunlight breaking through the clouds beaming down. The rotor blades still hadn't come to a complete stop, the pulsing noise swooshing and slicing the air, creating more wind.

James stood in front of us, waiting as a man dressed in a black suit exited the chopper. With bated breath, I watched the man fasten his suit jacket, not disturbed or fazed by the gusts of wind the rotor blades continued to produce. It was clear to anyone who watched this man walk across the helipad, shoulders squared with a confidence one could spot a mile away, that he fucking owned everything he touched. He exuded sophistication and power even from a distance. He had the same regal and majestic presence Elijah had—the same authority that beamed from his eyes as he regarded us. A six-foot-three powerhouse wrapped in a five-thousand-dollar suit.

James stepped in behind the man as he stopped a few feet away from us, the noise of the rotor blades quietening.

Something felt wrong. The way this man studied Elijah, then slipping his gaze down to me, regarding me no more than two seconds before turning his attention back to Elijah.

Elijah's grip on my hand tightened. "Marcello Saint Russo, what a surprise."

I immediately recognized the name.

"You should have told me you planned on paying us a

visit. Kind of risky, given our current circumstances, don't you think?"

Saint shot his cuffs, straightening his suit jacket. "Believe me, I wouldn't have risked it if it wasn't of the utmost importance." His voice was low, his expression hard and unreadable. Intimidating.

Elijah shifted, widening his stance. "Perhaps you can enlighten me, then, since your little unplanned trip has the potential to ruin this entire operation."

"I'm afraid I had no other choice." He glanced over his shoulder at James, the gun he pulled from his jacket pocket glinting under the slivers of sunrays. My heart ceased, my pulse racing and palms sweating. Everything turned hazy, fogged, like a dream.

A nightmare.

Elijah stiffened, forcing me farther in behind him, shielding me with his large frame.

"What the fuck is going on here, Saint?"

I couldn't think. I couldn't breathe, stone-cold terror slicing up my spine, and I had no idea what was happening.

"Why are you here?"

Saint smirked, eyes dark and gaze filled with malice. "I'm here for the girl."

CHAPTER TWENTY-THREE

CHARLOTTE

A few weeks later

There was always that split second of silence between hearing something and having your mind make sense of it. A fraction of time when there was nothing. No sound. No thought. No reaction.

I'd experienced a few of these moments in my life. Moments when I no longer felt my heart beat or my lungs expand. Moments when I wasn't alive, I merely existed, lingering in space within the absence of gravity. Yet, I was here, sitting in this chair, staring at the man across from me whose glasses would slip down his nose every five seconds, prompting him to push them back in place. The wall behind him proudly displayed the degrees he'd accumulated over the years, and judging by the wrinkles around his eyes, the grooves on his forehead, gray hair, and sharp widow's peak, he was at least sixty.

His finger tapped on the file in front of him, the sound oddly in tune with my pulse throbbing in the side of my neck. So many things had happened during the last few weeks, my life forever changed because of one man who came like a thief in the night, snatching me from my world and forcing me into his. A man who, despite my inhibitions and instincts, had me falling into his arms as if it were the only place I belonged. A man who claimed to have been seduced by my music only to have me seduced by the magnetism of a wicked darkness that dripped off him like liquid temptation.

I should have known better. I should have guarded my heart more fiercely, fought harder. But I didn't, and there were so many reasons I gave in so easily. Maybe because deep down I was intrigued by a man who felt so passionately about my music—music I was too afraid for the world to hear. Perhaps the knowledge of me being the object of his obsession fucked with my head and made me feel flattered in some twisted, fucked-up way. Or maybe I was just tired of being alone, desperate to have someone else to lean on other than myself. Perhaps that was what I thought Elijah could offer me. After all, who better to provide security and protection than a hitman who owned as much power as he exuded with every breath?

But now, as my mind slowly digested what I had just heard, word by word filtering through that one single breath of silence, I realized with a sinking feeling in my gut that I had made an ill-informed decision. I acted on my most vulnerable instincts, and now I stood on the brink of ruin with no hope of being saved.

Not by him.

Not by anyone.

Elijah lied. So many fucking lies and half-truths, I didn't know where the truth ended and the lies begun. But it was too late now. I flung myself into this black hole, and there was nothing I could do to escape the darkness.

I smoothed my palm across my belly, the two-thousand-dollar silk shirt unable to hide the poor, struggling New York cellist I once was.

The man across from me cleared his throat. "I know this must be a huge shock. But I can assure you there is light at the end of this tunnel."

"No." I looked up and straight at him, swallowing hard as a tear slipped down my cheek, my insides being ripped apart with every breath. "There is no light in any of this."

His thin lips pressed together, his gray mustache curving at the edges. He knew as well as I did that there was no end to this dark tunnel, and therefore no hope of any light.

I got up and straightened my skirt. "Thank you for your time."

He pushed his glasses back over the bridge of his nose and stood. "Of course. If there is anything I can help with, you have my number."

"I appreciate that. Have a good day."

He shot me a sympathetic smile. "Good day...Mrs. Mariano."

CHAPTER TWENTY-FOUR

CHARLOTTE

A few weeks earlier

Italy's winter cold had nothing against the chill that lingered in my spine. Elijah had been behind that closed door for almost an hour with the man who called himself Saint. He sure as hell didn't look like any saint to me. The man had malice and mystery plastered all over him—a lethal combination, in my opinion. Something Elijah had as well, but for some reason, I was drawn to his darkness, lacking the aversion I had toward the stranger who now occupied my thoughts as well.

I hadn't moved since they closed that damn door, my stomach twisted in knots as I rubbed my palms up and down my arms.

Elijah told me not to move. And Saint had instructed James not to let me out of his sight. I glanced up at the bodyguard who stood by the door, arms crossed and chest buff. The sheer size of this man was enough to make a person want to shrink into oneself. I was convinced he had intimidation bottled and used it as aftershave every goddamn morning, readying himself to fuck the world in the ass with a simple glare. But right now, I was more afraid of what was being said behind closed doors than the man standing in front of me like a giant brick wall.

I placed a hand on my belly, remembering what Elijah had said. "...maybe my seed has already started to bloom inside you."

God. I still couldn't believe how damn stupid I was. How irresponsible. What kind of person would I be if I brought a new life into this dark world I found myself in? What kind of mother would I be to a child when I was incapable of making good decisions for myself? Everything was twisted, turned upside down ever since Elijah took me.

Kidnapped.
Abducted.
Seduced.

Three words I never thought I'd put together in one sentence. One thought. Yet here I was, abducted, seduced, and maybe even in love if the flutter of nervous energy and the flicker of excitement inside my stomach was anything to go by.

God, this was all so fucked up. But I was a grown woman who knew better than to fight the inevitable—and falling deeply and completely in love with Elijah Mariano was undoubtedly unavoidable, if I weren't already.

James cleared his throat, and I glanced in his direction. "I don't suppose you'll give me an answer if I ask you how Elijah and Saint know each other?"

He merely lifted a brow in a silent yet extremely fucking loud *'no.'*

"Of course not," I huffed and leaned back in the chair. "Do you know how long they'll be? My ass is getting numb."

No answer.

"Can I at least go to my room and take a nap while these two catch up?"

"I'm sorry, Miss Moore. But Mr. Russo and Mr. Mariano made it clear you are to remain right here."

I scoffed. "You make it sound like these two men own me. Just," I held up a hand, locking my gaze with his, "let it be known that even though I'm here under questionable and extremely odd circumstances, I am still my own person. I still make my own decisions whether there are two men behind that goddamn door, discussing God knows what." I stood, my spine straightened and feet firmly on the ground, yet nowhere near to looking James in the eye. "I am a person, goddammit. And I am allowed to get my ass off this uncomfortable chair and go take a nap if I want to."

Determination clung to my every word, my squared shoulders broad with confidence. But James remained unmoved, glancing at me like a rottweiler would a chihuahua. It took one facial expression from him to tell me exactly what I was to him.

Insignificant.

Inconsequential.

Small.

My shoulders slumped, and I glanced down, defeated. "Ugh, I'm nothing but a goldfish in this sea of sharks, aren't

I?" I sat back down in the chair, massaging my temple with my thumb. "It's just a matter of time before I get chewed up."

James shrugged. But he might as well have said, *"Yes, you are nothing but fish bait dangling from a little hook waiting to be eaten."*

So many nights I spent staring at the ceiling of my crummy apartment, wishing that somehow, somewhere, there'd be *more* waiting for me. More happiness. More love. More life.

Within that space between when my mom died and Elijah stormed in, days were nothing more than this tiring war of survival from sunup to sundown. My life was one constant struggle to get from one moment to the next without sinking, without drowning. And what made it worse were all those thoughts of wasting away with no one out there to fight for me, to help me, to not let me lose myself.

People always said nothing was as scary as death. But I disagreed. There was nothing more terrifying than the kind of loneliness that could make you disappear without another soul even noticing you're gone. There would be nothing left of you. No memories. No thoughts. Not even the tiny space you occupied in this world. It would be as if you never existed. Never laughed. Never loved.

Nothing was worse than the fear of not leaving a mark.

If I had to die today, would my absence leave a scar on Elijah's heart forever? Or would it simply ache for a moment, only to be gone the next?

I let out a breath, rubbing my palm across my forehead. I was never like this. Never thought of having the kind of influence that would handicap someone else. A person who would rather be a source of another's pain than a distant memory that would eventually fade forever.

The selfish bitch in me preferred the scar—the disfigurement of what once was an oozing open wound. But I wanted him to feel something for me. Something intense. Feral. Like I felt for him. I craved to be his blessing and his curse.

CHAPTER TWENTY-FIVE

ELIJAH

The door clicked closed behind me, and I watched as Saint strolled toward his desk, the Italian fabric of his suit swooshing with every step. It was an important lesson I learned early on from my mentor. The man who saved me. Never take your eyes off a potential threat, no matter who it might be. It was within that split second of letting your guard down that a friend could turn into a foe.

He leaned back against the desk, gaze pinned on me. Two predators confined into one tiny space salivating for a fight.

I crossed my arms. "This unscheduled stop of yours wasn't part of the plan."

"And neither was the girl."

"She was a complication I didn't anticipate."

"Wasn't she?"

He studied me, eyes dark with suspicion while the silence pulsed with tension that could snap at any second.

Saint placed his hands on the edge of the desk, finger tapping on the wood. "I know who she is."

"I have no doubt that you do."

"Why her?"

"It's personal."

"I'm sure it is. Still, I can't help but wonder how this woman managed to become an unanticipated complication to a man like yourself." He leveled me with a pointed stare. "A man like the Musician."

And there it was. The threat. The split-second a friend could become foe.

I placed my hands in my pants pockets as I widened my stance, not backing down an inch. "This is killing you, isn't it? Not knowing."

He smirked. "I'm not going to lie. It does...*irk* me, not knowing how she fits into all of this. You know I don't appreciate surprises, Elijah. I don't like it when people hide shit from me."

"If it was my intention to hide her from you, do you think I'd let James live so he could inform you of my guest?"

He crossed his arms, puffing his chest like a goddamn peacock. "I suppose not. But I still don't appreciate being kept in the dark. I consider shit I don't know as threats—which is why I made it my business to know everything about everyone who has ties to my family and me."

"Bullshit," I scoffed. "You and I both know if you considered Charlotte a threat, you wouldn't have waited this long to come here. And honestly, was it necessary to make such a huge motherfucking entrance with that overpriced helicopter? A speedboat works just as well."

"What can I say? I like to make an impression."

"You like to show off."

"That too." His lips curled up at the corners. "What's the point of having so much money if you can't flaunt it to the world?"

"Good God. I thought having a family of your own would make you a little more humble, but it seems like you're still the same arrogant bastard you've always been."

"Not a chance. In fact, having a family of my own only made me more cautious. Protective. Deadlier."

I rolled my eyes. "You don't scare me, Saint. You never have."

"Do you think I scare Charlotte?"

"After flashing a gun around? Yeah. She's probably terrified of you—which I don't appreciate, by the way." I stalked closer, leveling him with a glare. "If you were anyone else, you'd be breathing out the side of your neck right now."

Seconds ticked by like bombs going off in quick succession, the tension between us mounting to a point where it was a mere matter of moments before it exploded. His brow dipped in the center, and my top lip curled into a silent snarl. He knew I was speaking the truth that the only reason he wasn't dead right now was because...well, I considered the man a friend.

A dear friend.

Family.

Saint smirked. "How much did it take for you not to punch me in the face when I landed?"

"A fuckton."

"God, I love fucking with you."

"You're an asshole, you know that?"

"Oh, I know."

We smiled, the tension shattered as we went in for a hug, Saint slapping my shoulder before leaning back. "She's going to kill you when she finds out we were fucking with each other."

I pulled a hand through my hair. "I'll just blame it on you since you started it."

"You played along, didn't you?"

"God, she's going to hate me."

We snickered, and I walked over to the cabinet, grabbing two crystal glasses, and poured us each some bourbon. I turned and handed him his drink before taking a seat on the leather couch. "Seriously, though, what are you doing here?"

"I had some business in Rome, finalizing a project with my father."

"Your father? You two getting along now, after everything?"

Saint took a sip of his whiskey before placing the glass down next to him. "I wouldn't say getting along. More like... trying to tolerate."

I smiled. "That's better than trying to kill each other."

"Maybe. I don't think our relationship will ever be what's considered normal between father and son."

"Well," I raised my glass, "he might be a son of bitch to you, but to me, he's the one who gave me a second chance in life."

Saint rolled his eyes. "If I have to hear how thankful you are for what he did, I swear to God I will hurl on my three-thousand-dollar leather shoes."

"Can't help it. I owe him everything. If he didn't," I sucked in a breath, "if he didn't intervene, God knows where

I'd be. I'd probably be rotting in a ditch somewhere, Roland's handprints engraved around my throat."

He took a seat next to me, and there we were, both staring out in front of us, sitting together like, well...brothers. "At least he was a good influence in one of our lives."

It pained me to witness how fragile his relationship was with his father. Of course, from Saint's point of view, I understood why. But it didn't lessen the appreciation I had for what his father had done for me. If it weren't for him, I never would have been saved that fateful night, taken to a better place with someone who showed me more love than my own fucking mother.

Saint glanced at me from the side. "If I have to be serious for a minute, my father is not a man with a lot of regrets. But not intervening and saving you sooner is one of his biggest failures and regrets."

"Rather late than never." I took a large gulp of whiskey, no longer feeling the sting of alcohol. "It wasn't always bad. Before my father died in that car crash, we were happy."

"My father doesn't feel affection easily, but I know he cared for your father. As cousins, they were close growing up." Saint scoffed. "When I was little, my father would bore me with all his childhood stories of him and his cousin Edgard."

"Edgard," I muttered while staring at my glass with the amber liquid. "I haven't heard someone say my father's name in quite some time."

"Okay," Saint stood, "let's not continue with this conversation since your past combined with mine is any psychologist's fucking wet dream."

I laughed. "Can't argue with that."

"So, tell me about the girl."

"You can't know everything, Saint."

"Of course I can. It's easy. Just open your mouth and tell me. Why is she here?"

I got up and straightened. "She needs protection."

"Well," he rubbed his jaw with his thumb and forefinger, "I vaguely remember your stay here on my yacht is because *you* need protection. And now here you are, offering that which you don't currently have to a girl I can't quite place in this equation."

"It's quite a conundrum, isn't it?"

"Don't fuck with me, Elijah."

"I'm not." I swirled the whiskey in my glass, contemplating how much Saint needed to know about how Charlotte fit into my current circumstances. There was no doubt that he already knew everything about her. It wouldn't surprise me if he knew her motherfucking blood type. But what he didn't realize was my reasoning behind having her here.

"Who is she to you?" Saint pushed for more information, making his presence heavier by squaring his shoulders.

I emptied my glass and placed it on the side table. "She's a debt."

"What kind of debt?"

"A debt I swore I'd repay."

"By protecting her?"

I nodded.

"From who?"

"The Bernardi family." My blood heated just thinking about them, about how they thought they owned everything and everyone, the fucking leeches who sucked everything good out of this motherfucking world.

Saint paced a few steps, still rubbing his jaw as the wheels turned inside his thoughts. "So, am I supposed to believe that the Moore girl being here is just a coincidence or an unplanned complication—as you put it?" He settled back, his eyes meeting mine. "Or would it be safe for me to assume that you needing my yacht to lay low for a while was bullshit and that she was part of this plan all along?"

I smirked and chose silence as my answer. Saint was a smart man, like me. There was no puzzle we couldn't solve. No problem we couldn't fix. And that was precisely what I'd been doing until now...fixing a fucking problem and ensuring I protected that which I had claimed ownership of years ago.

Charlotte.

But like me, you didn't get into Saint's good graces by spitting bullshit and reciting riddles. We were straight shooters.

I stepped up to him, not even fucking blinking as I looked him in the eye. I wanted him to see how damn serious I was. I wanted him to witness my resolve as I confessed both my weakest yet strongest vulnerability. "I love her."

Silence stretched between us—a taut rope tightening around our throats. That was what love was like for men like us. A cord that could either snap and let us plummet to our deaths or a chain that would take our last breath while our hearts exploded. Love was the one thing that could destroy us and leave us crippled. The one thing we couldn't control.

Saint cleared his throat. "I know firsthand how love can come out of nowhere and derail everything. And I am the last man to stand here and preach, reminding you what's at risk."

"Then don't."

"But she could get hurt."

I cocked a brow. "And your wife couldn't?"

"It's different with us."

"How? Explain to me how it's different from how your relationship started with you not giving a fuck about your wife. Me, on the other hand, I feel something for Charlotte. I want to protect her and not use her for my own gain."

"I'd watch what you say next if I were you." He stepped up, making himself seem taller to emphasize his challenging threat.

I matched it by moving closer, not backing down. "As you said, you are the last person to preach to me. So, here's a friendly warning. Don't."

Men could be family. Brothers. Uncles. Best friends. But all those close relationships meant nothing whenever wives, girlfriends, and women got brought up. It would make us turn from civil acquaintances to savage beasts.

Saint studied me while I refused to look away. "Does she know?"

I shifted. "She knows what she needs to know."

"That's a shitty answer."

"To a shitty question."

"I'm serious, Elijah."

"And so am I." The room seemed to get smaller with every passing second. "My past is just that. Past. Charlotte is my present. My future. There's no need to confuse one with the other."

Saint inched back, rubbing his fists together, the wheels

inside his head turning rapidly. "It's not her confusion I'm worried about here."

The back of my neck prickled with warning. "If you have something you want to say, just say it."

"Listen, Elijah. I am not the bad guy here, and I sure as fuck didn't come here to fight."

"Why did you come here, Saint? Why, after you heard I had Charlotte here, did you go through all the trouble to pay us a fucking visit?" I knew my anger was misdirected, that Saint and I had the type of relationship where we would never mean each other any harm. But I was on edge, my skin feeling too tight while my skull throbbed. It was like I waited for something terrible to happen, for shit to hit the fan, and I'd end up losing her. The thought alone had rage knocking at my chest, begging to be set free and devour everyone who got between Charlotte and me.

Saint straightened his black suit jacket, the epitome of calm composure. But I saw it in his eyes, the glint of his intention to tread on broken glass. To touch a subject we chose to avoid at all cost as a way to preserve our friendship.

"Do I have to be worried here, Elijah?"

"No," I spat out.

"Then why does it feel like I do?"

"Then I'd say married life has made you paranoid, worrying about shit you don't have to."

He shook his head then pointed to the door. "There's another woman's safety at stake here."

Anger simmered, and I pressed a finger against my own chest. "And you think I'd do anything to jeopardize that? Do anything to put Charlotte in harm's way?"

"If you love her as you claim, no. Not intentionally."

"What the fuck does that mean?"

Saint pulled a hand through his hair, black curls falling back into place. "I didn't come here to argue. I'm just concerned."

"About what?" I snapped. "Me? Or the girl?"

"Both."

I threw my hands in the air and let out a mocking laugh. "Just ask me what we both know you're dying to ask me. Go on." I dared him with a challenging gaze. "Ask me."

"Fine." He crossed his arms. "When was the last time you saw her? Huh, Elijah? When was the last time you saw Ellie?"

It was like a goddamn knife in my throat, slicing down to my goddamn chest. I stalked right up to him, stilling so close I could feel his goddamn breath on my face. "Do not fuck with me, Saint. You and I both know Ellie never existed."

CHAPTER TWENTY-SIX

ELIJAH

Past

His house was small but warm. It felt welcoming, like home.

It didn't reek of piss and rotten food. There were no dirty dishes scattered around the kitchen or smelly clothes lying on the couches.

The walls were clean, with no greasy hand marks and mold stuck to them. The man closed the door behind him. "You hungry, boy?"

I nodded.

"The bathroom is down the hall, first door on the left. Take a shower while I make us something to eat. There's a set of clean clothes for you on the bathroom cabinet." He placed the cello case in the jacket closet behind the door, and I was oddly curious about the guns he hid inside it.

"Will you teach me?"

He glanced at me in question.

I swallowed. "Will you teach me how to shoot?"

He shrugged out of his gray coat and hung it in the closet with his cello case, took off his striped beret and placed it inside as well before closing the doors. "That depends."

"On what?"

"Can you aim when you piss?"

I frowned. "What?"

"Can you aim when you piss? Or do you just," he waved his hand, "piss all around the goddamn toilet?"

"What does that have to do with you teaching me how to shoot a gun?"

He leaned down and looked me square in the eye. "If you can't control something as small as your dick, you can't control a gun, boy."

He patted me on the shoulder and brushed past me. "Shower. Now."

"I can," I blurted. "I can aim...you know, when I pee. It's just, in the mornings, it's a little more...you know."

He turned to face me again. "A gun doesn't care what time of day it is when you shoot it. It doesn't give a shit what the circumstances are when you pull that trigger. And that means you need to always be in control of it. No matter what. Once that bullet leaves the chamber, you make sure it always hits the target. Always."

He swung around and disappeared around the corner. I didn't know this man, I didn't know this house, and if I were any other boy, I'd probably be shit scared right now. But I wasn't. Not even a little bit.

It felt good to take a shower, to wash off the filth Roland's hands left on me. To get rid of the stench of neglect. They were gone. Both of them.

And Ellie.

The man who saved me shot Roland—the man who became my version of the monster under my bed. And me? I killed my mother. I could still feel the syringe in my palm, how I slowly injected the heroin into her arm. I could still see her face, her glazed eyes as the drug spread through her veins, killing her. Her apology right before she died meant nothing to me. Nothing. Because of her, Ellie was gone, and I had no idea what they had done to her.

Did they take her away?

Did they kill her?

I wasn't sure which one would be worse—my little sister being dead or locked up somewhere being hurt by monsters. It kept me up at night, wondering if she was under the same night sky as me, or whether she was looking down from Heaven. Maybe Heaven was better—for her, at least. If she were dead, I'd mourn her, cry for her, miss her. But she'd be safe, unharmed, and no longer hungry or afraid.

I sat down at the dining table, and the man placed a bowl of spaghetti in front of me, the smell of herbs and spices filling my nostrils and causing saliva to coat my tongue. I couldn't remember the last time I had a hot meal.

He took a seat at the other end of the dining table. "Someone will be coming by tonight. Someone who wants to see you."

"Who?"

"He's family." Gianni gestured to my plate. "Now, eat. You need some meat on your bones, boy."

I twirled the spaghetti around on the fork. I was

surprised I still remembered how to do that since the last time my mom cooked spaghetti was before my dad died. When Ellie and I were still beloved kids who got taken care of by our own parents.

"Thank you," I murmured as I kept my gaze down.

"For what?"

I glanced up. "For saving me."

The weight of my gratitude was right there in his eyes as he stared back at me, as if he knew I had never meant anything more than what I had said right now.

He simply nodded, rubbing his hands together as he leaned his elbows on the table.

I took a bite of the food, the tangy tomatoes with the subtle sweetness of basil exploding in my mouth. After that first taste, it was like years and years of going to bed hungry had rushed back, my stomach feeling like my throat had been cut off. I couldn't get the food into my mouth fast enough, and I turned from boy to savage.

"Hey, slow down, Elijah. The last thing we need is for you to choke to death."

I wiped at my mouth with the back of my hand. "How do you know my name?"

He leaned back in his seat, his eyes narrowed.

"You know me?"

He still didn't answer.

"That explains the clean clothes."

"How so?"

I placed the fork down. "I knew it was no coincidence, you having a set of clean clothes ready for me. All in my size."

He cocked a brow. "I have a son your age."

"No, you don't."

"How do you know I don't have a son?" He seemed curious as to how I'd answer, slanting his head to the side as he studied me.

I took a sip of water, my throat suddenly dry. "This is a two-bedroom house."

"You snooped?"

"I was just...taking a look around." My heart slowly started to claw its way up my throat.

"Well," he tapped his finger on the table, "the second bedroom is my son's."

For a moment, I hesitated, unsure whether I should say more or keep quiet. But, deep down, something told me not to mess this up. That this man sitting across from me was my last hope, and if I made the wrong move...I would have no hope at all.

My stomach tightened, and I looked down.

"Talk, boy. Say what's on your mind." Nothing was threatening about the way he spoke, no darkness hidden within his words.

I shifted in my seat. "The second bedroom," I started, nervously twirling my thumbs, "it doesn't look like a boy's room."

"How so?"

"It's too neat," I explained, my courage growing stronger. "It looks like there hasn't been anyone in it for years."

"Explain." He crossed his arms, seemingly intrigued as there was no sign of hostility. If anyone knew what anger and hostility looked like, it would be me.

I rubbed my fists together in my lap. "The shutters were closed."

"It's nighttime. Shutters should be closed at night."

"And there are no clothes in the closet."

"My son keeps all his clothes in the chest of drawers."

"There is no chest of drawers," I countered. "But there is a bedside table."

"And what of it?"

"It's covered in dust." I couldn't be sure, but I was certain I saw a hint of a smile tug at the edges of his lips, and it gave me the confidence to go on. "And so is the pocket Bible on top of it."

He leaned forward, his eyes narrowed. "How does the Bible on the desk prove that I don't have a son your age?"

I shrugged. "You don't look like a religious man. And it's doubtful that your son would have a Bible in his room when you don't have one in yours."

For the longest time, he studied me, not moving and not saying a word. The atmosphere grew heavy, and I started to regret being so candid and straightforward about "snooping" through his house while he thought I was taking an extra-long shower.

"Gianni," he said, not taking his eyes off me. "My name is Gianni."

I bit the inside of my mouth, my intense hunger replaced with nerves.

"You're very observant, Elijah. It's quite impressive."

I had my doubts about how sincere that compliment was—if it was a compliment at all. So, I simply nodded and avoided eye contact as I stared at the bowl of spaghetti in front of me.

"Why do you have a Bible in your spare room?"

"I use it as a...reminder."

"Of what?"

Gianni glanced at the table in front of him as if staring into open space. "My transgressions." He looked back at me, taking a visible breath. "Now, the man coming here tonight is the reason I got you out of that house."

I didn't respond.

"As I said, he's family. You don't have to be afraid of him."

"I'm not afraid," I blurted. It was important that he knew that. That he knew I wasn't afraid of him or anyone. I had spent too many days living in fear, wondering what Roland or my mom would do next. Every night I would sit in the dark, staring out the window at the sky, thinking it might be my last. The uncertainty of my fate, all the questions and fear surrounding Ellie's disappearance, ate at my insides, and there was no way I'd spend another day of life living in fear. I survived hell. I feared nothing.

Gianni nodded. "It's good not to be afraid. But remember, fear is the mind's best motivator when it comes to surviving. You can fear something and be brave at the same time, Elijah. The trick is not to let your fear control you."

My jaw clenched as I looked up at him, the wrinkles around his eyes betraying the secrets that came with his age. He looked older than my dad was before he died. I never had a grandfather. My mom's dad died before I was born. And from what I had learned through eavesdropping on conversations between my mom and dad, my dad didn't want anything to do with his dad. Something about the family business being too dangerous. That he was protecting Ellie and me by cutting ties with his side of the family.

A knock on the door startled me, and Gianni shot me a

reassuring smile, not saying anything about a simple knock scaring me right after I said I wasn't afraid.

My heart raced as I watched him open the door.

"Mr. Russo," Gianni greeted, standing to the side so the man could enter.

The man looked my way, removing the gloves from his hand. "This is the boy?"

"It is."

Mr. Russo approached, and I stood, trying my best to act unintimidated while my stomach slowly turned inside out.

A thick gold chain beneath the open collar of his shirt glinted under the light. But it was his eyes that seemed familiar to me. Crystal blue. Light but gleaming with an edge of darkness. Warning. Power.

"Elijah," he greeted. "I don't suppose you remember me?"

I shook my head while biting the inside of my cheek.

"The last time I saw you, you were just a baby." His expression softened. "You've grown up, and you look just like your father."

"My father?" My heart almost tore through my chest. "You knew my father?"

"I did." He crouched down in front of me, the hem of his black jacket touching the hardwood floor. "Your father and I, we were cousins. We grew up together." A kind of sadness clouded the blue of his eyes. "I'm sorry I wasn't there for you after he died. I should have come for you sooner, but I didn't think your mother would..." He glanced away as if the thought pained him. "Jesus." He straightened and turned around, pacing while holding his hands in front of his mouth. Even a child like me could see he struggled with whatever he was thinking at that moment. "I'm sorry, Elijah." He looked at me, and his apology made my chest hurt, causing tears to sting my eyes. "I'm sorry I wasn't there for you, but I am now. And you'll never want for anything again."

He rushed toward me and placed his hands on my shoulders—strong, big hands that squeezed tight. "I promised your father a long time ago that if anything should happen, that I'd take care of you. Unfortunately, life hasn't been kind to me the last few years, and I lost track of what was important. But I'm here now, and I plan on keeping my promise to your father." He touched my cheek, almost like a father would. "You'll be happy with us. I have a son your age. His name is Marcello. I'm sure you'll get along just fine."

Wait. What? I inched closer. "Am I going with you?"

"Yes." He smiled. "I'm going to take care of you the way you deserve to be taken care of."

"But I..." I looked at Gianni standing across the room, watching us. "I thought I was staying here with him."

"No, boy. Gianni just helped to get you out of that house, away from those bad people."

"But I want to stay." I shrugged out of Mr. Russo's hold and scrambled toward Gianni as I looked up. "I want to stay with you. Please. Let me stay here with you. I'll be good. You won't even know I'm here. I can cook. I can clean. I can work for extra money. I can do anything, but please," a tear slipped down my cheek, "please let me stay here with you."

I didn't know why I was so desperate to stay with Gianni. It wasn't like I knew him better than I did Mr. Russo. They were both just strangers to me. But there was something about the man who rescued me, something that made me want to stay close to him.

"Please, Gianni," I begged. "Let me stay here...with you."

Gianni looked over at Mr. Russo. "Elijah, why don't you watch some television while Mr. Russo and I go talk in the kitchen privately for a moment? Okay?"

A part of me wanted to beg him one more time so he could see how desperate I was to stay here with him. It was stupid, and I couldn't explain it. I just didn't want to go anywhere else.

Reluctantly, I nodded and sat down on the couch. The fabric was rough and the seat firm. Something told me Gianni didn't watch much television, which was great since all Roland did was sit in front of the TV, his hand in his pants and large belly showing from underneath his shirts which were two sizes too small. I hoped to God the devil didn't give him any mercy as he burned in hell right now.

Gianni switched on the television, turning up the volume so I couldn't eavesdrop. I pretended to watch the cartoon, pretended to like it while I anxiously waited for them. It seemed like hours, my stomach twisted in knots while my fate rested in the palms of their hands.

Gianni cleared his throat, and I jumped up, my gaze darting between the two men.

"Mr. Russo agreed that you could stay here—"

"Thank y—"

He held up his hand. "But it's not permanent," he continued. "At least, not yet. We'll give it some time, see how it goes. If it works out, great. If not, Mr. Russo here has a room waiting for you at his ridiculously large estate."

Mr. Russo frowned, and Gianni shot him a smug grin.

"Thank you." I swayed on my feet and cupped my elbow

with my other hand. "Sir," I looked at Mr. Russo, "you said you knew my father."

He nodded and came closer, waiting for me to continue.

"Do you...do you know what they did to Ellie?"

He arched a brow, glanced to Gianni and then back at me. "Ellie?"

I nodded.

"Boy...who is Ellie?"

"She's my younger sister. They did something to her. Roland and my mom. Roland, he..." I swallowed hard, "he choked me, and I passed out. When I woke up...Ellie, she was gone." Tears burned my eyes, my heart aching as if something squeezed it tight. "They, um...they acted like I was crazy, pretended that Ellie didn't exist. But they did something to her. I know they did." The more I spoke, the angrier the pain got. The more I missed her, wishing she was here now, with Gianni and me—knowing that we had finally been saved.

"Son," Mr. Russo sat down on the couch in front of me, "you didn't have a little sister."

"I did. I mean...I do. Her name is Ellie. She's younger than me. They did something to her. I know they did."

"Your dad never..." He wiped at his mouth with the back of his hand. "Elijah, is it possible that Ellie is your step-sister or half-sister?"

"No. No." I shook my head, my pulse racing. "Ellie is my sister. My real sister." My skin started to crawl, my thoughts scattered in a million directions.

This wasn't happening. Not again.

"Ellie is my real sister," I shouted. I didn't mean to, but my thoughts were so loud I had to raise my voice to hear myself speak. "She's my real sister, and I know they hurt her. They either took her away or..." tears slipped down my face, "or they killed her."

"It's okay, boy." Gianni rushed over and placed his hands on my shoulders. "It's okay. Calm down." He turned to face Mr. Russo. "Are we sure there was no girl?"

"Not that I was aware of," Mr. Russo muttered. "I know Roland had a girl—what was her name? Harley?"

"Harley?" I exclaimed. "No. No. That's Ellie. That's my little sister. Look," I moved closer, "I don't know what they did to her or what happened. All I know is that Roland didn't have a daughter. It's always just been Ellie. There is no Harley."

"Elijah, no." Mr. Russo's face fell as if it pained him to see me like this—so worried and desperate to find my sister. "Roland did have a daughter. She lives with her mom."

"No!" I yelled, and rage exploded from my chest as I grabbed the lamp that stood on the side table, smashing it on the ground. I couldn't stop myself—not while my insides broke into tiny pieces just like the porcelain lamp.

"Elijah!" Gianni's voice ricocheted through the living room, frightening my rage back into its cage. "Control," he snapped. "Get control of yourself."

His reprimand made my cheeks burn, and I could no longer look him in the eye as embarrassment flooded over me. So I slipped into the corner, my back sliding down the wall until my ass touched the cold ground.

"I think we should take him to a doctor. Get him checked out," Mr. Russo remarked, and I refused to look up. "We have no idea what kind of trauma this kid's been through. I'll arrange an appointment with a child psychologist first thing in the morning."

I pulled my knees up to my chest, burying my face against my arms, rocking like a crazy person. Maybe I was crazy. Maybe Roland and my mom were right.

"Give me a few days with the boy first," Gianni said. "Before we get doctors involved."

"Are you sure?"

"Yes. Just a few days."

Silence settled around us, and I still didn't look up. I didn't want to look at their faces, see the pity on their expressions while their thoughts and logic convinced them that I had been abused into madness.

"Okay," I heard Mr. Russo concede. "But if you can't get through to him, he's coming to live with us where I can keep an eye on his counseling."

His every word crawled down my spine, the thought of seeing doctors and getting counseling making me feel sick to my stomach.

The door slammed shut, and I heard Gianni's footsteps. "Look at me."

I clenched my jaw.

"Elijah, I said look at me."

I lifted my head, my gaze slowly slipping to where he sat on the couch, elbows on his knees and clutching his hands together.

"We need to talk, but first, you need to dry those tears and get control. Otherwise, talking won't do us any good."

I remained silent.

"Okay?" he urged, and I swallowed hard before wiping

the tears from my face. Angry tears. Hopeless tears. My tears.

"Now," he inched to the edge of his seat, "are you ready to hear what I have to say?"

I bit my lip and nodded, pulling my legs closer against my chest.

"I believe you."

My heart hiccupped. "You do?"

"I do. I believe you have a little sister and that her name is Ellie. I also believe that those monsters who did such a piss-poor job raising you tried to take her away from you."

I wiped my nose with the back of my hand. "Why? Mr. Russo doesn't believe me. Why do you?"

"Because I've seen her. I've seen Ellie."

I leaped to my feet, my heart about to tear through my ribs. "Do you know where she is? Is she okay? Can we go get her?"

"Calm down, boy." He held up his hands. "It was a while ago, and unfortunately, I don't know what they did to her. But I promise we will figure it out. If she is out there, I will do everything I can to help you find her. Okay?"

I rubbed the back of my neck, casting my gaze down to the hardwood floors, a single moment of hope causing an avalanche of disappointment.

"Elijah. I swear to you, if she's out there, I will find her. But you need to do something for me first. Now, look at me."

I did, and the second I looked into his eyes I could see his determination. I could see the trust, the belief, the bond.

"Sit down and listen to what I'm about to say."

I took a seat across from him, curious and scared at the same time.

THE VILLAIN

"Sometimes, we need to give the world what it wants in order to get what we want."

I frowned in question.

"Manipulation, if you want to call it that." He shifted. "You want to stay here with me, don't you?"

I licked my lips, my heart beating incredibly fast. "Yes, sir."

"You want to find your sister?"

"Yes. Sir."

He tilted his head to the side, his salt and pepper hair touching the top of his ear. "Then you give Mr. Russo what he wants so you can get what you want."

"I don't understand. How—"

"It's simple. He feels guilty for not coming for you sooner, so he's going to want to be involved every step of the way. Overcompensate by giving you the care he thinks you need," he shrugged, "and right now, he thinks you need to see a psychiatrist. So what you have to do is not give him any reason to believe that you need counseling. That you are happy here with me. Stable."

My top lip curled. "So, I have to lie? Pretend that Ellie doesn't exist?"

"Exactly. If you don't, he will take you and force you to see a doctor. If you give them any reason to think you're crazy, they will treat you like you're crazy. And that, dear boy, will take away every chance you have of ever finding your sister."

My head hurt. But in some twisted way, what he said made sense. Mr. Russo already wanted to take me away from here, and right now, here was the only place I wanted to be.

He stood, his six-foot frame towering over me. "From

today, you never mention Ellie's name to anyone but me, understood?"

In my mind, I could still see her face as if I had seen her five minutes ago. Her cute little smile, her blonde ponytail bobbing as she jumped around, laughing. She was the only part of my life that made sense. It was because of her that I held on, never giving in to the darkness Roland and my mom threatened to drown me in. So if pretending was what I needed to do to find her, then that was what I'd do.

I got to my feet and looked up at Gianni, knowing that this was the day my life would change forever. "Understood."

CHAPTER TWENTY-SEVEN

CHARLOTTE

Present

The door creaked open, and I leaped to my feet as Elijah walked out.

"Everything okay?"

"Everything's fine." He shot me a half-smile, but it didn't fool me. "Just two friends catching up."

"You don't look like a guy who just spent an hour catching up with an old friend."

Elijah snaked an arm around my waist and turned to face Saint. "Will you be staying a few days?"

"Wish I could. But even though my wife is basking in the lap of luxury at the hotel in Rome, she'd be really pissed off if she knew I was staying on The Empress without her." He glanced around. "We got married on this yacht, so we have some…" he cleared his throat, "fond memories of our first time together on this beauty."

"Jesus, Saint." Elijah rolled his eyes. "We're all adults here. You can just say that you fucked like rabbits on this yacht."

"Among other things." Saint smirked and buttoned his suit jacket, the confidence he exuded bordering on arrogance. With Elijah clutching me against him and Saint staring me down with his crystal blue eyes, it was hard to fucking breathe because their presence alone sucked all the air out of the room.

"Charlotte." My name rolled off Saint's lips like honey, yet there was a certain look in his eyes as he pinned my gaze. A warning. A glimpse of caution. "Maybe you and Elijah should join my wife and me for dinner one night. It would be great to get to know you better."

"Um," I wiped my palm down my leg, "that sounds great. What do you think, Elijah?"

"I think there are more important matters at hand than a simple social dinner." His words were clipped, his tone stern.

Saint slipped his hands in his pants pockets, the two men staring at each other as if they could read each other's minds, making me feel like I was the third wheel here—a voyeur on whatever the fuck was going on between them.

"Come on, Elijah." Saint held out his arms. "This is Rome. You don't bring your woman to this beautiful city and not show her around."

Elijah widened his stance, the lack of amusement painfully evident in his expression. "I'll consider it."

"Good. Great," Saint said and held out his hand toward

me. "It was great meeting you, Charlotte. Take care of this guy. God knows, he needs it."

"Oh, I highly doubt that." I glanced from Saint to Elijah. "Something tells me he can take care of himself just fine." Of course, he could. The man was a goddamn hitman for the mafia—if anyone could take care of themselves, it was Elijah. But I wasn't sure how much Saint knew about Elijah's profession, so I chose not to say too much.

"Elijah." Saint nodded in his direction. "You and Charlotte are welcome to stay on The Empress for as long as you like."

"It will only be for a few more days."

It will?

Saint straightened his jacket. "Don't underestimate the Bernardis. Make sure it's safe to travel before you decide to do so."

Elijah pressed his lips in a thin line, and I could practically feel the tension ripple off him. "You don't have to worry, my friend. I know how to handle the Bernardis."

"I'm sure you do."

For a second, their gazes remained fixed on one another—a stare-off of giants. What the hell was going on?

Saint turned and nodded at James before both of them walked up to the deck. Once they were out of earshot, I shrugged out of Elijah's hold and turned to face him. "What was that?"

"What was what?"

"That. You and Saint."

He pulled a hand through his hair. "I told you. We're good friends."

"It sure didn't look that way."

"Saint and I have known each other for years. We have a...weird relationship."

I scoffed. "No shit. For friends, it sure looked like you'd rather beat each other up than shake hands."

He placed his hands on his sides, sighing as he looked up at the ceiling. "I was just a little on edge because of Saint's unplanned visit."

"Why, though?" I frowned. "It's his yacht."

"And this is your life on the line. I told you, we can't afford to take any risks. And him coming here is a risk."

"Why is it a risk?"

He grabbed my shoulders and pulled me closer, almost lifting me on my toes. "Everything that's not part of my plan to protect you is a risk. Our first mistake will be underestimating the Bernardi family and their fucking desperation to get to you. I will not take any chances, Charlotte." He brought his face inches from mine, his breath warm and eyes burning. "Not with you."

His grip tightened around my arms, and I could feel the blood rushing to my skin, my heart pounding against my chest as Elijah's expression darkened. "Don't you get it? You are my number one priority."

"Because of a debt." The words slipped from my mouth, and I hated how insecure it sounded. But I couldn't stop myself. "That's what I am, right? A debt. That's the reason you're so desperate to protect me."

He let go of my shoulders, stepping back, eyes leveling me with a gaze so dark I felt its chill inside my veins. "Is that what this is? You're insecure and trying to get some kind of affirmation from me. For what?" He shifted closer. "To get some sort of commitment? To feel wanted? To know that you're no longer my captive?"

I saw the challenge in his eyes. The malice. In that study with Saint, whatever went down had him riled up, and now I was on the receiving end.

Putting one foot in front of the other, I took a step that brought our bodies a breath apart, my neck craned back so I could look him in the eye. "Maybe I want affirmation that the man I share a bed with sees me as more than just a debt. Maybe I want to know that the man I allow to fuck me every goddamn night isn't just using me as a pastime while we're stuck on this yacht."

The expression on his face turned to stone, and as he moved forward, I had no choice but to step back. "You *allow* me to fuck you?"

"You know what I—"

"Is that what you've been doing every time I slipped my cock into your cunt? You *allowed* me to fuck you?"

My heart started to beat incredibly fast. "That's not what I meant."

"You spread those thighs of yours, your pussy dripping while you pant for me to fuck you—yet now you say you *allow* me to be inside you?"

"Elijah—"

"There's a difference between allowing something and wanting it, Charlotte." My back hit the wall, and he cocooned me. "A huge motherfucking difference."

"I know that."

"No. I don't think you do." He leaned his head to the side as he dragged a finger down my cheek, his predator gaze studying me as if he couldn't decide where to start tearing me apart. "Should I show you? Teach you the difference?"

"I didn't mean it like that, and you know it."

His fingers bit into my jaw as he forced my head to the side, causing me to flinch as he leaned in, lips touching my ear. "I think I should show you the difference by fucking you as my captive rather than my guest."

"Elijah—" His arms roped around my waist and lifted me over his shoulder. "Elijah, what are you doing?"

"Exactly what I said. I'm going to show you how a psychopath fucks his captive."

He carried me into my room, slamming the door closed behind us with his foot.

"Elijah, don't."

"Now would be a good time for you to close that mouth of yours." He dropped me on the bed, but before I had a chance to move, his fingers tore through his shirt, buttons bouncing on the floor around us. "Unless you want to taste my cock on your tongue."

Somewhere really far back in my mind, I knew his words were meant to intimidate, to scare me into submission. But this twisted side in me loved every dirty word he spoke. And the sight of him, his firm abs, and the delicate music notes inked onto his skin—it took my breath away. It did every time we were together, and all I wanted to do was trace my fingertips around his chest, feeling his velvet skin against my palm as I laid it over his heart. Even now, while he towered over me like a threatening storm, I still wanted him. My body still craved him. My thighs were already burning with the anticipation of feeling him between my legs—feel him move as he pumped in and out of me. But there was something different in his eyes tonight—as if a starved beast was looking down at me, bloodlust oozing from his gaze.

He stepped up, cupping my chin in his palm as he forced me to look up at him. His touch was tender, his finger gently brushing across my bottom lip. It was a moment that warmed my heart...until he wrapped his fingers around my throat, tightening. I clasped both hands around his wrist, gasping for air. "Elijah..."

"You're a beautiful woman, Charlotte. The kind of beauty men like me would kill to protect and keep." He forced me to my feet, still squeezing the air from my lungs. "But insecurities can spoil that beauty. Turn it rancid." He pulled me closer, his lips brushing against mine, causing me to crave his taste. "It's pathetic. Unbecoming."

My cheeks burned as embarrassment rushed to the surface. Finally, his grip loosened enough for me to be able to speak. "Under normal circumstances, any woman needs security when it comes to a man. And, given how fucked up our situation is, I think me having some insecurities is understandable."

"Don't fool yourself, my little cellist. It's the fucked-up part in our situation that you crave the most."

"You don't know me."

He leaned forward, and I closed my eyes as he dragged his tongue up the side of my face. Warm. Wet. Wicked. "I told you this before. No one knows you as well as I do. And after our few weeks together, I know you...inside...and out."

"So you think."

A grin settled on his face, his lips glistening. "On your knees."

"Excuse me?"

His hand enclosed around my throat, choking me, allowing me no air to breathe. "On your. Fucking knees."

With my palms around his wrist, Elijah forced me to the ground. It was there in his face when I glanced up at him in panic. The darkness. The wicked intent. His need to dominate absolute.

The wooden floors were hard beneath my knees, my lungs burning and body screaming to take a breath. Sweat beaded down my back, and pressure throbbed behind my eyes.

"I'm going to loosen my grip now. If you scramble away, try to run, I will tie you down and fuck your mouth so hard you'll gag and choke while I shoot my cum down your fucking throat. Understood?"

There it was. The heat. The need. The undeniable desire to be owned. It consumed me, burned inside my belly while my pussy ached. It was sick and twisted—a black hole that fed on the depravity that pulsed between Elijah and me. I hated it. But I loved it. I despised it yet craved it like my next breath.

The moment his hand left my throat, I gasped for air, the oxygen burning my lungs. I touched my neck, the sting of his grip still lingering on my skin. "Why are you hurting me?"

"Isn't that what a psychopath does to his captive? Hurt her. Use her. Fuck her."

The sound of him unbuckling his belt caused me to quiver, not knowing what to expect from him. Not while he was like this—consumed. Possessed. Unpredictable.

Exhilarating.

Like a prowling predator, he moved in behind me, taking both my hands in his. I gasped when I felt the bite of leather on my skin as he fastened his belt around my wrists. My instinct to fight fused with adrenaline, but there was something more potent that burned in my belly—something wicked and tainted. Something that had me wanting everything he had to offer. Thrilling pain and aching pleasure.

Dark eyes gazed down at me as he stepped back in front of me and unzipped his pants, licking his lips as he slipped his hands inside, pulling out his cock. It was impossibly hard, his fingers wrapping around the thick girth, and all I could think about was how it felt to have him inside me—how exquisite it was to feel him move in and out of me while my pussy was slick with need.

He pumped his length once, stroking across the tip of his cock. A part of me feared the man in front of me, yet another part lusted for him. Admired him while I knelt on the floor, forced to look up at him, his naked body contoured and defined to perfection.

"There is something about a woman on her knees that just seems so fucking right."

He grabbed my hair, yanked my head back and brought his cock an inch from my mouth. I could smell sex on him, the exhilarating anticipation of fucking and savagery. Every thought inside my head tried to convince me that I should hate this. That I should be appalled by the unforgiving way he treated me. But I didn't. It was quite the opposite—my body humming with adrenaline and lust, my senses heightened as I craved more.

"I'm not your captive." I tried to sound horrified, scared when, in fact, I was exhilarated. As much as he wanted to hunt, I wanted to be hunted. I wanted to be the prey...his prey.

His lips curved in a wicked grin as if he knew. He thrust his hip, the tip of his cock brushing against my lips. Fire erupted in my belly, my body electrified with the energy that crackled between us.

"Lick it."

I didn't move.

Playing.

He yanked my hair, causing my scalp to burn. "I said lick my motherfucking cock."

I wanted to defy him, keep on fighting him until the beast broke free, but I craved his taste too much. While I looked up at him, meeting his dark gaze with my own, I opened my mouth. He bit his lower lip when my tongue touched the tip of his dick, licking leisurely circles around it. The naïve little masochist that I was tried to savor it, tried to play with the beast. But I should have known better. I should have known that my sexual prowess was no match for his mastery.

With a snarl, he thrust his hips and plunged his cock into my mouth, forcing me to take every inch of him, giving me no time to open my throat or hollow my cheeks to accommodate him. I gagged, but he only tightened his grip in my hair more—pushing deeper, harder, mercilessly pumping his length in and out of my mouth.

My eyes teared up, and spit dripped down my chin as I struggled to take him. His taste exploded on my tongue and consumed my tastebuds, and a half-cry, half-moan slipped up the back of my throat.

"See, now that's what a captive's face is supposed to look like when her mouth is stuffed with cock." He wiped at a tear with his thumb before placing it in his mouth. "Tasting a person's tears is as close as you'll come to consuming their soul."

The words 'fuck you' got lodged in my throat as he pushed my head forward, flexing his hips, filling my mouth with his length. I gagged again, and this time my back arched with the reflex.

"You need to slack your jaw, princess. Or you'll be choking on your vomit instead of my dick."

While I tried to open my mouth wide enough, slipping my tongue around the ridges of his girth, my thighs trembled as my pussy throbbed.

"God, your mouth is like velvet around my dick. But as good as it feels, it doesn't come close to having your pussy clench my cock."

I moaned, and he grabbed the base of his length, pumping it in his palm as he fucked my mouth. It was a vile act of dominance, the way he forced and controlled me. But there was no denying how fiercely my body burned for it. How it hungered for more.

More pain. More dominance. More of Elijah's wicked kink and sordid lust.

"You want security, do you, my little cellist?"

I glanced up at him, barely able to breathe as I sucked him between my lips, my panties wet and slick with jaded lust.

"You want me to mark you as mine?"

Yes. Yes, I did. I wanted to be his. I wanted to know that even when his debt was repaid, he'd still want me. He'd still own me. I never wanted another man's touch ever again. Only his. Always, only his.

I nodded and licked around his swollen length when he

pulled at my hair, yanking my head back. His cock slipped from my mouth with a pop, and he groaned as he sucked air through his teeth, shooting his cum on my face, the warm liquid sticking to my cheek and chin.

It was degrading. Humiliating. But he did what I wanted him to do. He marked me, and by doing so, he made me feel more alive than I ever had. My body, my mind, my soul, everything was set alight by this man, even if everything about him, about us, was distorted and twisted. Deep inside, if I had to be honest with myself…

I wouldn't want it any other way.

CHAPTER TWENTY-EIGHT

ELIJAH

The twisted son of a bitch in me had always fantasized of seeing her on her knees, vulnerable and entirely at my mercy. I'd wanted to play this little game with her ever since I dragged my finger through her slick pussy for the first time. But I wasn't sure she'd be able to handle it. There was a fine line between a man's hunger for carnal lust with a woman he cared for and a serpent's appetite for fucked up fuckery with every pussy he can get his dirty hands on. I wasn't sure if she'd be able to distinguish between the two when it came to me. Knowing what I felt for her, believing it while I opened the gates of my depraved desires.

And, Jesus Christ, did she exceed all my expectations. I took a huge motherfucking risk by playing this game—but she played it just as hard, and I fucking loved it.

I let go of my cock, now limp and wet from her spit. I touched her chin, wiping my cum along her lower lip with my thumb. "How do I taste?"

Her eyes were red, but her irises bright with ecstasy as

she licked her lips, tasting me on her tongue. "Good," she whispered, her hair a tangled mess around her face.

I helped her to her feet, her hands still tied behind her back. I took the hem of her shirt between my fingers and lifted it, wiping her face clean of my cum. I'd be the world's biggest fucking liar if I said I didn't like seeing my jizz staining her pretty face.

Her cheeks had a healthy pink glow, her lips glistening with temptation. Her body was quivering, and I could smell her arousal, sense her need to come. And even though I still felt the aftermath of my orgasm lingering in my balls, I was far from done with her.

The fabric of her shirt required no effort to be torn down the middle, exposing the flawless skin of her stomach and enticing swell of her breasts.

The torn material pooled around her feet, and I swirled a fingertip around her pebbled nipple. "God, I love your tits."

Her eyes closed as I squeezed her breast.

"On the bed. And on your knees."

"But my hands."

"What about them?"

"They're still tied."

I grabbed her elbow and turned her around, pulling her naked back against my bare chest, snaking my hands down her front, slipping inside her shorts, helping her shimmy out of them. The second I dragged a finger through her slit, I groaned in appreciation of how fucking wet she was, her pussy weeping for my dick. "I know your hands are tied," I whispered with my lips against her ear, slowly easing her forward toward the bed. "And that's why your pretty face will just have to be firmly planted on those silk sheets."

The most beautiful yelp crossed her lips as I pushed her, forcing her down on the bed. I grabbed her ankles and forced her to lean on her knees, her cheek flush against the crisp navy-blue linen. I took a step back, admiring the view of her ass in the air, pussy lips spread, and hands tied. The perfect fucking picture of submission—a woman, surrendering her body to a man. If only she knew how goddamn beautiful she was. The potent perfection that radiated from her every minute of every day.

"You have no idea how perfect you are, do you?"

"Every woman has her insecurities."

"Well, you shouldn't have any." I placed my palm on her ass, gently easing it down her thigh. "It's ironic how every time you hold that bow, leaning the cello against your heart, you strive to find perfection—yet you are perfection, Charlotte." I eased a finger through her wet folds, her moan a fucking melody to my ears. "You've spent your whole life trying to find perfection when it's been staring back at you for so fucking long."

"I'm not perfect." Her lips brushed against the silk sheets. "Especially when I'm with you."

I stilled. "What does that mean?"

"It means that when I'm with you like this, my body, my thoughts all delve into this dark place." She closed her eyes, taking a visibly deep breath. "And I like it. I like being in the dark with you, Elijah. I love how my body feels when I submit to you. How my skin burns when your touch hurts. How my lust ignites when your words are harsh."

Sure as fuck, her words slammed right in my chest and crashed against my balls, turning my dick to fucking stone. "So, how does that not make you perfect?"

"Because...because how can I be good, perfect, when I crave to be fucked by a man who kidnapped me, held me against my will? How can I be perfect when..." her throat bobbed as she swallowed, "when I'm in love with a man who kills people as easily as taking his next breath?"

And that was the moment my entire goddamn world changed. Her words, her confession of love, it was instantly engraved in my soul, my heart becoming too big for my fucking chest.

"You're in love with me." It wasn't a question. It was more like that pinch one needed to make sure you weren't dreaming. I knew I had been in love with her since the first moment I heard her play the cello, but I never thought of the day she'd say those words, feel the same way about me as I did about her.

"I am," she whispered, a silent tear lapping from her cheek onto the sheets.

I licked my lips, and suddenly having her tied up in this exact moment felt wrong—so I grabbed my belt, ready to untie her, but she jerked away.

"Don't. Whatever you planned on doing...I want you to do it. I need you to do it."

It was there in her voice, her desperation, her plea to play. To do wicked things while we danced in the darkness. Jesus Christ—there was no doubt just how obsessed I was with this woman. Not after this.

"Okay." I moved my hand from her wrists, down her side to cup her breast as I got onto my knees next to her, the mattress dipping under my weight. "But I think you need to hear me say one thing before we continue."

She bit her bottom lip, her hands tugging against the leather.

I tasted her skin as I traced my tongue along the curve of her back, placing a kiss on her naked shoulder and leaning down, so my lips touched her ear. "I'm in love with you, Charlotte Moore." She sucked in a breath. "I've been obsessed with you since that first time I heard you play." Her body squirmed, a subtle moan wafting from her lips. "You have possessed my every thought, every dream, every filthy fantasy for so fucking long. This right here, you like this, us...this is what I want. What I crave. What I need. And now that I have this—have you, I think it's only fair you should know that..." I licked around the shell of her ear, her body shuddering and skin hot, "there is no chance in hell I'm ever letting you go. Ever. Do you understand the magnitude of that? Of what I just said?"

She nodded, and I moved back, brushing my hand around her thigh to touch her sweet, needy little cunt.

"See," I slipped a finger inside her, and she pushed her greedy hips back, "I don't think you do. I don't think you understand just how fucking serious I am when I say I'm never letting you go." The sound of her arousal sucking my finger into her pussy made my balls tight and my dick hard. My thumb found her clit, and her knees quivered. "Not even if you ask me. You can beg, you can plead, you can scream, and fucking cry—not even your tears will have the power to convince me to let you go." I drew my finger out of her and spread her arousal up between her ass cheeks, applying the slightest amount of pressure at her tight little hole. She gasped, and her entire body went rigid, a telltale sign that no man has ever touched her there before.

Good. In time, it would be mine. But not today.

I positioned myself behind her and could see the trail of goosebumps on her skin, kissed with a glistening sheen of sweat and heat. The tip of my cock touched her swollen cunt, her body so hyperaware of every single touch it trembled before me, her hips leaning back in an attempt to take me, to have me fill her so she could shatter with the release she so desperately needed.

"Do you understand what I'm saying, Charlotte?" I held my dick and brushed it along her ass, painting her skin with my precum, teasing the fuck out of her. "There is only one thing that could ever take you away from me." I steadied myself at her entrance. "One thing that not even I can escape. Death." The sheets ruffled beneath my knees as I plunged into her—deep, hard, impaling her body and owning her pussy with one hard thrust. Her moans slammed against the ceiling, crashing against the walls around us, her shoulders forced against the mattress. The heat of her greedy pussy wrapped around my cock, clamping down, allowing me to feel her inner walls and the slick friction of euphoria I could only find between her legs.

"You hear that? The only way you can get rid of me is if death comes for one of us." I reared back and speared back into her, hitting the deepest part of her. "Other than that, you're mine, and I'll slit the throat of any person who dares to take you away from me." Saying it, envisioning it, thinking about the blood of my victims coating my hands, crusting around my fingernails—all for the name of love, the love I had for my cellist—it made my dick throb and balls ache, lust scraping at my spine with its wicked intentions. "You know," I reached around her hip, arching my back as I found her clit.

"A part of me wished someone would just look at you funny, so I have half a reason to slice him open from nose to navel, reach inside his chest and squeeze the last bit of life from his rotten heart. Maybe then you'll realize how fucking important you are to me. Far more than some debt a thankful little boy felt he had to pay."

"Dear God," she moaned, pushing her face deeper into the sheets, her hips pushed out toward me, making her pussy bloom while I fucked her.

"You like that, don't you? Thinking of me spilling blood for you, pulling out a man's heart all in the name of love."

"I guess that makes us both fucked up." She squirmed, trying to match my every thrust as much as she possibly could with her hands tied behind her back.

Sweat beaded around my temples, my heart racing as if it could tear from my chest, my body rigid as tension gripped every muscle, ready to pump my release into her.

"I need you to come," I ordered through my rapid breaths. "And I want to fucking hear you."

"Elijah." Her lips parted, eyes closed, and lips glistening. "Harder."

Snaking my arm around her waist, pulling her tighter against my pelvis, skin slapping on skin, I pressed down on her clit, working her pussy as if my fucking life depended on it. "You better come on my cock before I cream this cunt of yours, cellist."

Her moans grew louder as I pistoned harder, faster, mercilessly in and out of her. My balls smacked against her skin, and I bit my bottom lip, tasting my own blood while I fought for control, wanting her to come. But, Jesus, I was on the edge, my body ready to tip over. That was when I let go of her waist, reached for her hair, fisting the dark strands, and pulled her head back, causing her to scream. God, her screams. It was beautiful.

"That's it," I bit out, pulling her hair harder and fucking her cunt faster. "Scream for me, baby. Let me hear your pleasure."

"Elijah. I'm coming." And then I felt it, her pussy throbbing around my cock as she climaxed, her walls sucking me in deeper as her entire body trembled. Sweet, violent moans of ecstasy filled the bedroom, and I never wanted her to stop. I loved hearing her scream my name and watching her come undone because of my cock.

As her screams quieted, my orgasm snapped from my spine and slammed against the tip of my dick, jerking and throbbing as I spilled my load inside her. It was so fucking intense, every muscle in my body ached.

My cock was still twitching when I reached for the belt around her wrists, untying it. She fell forward, and I groaned as I slipped out of her, instantly mourning the loss of her slick heat.

I lay down on top of her—her back against my chest, her ass spooning perfectly against my cock. I eased the hair from the side of her face, both of us still breathing rapidly. "Don't ever doubt my intentions when it comes to you. Do you understand me?"

She clutched the silk sheets between her fingers, her wrists red from where the leather had bitten into her skin. "Yes," she whispered, her voice almost inaudible.

"You're my cellist," I rasped against her ear, "my obsession...my requiem."

CHAPTER TWENTY-NINE

CHARLOTTE

The sound of his rhythmic breathing calmed me. The early sunrise peeked through the round windows, casting shimmering rays across the room. It was going to be a beautiful sunny day in Italy today.

Italy.

God. I had never gotten the opportunity to travel, and here I was off the coast of Italy on a yacht, yet unable to explore and experience one of the most romantic cities in the world.

I hate Murphy.

My thoughts drifted to my grandfather and what Elijah had told me about him. Just like Elijah, Gianni Guerra was a hitman for the mafia. A killer. A contractor. A soldier for this Bernardi family Elijah was so hellbent on protecting me from. I didn't know these people. I didn't know my grandfather. I didn't even know Elijah until he stormed in and placed himself right in the center of my life. A man who was raised by my grandfather, trained by him to be a killer. And judging by the number of music notes inked on Elijah's skin, I'd say he did a fucking brilliant job.

I slipped my arm from underneath the pillow, and I felt that all too familiar stiffness in my hand. It ached, my fingers burning as I moved them, trying to warm them up and get some blood flowing. It was probably too much to ask to have a sunshine day *and* a pain-free one as well.

Elijah tightened his hold around my waist, pulling me closer. His cock stirred and hardened against my ass, his palm cupping my breast.

I smiled. "Good morning, Mr. Mariano."

"Oh, it's a good morning indeed." He traced his lips against my naked shoulder, peppering kisses along my skin. "There is no better feeling in the world than waking up and finding you here next to me. Naked and ready for me."

He squeezed my breast, rolling my nipple between his fingers, stirring to life a new flame inside my core. But as much as my body craved to be used by him once again, my mind wandered to the streets of Italy, to Gianni currently behind bars in prison somewhere.

"I want to meet him."

He stilled, his hand paused on my breast.

"I want to meet my grandfather, Elijah." I turned on my back so I could look at him. "Please."

Those lustrous amber eyes I found myself lost in over and over again turned dark, the sexual tension snapping in half, leaving his body cold and his expression ice.

"I told you, it's not safe." The sheets swooshed as he abruptly got out of bed, and I sat up on my elbows, watching him pull on a pair of pants.

"I know. But isn't there a way for us to make it safe? I don't know, change my name, color my hair, something." Despondent and frustrated, I lay back down, staring up at the ceiling. "He's the only family I have left, and besides wanting to meet him, I'd love to..." My voice trailed off.

"Love to what?" Elijah stilled and studied me. "Love to what, Charlotte?"

I sat back up, clutching the silk sheet in front of my chest. "I've never been anywhere my entire life, and now I'm here in Italy, yet...I'm not."

"What are you saying?"

"I'm saying," I brushed the curls from my face, "I want to go and see Italy instead of being stuck on this damn yacht. I want to join Saint and his wife for dinner, and at least pretend for just a little while that everything is normal."

"We are stuck on this yacht for your protection. This is not a fucking trip around the world." He stomped to my side of the bed, dark eyes glowering down at me. "I didn't bring you here so you can explore Italy and sight-see."

"I know that—"

"If you knew that, why are you saying this to me now? I thought you understood."

I grabbed the sheet and shot to my feet. "You know what...no, I don't understand. Everything you've told me has been so damn vague, it's impossible for me to piece it all together."

"What?" He scowled.

"I'm serious. Honestly, I don't care whether you're vague on purpose or not. I don't care if there are things you're not telling me. I just want to meet my grandfather and not be stuck on this yacht when Rome is right there." I pointed out the window on my left, the waves rippling across the ocean outside.

Elijah roughed a hand through his disheveled hair, rubbing the back of his neck before pointing in the other direction. "It's that side, actually."

"What is?"

He lifted a brow. "Rome. It's that way."

"God," I huffed. "I don't care, Elijah. I just can't believe that life would be so hellbent on fucking me in the ass by bringing me halfway across the world and not have me see at least some parts of Italy."

His expression softened, yet his gaze remained pinned on mine—a moment of tenderness and affection flashing in his eyes. His palms were warm as he cupped my cheeks, stepping closer. "Firstly, if anyone is fucking you in the ass...it's me."

"Stop." I couldn't help but smile and tried to look away when he forced me to meet his gaze.

"Secondly," he licked his lips followed by a tick in his strong jaw, "what kind of man would I be if I didn't at least show half of this romantic city to the woman I love?"

The woman I love. Four words that had the power to melt any defiance I might have had.

I leaned into him, placing my hands on his chest—his skin warm with the subtle brush of chest hair against my palms. "Thank you."

"Don't thank me yet. Thirdly—"

"Oh, no." My excitement wavered as I let my head down.

"Thirdly," he emphasized before placing his hand

beneath my chin, lifting my face so I could look him in the eye, "I can't promise that you'll be able to see your grandfather."

"Elijah—"

"Besides the fact that it's not safe, Gianni is under state protection until the trial has run its course. Most probably even after that. Maybe forever."

"He's all I have left."

"I know." He touched my bottom lip with his thumb. "Which is why I'll do everything I can to make it happen. But I can't make any promises."

To say that he'd try was better than to have him give me a straight-up no. The hope of meeting the only living relative I had left was better than having no hope at all.

Lifting myself on my toes, I kissed his lips softly before licking his taste off my own. "Thank you."

His dark brows slanted inward. "Oh, you'll be thanking me...tonight. Naked."

"You know, for a man who kills people for a living, you are such a guy."

"A man has his needs."

"Uh-huh."

"Okay," he stepped back, "apparently, I have travel arrangements to make, and a huge fucking protection detail to plan."

I was impossibly giddy with excitement—minus the daunting knowledge of some mafia family who wanted to get their hands on me and do God-knows-what to me.

A stabbing pain jolted up my fingers, into my right hand, and I tried to shake it out, fisting my fingers.

Elijah stilled as he reached the door, glancing back at me with a pained expression. "If I were a man who believed in miracles, in God...I'd pray for Him to rid you of that cross you have to bear."

"I'm fine, Elijah. It's—" But he was out the door before I could say anything more. It had been so long since there was someone in my life who cared so much about me that my pain became his. It was bittersweet having someone care so deeply for me.

I took my time showering, getting dressed, blow-drying my hair, and adding a touch of make-up. Even though the sun was shining, autumn meant an early winter chill would be in the air, so I opted for black denim jeans and an oversized white turtleneck. It took a moment's glance in the mirror to convince me that I would never be able to play the part of an affluent, high society, glamor girl. A rich man's wife. A mafia wife.

My stomach turned. Every now and then it hit me that my life had become a live action movie. A goddamn *Sopranos* episode with mafia bosses and assassins, my grandfather being a part of that world. The man I shared a bed with too.

There was no use denying it or trying to fight what I felt for Elijah. Whatever the future held for me, for us...all I knew was I wanted him to be a part of it. No matter what the cost, or the sacrifice.

The cello case caught my eye, and there was this overwhelming urge inside me to play. To lose myself in the music. To find silence just for a short while.

Every time I touched the neck of a cello, the feel of the

smooth finish would remind me of how deep my passion for music ran—how firmly it was engraved into my soul. The bow, the strings, the earthy scent of resin—this majestic instrument and its power to create flawless vibrations and timeless tenors were the oxygen in my blood. It was the one constant in my life.

I closed my eyes as the cello's neck rested against my heart, hyperaware of the weight of the bow in my palm. With my feet flat on the ground, posture firm and breathing steady, I waited for the music to pour out of me and resonate on the instrument. Only, it didn't come. Not while my fingers ached and my palms burned. A two-and-a-half-pound bow suddenly weighed a ton, and I was barely able to keep it steady.

God, no. I wanted to play. I needed to play. My soul yearned for the melody while my mind craved the silence. But my body had declared war against my needs—its weapon, rheumatoid arthritis.

Frustration pulsed in the back of my head while I desperately tried to bite back the tears. It wasn't the first time I couldn't play because of my hands, and it wouldn't be my last. Yet every goddamn time it fucked with my head—slicing a part of my soul from my bones. As if it wasn't enough not being able to play in front of people, I had to have this crutch forced on me as well.

Try again. I could hear her say it. My mom, standing behind me, urging me to try again after I had failed to find that perfect vibrato for over two hours.

Never give up.

If you want it bad enough, it will happen.

Every dream has its sacrifices. You either make those sacrifices and live with the consequences, or live without the dream.

"With it," I whispered. "Not without."

I lifted my shoulder, inhaling deeply, steadying the bow. I tried. God knows, I tried. But the pain was too debilitating and far stronger than my love for music. Today, anyway.

A tear slipped down my cheek as I lowered my arms, and as I opened my eyes I stared right at him. Elijah. Standing by the door, watching me, his expression a reflection of my pain.

There was no way I could have hidden what I felt at that moment. Frustration. Disappointment. A longing to do what I loved without limitations. Even knowing how it affected Elijah couldn't stop all the feelings from sweeping over me.

I cried, dropping the bow to the ground. Elijah was at my feet, replacing the cello with his comforting presence, wrapping his arms around me and pulling me down to the floor with him, cradling me against his chest.

My solace. My peace. My protector.

A gentle stroke of his hand brushed at a curl that clung to my wet cheek. "I'd fight the devil for you, Charlotte. And I'd go on my knees before God...for you."

The power that resonated from his words slammed against the deepest part of my soul. To hear a man like him who thrived on power, putting his faith in no one but himself, say that he'd surrender for me was such a defining moment, my heart could burst. This was him revealing that he loved me without telling me. Erasing those three words and replacing them with a piece of his soul. Along with the affection I already had for this man came a sense of appreciation, thankfulness...relief that I no longer had to bear this cross alone.

I nestled my face into his chest. "Where have you been all my life?"

"I've always been there." His fingers weaved through my hair. "You just never saw me."

CHAPTER THIRTY

ELIJAH

There was a storm brewing in the dark clouds outside. I could smell the rain, feel the looming thunder coming from the distance. Maybe it was the universe's way of telling me that I had made a massive mistake by bringing Charlotte here.

Roma. It was a beautiful city that spoke to my soul whenever I was here, walking its streets and watching its people. Knowing how magical this city was, I couldn't deny Charlotte's desire to experience it herself. Yes, my first priority was to keep her safe and out of the hands of the Bernardis. But her happiness had become my priority as well the second I told her I loved her.

Soft hands snaked around my middle from behind, and I closed my eyes, relishing the feel of her. Her presence. Her peace.

"Did you enjoy the spa bath?"

"Hmm-mm. Totally ruined a normal bathtub for me."

I snickered, loving the thought of pleasing her. Even if it meant soaking in a bath for an hour.

"Thank you," she whispered, leaning her head against my back.

I placed my hand on top of her twined fingers. "I would do anything for you, Charlotte. Never doubt that."

The gentle pitter-patter of rain against the windows dwindled the silence. Secretly, I was thankful the weather didn't allow any sightseeing today. It gave me one more day of being able to protect her within the confines of four walls.

"This hotel room is amazing, Elijah." She maneuvered her body around mine to stand in front of me, her hair wet, her naked body wrapped with a plush white towel. "But a simple cabin, or even a tent would have sufficed."

"A tent in Rome?"

She snickered, and her cheeks blushed.

I tucked a strand of hair behind her ear. "You deserve the best of everything. And this is the best hotel in Rome."

"You know," she smirked, "for someone who supposedly stalked—"

"Observed."

"*Stalked* me...for years, I sometimes get the feeling you don't know me at all." She tightened her hold around me, and my cock stirred. "It's not about money for me, or the fanciest food or most expensive hotels. For me...it's about moments. Memories. The perfume."

Perfume. The keeper of memories. The reason she had been buying herself the same brand of perfume for years—a reminder of her late mother.

I touched her chin with a gentle nip between my fingers. "I don't know what it's like to have fond memories of a mother, but I imagine it can't be easy missing someone like that every day."

The soft light of a single sunray that broke through the thunderous clouds touched the blue in her eyes, her unshed tears glimmering, igniting this deeply rooted need inside me to make it right. To comfort her and slay those motherfucking memories that broke her heart over and over again. But I wasn't like her. I didn't know how to comfort, how to sympathize or encourage. All I knew how to do was to hate and kill. I had been programmed not to care—a hardened man who didn't give a shit about anyone else's suffering. If I had to care about other people, their feelings, their pain, I wouldn't be in the profession that I was. I wouldn't have been able to secure owed debts or exact the revenge my clients craved. I'd be too busy searching for unicorns and fucking rainbows in the eyes of my victims, trying to find some sort of redeeming quality that would give me a simple reason *not* to slit their throats.

No. I wasn't that man. But for her...I wanted to be.

A simple nudge of my finger lifted her chin so I could kiss her. There was no resistance from her, her lips parting and tongue welcoming me into her mouth, allowing me to explore and taste.

It was an instant high every time our mouths latched and desires collided. Her kiss was honey—an amber sweetness that overwhelmed my tastebuds, causing me to want more while knowing I'd never have enough. Charlotte was my ecstasy, the drug that rushed through my veins, corrupted my mind, and clung to my skin.

Taking everything she offered by opening her mouth filled my heart and enticed my body, tempting me with hers simply by being close. How could I ever be the kind of man she deserved—anything other than a monster? Nothing about me was whole. I was just an empty vessel held together by a thousand broken parts left behind by a boy I had chosen to leave in the past.

While I was with her, touching her, kissing her, hearing her fucking breathe next to me, something felt right. Somewhere between all those broken pieces was something whole...and it was her. But whenever our heated breaths mixed it created this fucking toxic hunger that made my control non-existent. And I didn't give a fuck about being the man she needed, being the better man who would put his woman's feelings above his own. All I cared about was burying myself in her, feeling her from the inside, hearing her screams of pleasure, the vibrations slithering across my skin. That was all I wanted.

Fuck this debt.

Fuck the Bernardis.

Fuck Italy.

And fuck that goddamn cello that lured me into her world, because now I had dragged her into mine. That was what monsters like me did. We took. We corrupted. We ruined. Give us a rose, and the petals would wither instantly while the thorns bloomed.

I snaked my hands around her waist, cupping her ass, lifting her on her toes, pushing her against my hardened cock. "Turn around."

She stilled and inched back, but I pulled her closer, forcing her to take my tongue. It fucking burned inside me, my blood nothing but flames that scorched my veins.

A growl vibrated from my throat as I reached up, fisting

her wet curls between my fingers, tugging hard as I licked down her jaw. "I said turn the fuck around."

It was so easy for me to pluck the towel from her body while I forced her to turn, giving me the splendid view of her naked back, that enticing curve that trailed down toward her firm ass.

I bit my lip thinking of all the fucks I didn't give in that moment—my mind and body completely consumed with this woman.

My hands settled on her waist, her skin hot even though her body trembled. "If I had my way, you'd walk around naked every minute of every goddamn day." I eased her forward, toward the window that looked out at the wintery scene of the city of Rome. "I would have you thoroughly fucked, that cunt of yours possessed with a permanent ache to remind you who you belong to."

A soft whimper brushed past her lips, and she reached up, weaving her fingers through the hair at the back of my neck. I palmed her breast—round, firm, her nipple hard and begging to be sucked.

"Elijah," she whispered as I brought her one step away from the window, "people will see."

"Let them." I wiped her wet curls from her shoulder, peppering wet kisses along the flesh of her neck. "While most men would gouge out the eyes of those who see their women naked and panting while getting fucked, I want every goddamn man out there to watch me fuck you. I want them to see your body quiver as I pound into you, witness how your body surrenders to me as my cock fills your cunt." Another nudge and her body was flush against the cold window. The sound of her gasp made my dick twitch and my balls ache.

Reaching between us, I unzipped my pants, fisting my length as I dragged the tip against her naked ass, down the slit, dipping between her thighs, groaning as her arousal coated my cock. Slick. Warm. My ultimate fucking undoing.

"I wonder how many people are out there now, watching us," I rasped against her ear. "I want every fucking man and woman in this entire sick, twisted, fucked-up world to know you belong to me. That this pussy," I jerked her hips back and plunged into her without warning, her warm breath misting the glass as she cried out, "is mine. Just mine." I pulled out of her entirely before slamming back into her, and she placed her palms against the window as another moan escaped her.

Consumed with her heat tightly gripping my cock, I shed the skin of a lover and embraced the instincts of a goddamn animal. Primal. Starved. Ready to be sated.

Leaning back, I looked down to where I entered her, my cock disappearing inside her, slipping out and glistening with her slick lust wrapped around my length like motherfucking silk. Jesus—the sight alone had me heading to the edge way too fucking fast.

"Do you know what you're worth, Charlotte?" I bit out, chained with toxic lust—an angered hunger that took control of my body. "Do you know what I'm willing to do to keep you?"

"No." She whimpered, but she was lying. It was there in the slight tenor of confidence in her voice, her willingness to play her role perfectly for me. Her role as prey.

I bit my bottom lip, fisting her hair and forcing her face

harder against the glass. I stilled inside her, and her hips swayed as her body demanded the decadent friction of my cock against her inner walls.

My hand gripped her hip, keeping her from moving. "You are worth a thousand last breaths. A million fucking slit throats. That's what I'll do for you, my sweet cellist," I rasped against her ear and licked down her neck. "I will kill every man who merely thinks he can desire you, touch you, kiss you...fuck you as I do."

"Please, Elijah," she pleaded. "I need you to move."

"I know you do." I inched back, easing out of her, giving her just the tip. "But I like you like this. I like to see you crave my cock, desperately wanting to get fucked." I tightened my grip on her hair. "Hurt, and used."

"Please." She tried to move against me, tried to force my dick inside her, but I inched back even more, loving the torture I inflicted on her willing body and needy cunt.

"Look out the window. How many people do you think are watching us right now? Looking at your tits squeezed against the windows, your naked body brushing against the glass." A tremor wracked through her as I eased back inside her, little by little, allowing her pussy to wrap around my length. "I wonder how many men are jerking off right now while imagining it's them fucking you. How many women wish they were you, getting fucked."

"That's the problem," she whispered, trying to glance at me over her shoulder, a glint of defiance in her irises. "I'm not getting fucked right now...am I?"

A growl ripped from my throat as angered lust wrapped around my cock, the throbbing ache forcing me to spear inside her so fucking hard, she cried out and swallowed her own motherfucking words.

My thrusts started slow, but deep. Real fucking deep, my cock buried to the hilt inside her. Thrust after thrust, the ecstasy intensified, every muscle in my body wrapped in a goddamn vise, demanding a release. But I didn't want it to end. I wanted to be inside her for the rest of my motherfucking life—live in the paradise I could only find between her legs.

I let go of her hair and slammed my hands next to hers on the window, my palms flush against the glass as I cocooned her. "Tell me, Charlotte," I thrust deep and hard, lifting her on her dainty fucking toes, "would you worship next to me in Heaven? Or rule alongside me in hell?"

"Hell." She breathed, answering without hesitation. "I'm going to hell with you."

Jesus fucking Christ, that was the last push I needed to ram me over the edge, my climax ripping my goddamn body apart as I spilled my seed into her.

She cried out as she came with me, our cum gushing down her thighs and ruining my Armani suit pants in the process. But I couldn't care less, the sound of her pleasure and the sight of her rapid breaths clouding the windows worth far more. It was fucking priceless, seeing her like this. Jaded and out of control—a stark contradiction to the controlled woman I'd watched for years, seeking perfection as she played the cello. This was what made her mine, the fact that I got the version of her no one had ever seen.

The Charlotte Moore no one would ever have the pleasure of seeing.

No one...but me.

CHAPTER THIRTY-ONE

CHARLOTTE

"Tell me about her."

"About who?" Elijah stepped up behind me, easing up the zipper of my dress.

"Saint's wife."

"Milana." He brushed his palms down the sides of my arms. "She's lovely. The exact opposite of Saint."

"Opposites attract. Like us." Our gazes locked in the mirror, a silent moment that conveyed so much without a word being spoken.

He placed a tender kiss on the nape of my neck, and I closed my eyes as his warm breath caressed my skin. "I think it has been proven time and time again that you and I," he glanced up at our reflection, "aren't that different after all."

The air was suddenly laden with tension, my body hyperaware of how close he was. The soft fabric of his suit jacket touched my arms, and for a second I regretted insisting that we accept Saint's invitation to join them for dinner. I'd much rather be Elijah's fuck toy right now, than his plus one.

God. He was right. We weren't that different—not since I chose to embrace my most wicked desires Elijah so expertly awoke.

"You look beautiful."

I shivered as his hands traveled over my waist, fingers stroking the fabric of my midnight-blue dress. The full-length, halter-neck chiffon dress wasn't something I'd choose for myself. Not because I didn't like it, but simply because I couldn't afford the price tag on the Vera Wang evening dress. But Elijah had insisted that I choose at least three dresses from the collection he had brought to our suite from the hotel's boutique. From the three, I could see by his wicked grin this was the one he fancied the most.

I eased my palms down the silk. "I'm not used to dressing up like this." I glanced around, the four-post bed and its white drapes the center-point of this vastly luxurious room. "This is all..." I let out a breath, "this is all so much to take in. To get used to."

"Is it something you want to get used to?" He studied me from underneath his lashes, his gaze intense and curious.

"What do you mean?"

He shot his cuffs, straightening his navy suit jacket. Elijah pinned me with his gaze, shoulders squared as his dominant presence engrossed me. "I mean, if you had a choice right now—which you don't," his head slanted to the side, "would you pick this life...with me?"

There was no correct answer to this question. Countless nights I had lain awake thinking about it—whether, if given a choice, I'd choose him. The truth was a mindfuck, but the lie was even worse.

The weight of it made me look down, afraid I might get lost within the swirl of his dark irises—a dark vortex I had given up on fighting yet still feared.

"It doesn't matter." I turned to look at my reflection again. "We're too deep into this for my answer to change anything."

"If I demanded it?"

I twined my fingers together in front of me. "Would you?" I faced him. "Demand an answer?"

"I might."

"Will you be able to handle the answer?"

He shrugged. "That depends whether I like it or not."

I licked my lips, nervous tension settling in my shoulders. "What would you do if you...didn't like it?"

"I'd still keep you." There was no hesitation, and no doubt about what his intentions were if I had answered no, saying I wouldn't choose this world, living this life with him.

"Then there's no reason for me to give you an answer, is there?"

He picked up the bottle of perfume that stood on the bedside table, tracing his fingers along the delicate glass bubble before handing it to me. "Maybe it would make me feel like less of a monster if I knew you'd pick me."

It was one of those pivotal moments that changed the sequence of my thoughts, as if it lifted the veil that blinded me all this time.

Elijah Mariano had so many layers to him, so many complexities that it was easy for me to look past it all, only seeing The Musician. The man who kidnapped me. The man who seduced me, and ultimately stole my heart. But for the first time, I saw a man who needed security as much as I did. Who needed reassurance as to how I felt about him. Even though he made it abundantly clear that whether I felt that way or not, he wouldn't let me go—which I believed—deep down he wanted to know that when given a choice I'd choose him. Like me wanting to know that I was more to him than just a debt he needed to settle.

Elijah turned to walk away when I called out, "Ask me again."

He stilled and slowly faced me.

I swallowed. "Ask me again."

Silently, he studied me, and my heart raced wondering about what he was thinking.

He rubbed his jaw with his thumb, taking a step closer. "If you had a choice," he lifted his chin, "would you pick this life with me...willingly?"

"Yes." There was no use in denying the truth. "I would choose you, Elijah. Even though my head is telling me it would be the worst decision of my life, my heart is convinced that I would have no life without you."

The muscle in his jaw pulled taut, and I gasped as he rushed forward, cupping my cheeks tightly in his palms and capturing my lips with a desperate kiss. I was sure I felt the ground crack beneath us, and we fell. It was no longer gravity keeping me grounded. It was his kiss, his touch, the way he consumed and electrified me at the same time. His tongue dueled with mine, claiming my mouth with one hungered sweep after the other.

I kissed him back, not because his onslaught left me no

choice, but because I wanted to. I wanted him to feel what I felt, needed him to taste my surrender as he devoured me with one heady kiss that left me breathless.

His lips tore from mine, and our foreheads touched as he refused to let me go. "Promise me," he whispered. "Promise me you will never leave me, no matter what."

"Elijah—"

"No matter what, Charlotte. Promise me."

His thumb brushed along my wet lips, and I closed my eyes, my heart beating a staccato rhythm inside my chest. There was no use even trying, an unnecessary energy vacuum for me to even try to think of a reason I wouldn't do this.

"I promise," I whispered, placing my hands on his wrists as he held my cheeks. "I promise I'll never leave you."

"Then marry me."

My heart stopped. "What?"

"Marry me." He shifted, bringing his body flush against mine. "Marry me tonight."

I scowled and inched back. "Elijah, what are you doing?"

"I'm proposing."

"I know that, but why...how...no, Elijah, that's insane."

"Give me one reason we shouldn't get married."

"I can give a thousand."

"Fine." He licked his lips. "I'll give you one reason we should get married, then."

"One?"

"Yes. One." He kissed me then placed a warm palm on my chest. "Because among those thousand reasons you think we shouldn't get married, your heart still says we should."

I swallowed hard, finding it difficult to breathe with the

immense weight of this moment. There was no doubt that he owned my heart. My body. My mind. I was his in every way that mattered, and the only thing—no, the only thought that kept me from saying yes was this voice inside my head that kept whispering how fucked-up and distorted everything was. My life had been derailed since the moment he whispered my name in the Alto Theatre. Like a hurricane, he stormed into my life, and he took everything he could. Everything. If he were the devil, he'd most likely have taken my soul too. But I couldn't think straight. There was no way I could sort through my thoughts.

I gently shook my head. "No, Elijah. I can't marry you."

His throat bobbed as he swallowed, and I hated the shadow of disappointment in his eyes as he stared at me as if I had just ripped his heart out.

"I can't marry you because—"

"Of the thousand reasons?"

"No." I sighed. "Because you so utterly enthrall me, and I'm so consumed with what we have, it's impossible for me to make a rational decision when it comes to you. Don't you get it, Elijah? Your presence in my life, the way you possess me makes it hard for me to remember who I really am. To be...me."

It was excruciating to stand there while he merely stared at me, not saying a word as if I had stolen his last breath. I didn't dare say anything else, my hands trembling and heart pounding. Elijah's presence swept through the room, suffocating me in his silence while my heart cursed me for saying no. For creating a scenario where he'd be hurt enough to forget about what we shared and be reminded of what I had always meant to be for him. A debt.

He licked his lips, and all I wanted to do was kiss him. I wanted to have his arms around me while I poured everything I felt for him into one damn kiss. But I couldn't. A simple kiss wouldn't be able to mean more than my rejection of his proposal.

"Okay," he muttered. "Make sure you're ready for dinner in ten minutes." He stormed out, and I wanted to go after him, my heart pleading with me to run and tell him yes. Shout it from the goddamn rooftops, yet something stopped me from doing that. The rational side of my mind thought through the haze of this intense connection Elijah and I shared.

I sucked in a breath as a tear slipped down my cheek, and I wiped it away, squaring my shoulders and steeling myself against the ache that had my heart bleeding inside my chest.

"I did the right thing," I whispered to myself. "But why doesn't it feel like I did?"

My reflection in the mirror mocked me. I was no longer the girl who played cello in front of an empty audience. I was no longer the Charlotte Moore who cared for nothing else but music. Whether I married Elijah or not, he had changed me forever, and nothing could change that. If I had to return to my life as it was before him, I still wouldn't be her.

This woman in the mirror wearing the expensive dress, with her hair styled in the perfect updo—not a strand out of place—this was me. The woman whose heart bled out on the carpet because she had just rejected a man who offered her a relationship society had dubbed abnormal and toxic. It was a kind of relationship that offended others, yet it made me soar with more freedom than I had ever experienced before.

My chest rose and fell as I took a deep breath, and my gaze fell on the music box standing on the nightstand. That little box carried such a tragic story of a brother who loved his little sister so unconditionally. A boy who couldn't save his sister being snatched by the unknown, and he had to live with that his entire life. Brushing my fingers along the box, I wondered if he'd ever find her.

I opened the box, and the music started to play, the little ballerina twirling around and around. Inside laid a little pocket Bible which I overlooked before, snug within the confines of the box.

"Ready?"

I jolted and closed the box, setting it down. "Yes."

"Let's go." His voice was ice, his demeanor cold. It wasn't my Elijah who stood before me. It was him...The Musician.

Elijah and I made our way to the hotel lobby in silence, my heart pounding with the uncertainty of where this left us, how things would be between us from here on out.

I was on my way to the hotel restaurant when he grabbed my elbow. "This way."

Unsure, I glanced around. "Where are we going?"

He didn't answer me and simply led me in the opposite direction through a double door that took us down a hall. "Elijah, where are you taking me?"

Tightening his fingers around my elbow was his only answer. We walked out into an underground parking area, a silver Maserati idling in front of us. A man dressed in a black suit handed Elijah the keys, and he let go of my arm.

"Get in."

"What? Where are we going?"

THE VILLAIN

He held the door open for me. "Get in the goddamn car, Charlotte."

Our eyes met, and I kept his gaze for a second, a storm raging in his irises—a storm I was afraid I wouldn't survive. But I got into the car anyway.

The door slammed shut, and I watched as Elijah rounded the front of the car, my pulse racing impossibly fast.

"Where are we going?" I asked as he got in behind the wheel.

"You'll see."

Lights ignited the narrow streets, boosting the hues of romance that echoed off the tall buildings. Crowds of tourists and locals alike walked on the sidewalks—people laughing, couples kissing, the atmosphere almost electric in the city's vintage ambiance. It was far more beautiful than I ever could have imagined. No television show or magazine picture did this city justice. Words couldn't describe the sight of Rome under the stars. The sky was clear of the clouds and rain we had just that morning.

The silence in the car was excruciating as Elijah sped down the streets of Rome. I glanced at him, his silhouette dark as he clutched the steering wheel with his strong hands, veins bulging with the strength that ran through his blood. There was no denying it, Elijah Mariano was a force of power and primal instincts. I was convinced that if God had never made humans and the Earth was only intended to be roamed by divine beings, Elijah would have had his own corner to rule.

My skin prickled as Elijah met my gaze, and I quickly looked away, only to see the colossal building in the distance, getting closer and closer as we kept driving.

"Is that the..." I leaned forward, placing my hand on the dash. "Is that the Colosseum?"

"Yes."

Chills erupted in my spine, spreading to every corner of my body. "My God," I breathed as I took in the sight. The majestic building painted with beautiful golds of splendid lights was breathtaking. I couldn't take my eyes off it, its imperial presence demanding my attention. "It's beautiful."

A dialing tone sounded, and I realized Elijah was making a phone call.

An unfamiliar voice answered. "Sir?"

"Is it done?"

"Yes, sir."

"Good. We're here."

The phone call ended, and Elijah parked the car, switching off the engine before getting out. I leaned over. "Elijah—"

My door flung open, and he reached out his hand. "Come on."

"Are we?" I was dumbfounded. "Are we going in here?"

"Not if we stand out here all night. Get out of the car."

I lifted the hem of my dress so I wouldn't step on it as I took his hand, getting out of the car. "Oh, my God. I can't believe this." In awe, I kept my gaze on the building, the grandiose structure appearing alive against the backdrop of night, the moon casting an elegant hue across the massive architecturally complex building.

"What are we—" I turned to find Elijah staring at me, his eyes soft, gentle, as if admiring something he had never seen before. I stilled. "What are we doing here?"

He took my hand, the expression on his face unreadable. "Finding another reason."

"Wha—"

"Just come with me." He led me toward the building, the early winter chill wrapping its cold tendrils around me, making me shiver.

The exterior of the building consisted of numerous triumphal arches which aesthetically made the building seem less bulky. The triumphal arches reflected the spoils and riches for the crowd it was originally built for. And walking through them, glancing around and taking in the magnificent stone and architecture, I could practically feel the energy of the crowds that used to gather here to watch the gladiators, hunters, and the numerous blood sports that took place right here in this very arena.

"I literally have no words." I gaped at everything around me, finding it impossible to take it all in. "Never in my wildest dreams could I have imagined the kind of magic that lingered in these corridors. The history. The stories these walls could tell. Do you think there—" I paused at the sight of the cello leaning against a chair which stood beneath one of the arches. "What is this?"

"Exactly what it looks like." Elijah traced a finger along the neck of the cello, his other hand tucked into his pants pocket. "I want you to play. Here," he waved his hand around, "in one of the most magnificent amphitheaters in the world."

"Elijah. This is...I don't have words."

"Good. You don't need words." He picked up the cello and held it out to me. "All you need is music."

I glanced around. "Are we alone here?"

He shrugged. "Maybe. Maybe not."

"You know I can't—"

"Stop saying you can't, and just play, Charlotte. For once, stop giving a fuck about what other people think, and just do what you want to do."

We stood there, eyes locked and hearts beating, this indescribable pull between us pulsing like a life source.

I took the cello from him, holding my breath, hoping the haunting pain wouldn't ruin the moment. But it didn't, and I let out a sigh of relief as I picked up the bow, loving the feel of it in my hands. The chair creaked as I sat down, lifting the skirt of my dress over my knees. Elijah's gaze cut to my legs, lingering for a moment before he looked me in the eye again. I removed my shoes, wanting to feel the ground beneath my feet, and I straightened my back—a firm posture, yet my body relaxed.

The neck of the cello rested against my shoulder, my heart already feeling its weight beneath my chest. The pine scent of resin allowed my mind and body to tune in to this majestic instrument—a colossal beacon in my life just like this ancient building was to the world.

Leaning my head to the side, I let out a breath as that brief moment of silence ensued—the time where I found peace from every storming thought, every worry, and every doubt.

I brushed my fingers along the strings, feeling it beneath my fingertips, allowing the music in my soul to flood through me so I could set it free.

I didn't know what I would play until that very second I eased the bow across the strings and the sound slowly, gently started to move me. *Edelweiss*. It was the composition my soul demanded, and it flowed down my spine, the deep yet soft sound reaching inside my chest. The music within me escaped, echoing off the strings as I continued to ease the bow. As I moved my fingers up and down the neck of the cello, the vibrato kept me here instead of sweeping me away as it always did. The sound, the harmony, it allowed me to stay right here, with him. Elijah. The man I could feel in my veins, my blood calling out to him as the music grew stronger, the cello and I moving as one. The crescendo ignited, and this was always the moment when I laid my dreams at my feet, baring it all to the world—but this time it was different. The resonating tenor cleared my mind, and I realized this time there was no dream to stem from the magic of music because...*I opened my eyes*...my dream was standing right there.

I stopped playing, my eyes pinned on Elijah, who stared at me as if I was his last hope. There was no darkness in his irises, no malicious intent splayed on his expression as he regarded me.

"I love you, Charlotte." He stepped closer. "I've loved you since that day I heard you play this same song. I might be a monster in this world," he held out his hand, and I took it, standing up, "but I want to be a colossus in yours."

I smiled at his choice of words, my heart feeling like it would break free from my chest as the love I felt for this man became utterly profound and unmistakable. He was right. I had to stop entertaining thoughts society had programmed us to think.

This is wrong.
This is twisted.
This is madness.

How can this be love when it hurts?

Well, it could. It could be love and hurt at the same time. It could be utter madness yet the sanest thing I had ever done. And it could be the biggest mistake of my life, or the best decision I ever made.

"Yes," I whispered, finally allowing my heart to drown out my thoughts. "I'll marry you."

CHAPTER THIRTY-TWO

ELIJAH

A wise man once told me that there was only one way any man could find peace, and that was by finding the woman who held his heart. Until then, a man merely drifted aimlessly through life not knowing the meaning of the word "home."

That was her.

Charlotte was my home. It was in her arms that I found peace from the memories that tempted the bloodlust—a hunger sated by the pull of a trigger, witnessing another man's last breath. But with her...I experienced peace. A kind of comfort I had never known yet yearned for in the deepest corner of the humanity I'd forgotten I had.

My heart swelled inside my chest with a warmth that filled all the empty spaces inside my soul—every crevice, every hole, every corner that laid dormant and dark for so fucking long. It was as if I had never lived before this very moment—but only existed, waiting for her.

I rushed toward her, my arms wrapping around her body

like a vise, pulling her close and kissing her hard and desperate—as if she was the cure to the disease that had festered inside me all these years.

Her subtle moan fused with our kiss, and I wanted to stop time. I wanted this moment of complete serenity and delectation to last forever and a day. This woman had become my life, which was why I had to take this chance. Bring her here and convince her that she belonged with me, forever...until death us do part. And now that she had said yes, I wouldn't let another hour pass without her being mine—in heart, body, soul, and by law.

I leaned back, letting out a groan as our lips parted. Without taking my eyes off her, I called over my shoulder, "You can come out now."

Saint and his wife appeared, Milana wiping a tear from her cheek. "That was beautiful. Your talent is beyond amazing."

"I have to agree with my wife here," Saint chimed in. "It's been a while since I heard someone play the cello as flawlessly as you did just now."

Charlotte's cheeks turned flaming red, her eyes wide as she cut her gaze from them to me. I merely nodded, knowing she was dumbfounded and probably horrified that they had been listening to her. Gently, I touched her chin, brushing a tender finger along her jaw. "The world needs to hear your music, Charlotte."

Father Gillian, a local priest, walked up behind Saint, and I nodded toward him in acknowledgment. He had owed me a favor since I had taken care of a problem he had five years ago. A problem I made disappear without question. And today, I called in on that favor.

Charlotte frowned. "What's going on?"

"You agreed to marry me."

"Yes," she replied slowly.

I brushed a curl that had escaped her elegant updo behind her ear. "And that's what we're going to do. Right now."

"What?" She stared at me in question before cutting her gaze toward our guests. "Now? Here?"

"Yes, now. Right here." I took her hands in mine. "You're mine, Charlotte. There's no need to delay the inevitable. Whether you marry me now, or next week. You're going to marry me. I just choose now rather than next week."

"But...but," her cheeks blushed the most beautiful shade of pink, "I don't...we don't—"

I pulled her close and placed a palm against the side of her neck, brushing a thumb across her lips. "You can't think of one single reason for us not to get married right now...can you?"

"Well...um." She placed a palm on her forehead, glancing at Father Gillian. "Well, no. But—"

"But nothing. I'm not waiting another day before making you my wife. I love you, Charlotte. That won't change, so there's no use in waiting."

She bit her lip, her eyes alert and confused. But there was a shimmer of excitement in her crystal blue irises.

I leaned closer, dragging a finger down her neck before placing a gentle kiss below her ear. "Marry me, Charlotte Moore. Now."

She trembled, and her warm breath caressed my cheek, the vein in her neck pulsing rapidly. "Okay," she whispered, and I was sure my heart would explode.

I smiled, taking her hand, bringing it up to my lips, her scent of gentle jasmine intensifying the already potent love I felt for this woman.

Father Gillian stepped up. "Are we ready to start?"

The moment she smiled at me, I nodded. "We are. Oh, and Father," I glanced at him, "skip to the important parts."

"Of course." Draped around his arm was a long velvet ribbon, and he took it in his hand. "As per the groom's request, we will perform the handfasting ceremony. Now, join your hands, and with your hands, your hearts."

Charlotte stared at me, confused, and I reached out, crossing hands—taking her right hand with my right, and left hand with my left. Our relationship had been everything but conventional, and I wanted us to be bound and joined in every way possible. And what better way than being bound together before God?

Father Gillian started winding the white ribbon around our hands while we never took our eyes off one another for a single moment.

"These are the hands of the one you love and adore. On this day, you promise to love and honor one another for all your days. Reaching out to the one you love, may you find strength. Standing side by side, may you find partnership. Sharing responsibilities and chores, may you find equality and ease. Helping each other in daily life and works, may you find fulfillment. Loving each other through dark and light times, may you find power. Look deeply into one another's eyes now, and promise always to see one another through the eyes of love. As you hold hands, may you warmly hold one another's hearts. Our wish for you is that you build an extraordinary life

together. May your marriage be all you two would choose it to be."

I felt every word, prayed it, even. She was the woman I adored, the one I vowed to love and honor until the day I took my last breath. In her I found my fulfillment, my light, my strength. And there was no other way I'd ever look at her other than as the one I loved with all my goddamn heart.

With the ribbon draped around our hands, binding and unbreakable, I experienced this divine moment where, for the first time in so very long, I believed. I believed in goodness, love. I believed in God, because there was no other way to explain the whirlwind of emotions that crashed against every bone in my body.

The priest took a step back. "Do you, Elijah Mariano, take this woman to be your lawfully wedded wife, to have and to hold from this day forward, for better, for worse, for richer, for poorer, in sickness and in health, until death do you part?"

"I do."

A tear slipped down her cheek, and she smiled as it lapped over her beautiful heart-shaped lips. Her palm squeezed mine beneath the velvet ribbon, and I tightened my hold on hers.

"Do you, Charlotte Moore, take this man to be your lawfully wedded husband, to have and to hold from this day forward, for better, for worse, for richer, for poorer, in sickness and in health, until death do you part?"

For some reason, I stopped breathing, waiting for her to say the two words that meant more to me than all the riches in this entire goddamn world. Two words that had the power to break me as easily as they could make me whole.

Her hand trembled in mine, her gaze soft and eyes filled with so much emotion I could practically feel it wrap around me.

"I do." More tears trickled down her face, and I didn't wait for the priest to say the words. I fucking kissed her, pressing my desperate lips against hers, tasting her tears on my tongue.

"I now pronounce you man and wife. You may kiss the bride."

But I was already kissing her as if she held the oxygen I needed to stay alive. With our hands bound and our lips locked, I poured every ounce of love a man like me was capable of feeling into that kiss. If all the words disappeared today, I wanted her to know how much I loved her simply by tasting my lips on hers.

"I love you," I said against her wet lips, every word stemming from the most vulnerable corner in my heart. "I love you so much it fucking hurts."

Father Gillian cleared his throat at my use of the f-bomb, and Charlotte snickered.

"Okay, lovers," Saint intervened. "Let's not make the priest spill his entire bottle of holy water on the two of you."

I turned to Father Gillian. "You've taken care of the paperwork?"

He nodded. "Everything is taken care of."

"Thank you, Father."

We gave each other a knowing look—a debt paid and settled, never to be spoken about again. With that, he turned and left just as Mila, Saint's wife, started unwinding the ribbon. "Congratulations, you two."

"Charlotte, this is Milana Russo. Milana," I smiled, "this

is my wife, Charlotte."

"It's nice to meet you, Charlotte," Milana greeted politely.

"Come on, wife," Saint reached out and snaked an arm around Milana's waist, "let's leave the newlyweds. Elijah," he shot me a pointed stare, "see you two at the hotel for dinner?"

"Yes. We're right behind you."

"Hmm-mm." He gave me a knowing look before ushering his wife through the arches in the other direction.

Finally alone, Charlotte and I remained in this bubble we had just created, the entire world around us blocked out by the ancient walls that surrounded us.

She scowled. "You knew I was going to say I'll marry you?"

"I hoped."

"Bullshit. Arranging a priest, witnesses. That was a pretty bold move."

"What am I if not bold?"

Charlotte held the velvet ribbon in her hand. "I think that was the fastest wedding in the history of mankind."

"Not as fast as Saint and Milana's wedding, I can assure you."

"One day I'd love to hear their story."

"One day." I stepped closer. "But first," I tipped her face up to mine with a gentle touch of my hand to her chin, "there's one last thing we need to do to officiate this marriage."

"Elijah," she gasped. "Here?"

I gave her a devilish grin. "Right fucking here. Pun intended."

CHAPTER THIRTY-THREE

CHARLOTTE

It happened so fast, it felt surreal.

Did Elijah and I just get married? The priest, the velvet ribbon, and those beautiful words weaved together with the magic of the ancient ground we stood upon had me soaring in this dream-like state while the energy of a joy I had never experienced before filled me up.

Elijah's arms wrapped around my waist, his hard length rubbing against my stomach as he pressed me tightly against him, grinding his hips, making his intentions known.

His kiss was fire, an act of love steeped in the deepest pools of passion, claiming my mouth as if he tasted me for the first time.

Slowly, his fingers swirled behind my back as he wound up the fabric of my dress. "Since this is our wedding night, I'm going to give you the choice."

"What choice?" I breathed against his wet lips.

With a gentle stroke of his cheek against mine, his five

o'clock shadow brushed against my skin. "Whether I take you back to the hotel and make love to you all night."

"Or?" I leaned into him, swept away and drugged on desire.

"Or..." A greedy hand slipped from my waist to cup my breast, and I arched my back, "I fuck you right here, right now...hard and fast."

A gasp slipped past my lips as I pushed my body forward, deeper into his touch as he kneaded my breast, pinching my hardened nipple scratching against the silk of my dress.

"It's your choice, wife."

My insides coiled. *Wife.*

There was a devilish glint in his eyes as he stared at me, giving me a glimpse of his hunger—a desire to get burned to fucking ash. And God knew, I was right there next to him, ready to be consumed by the flames.

I slid my arms around his neck, leaning into him, placing my lips against his throat, feeling his Adam's apple bob as he swallowed, his hand snaking up my back. "As a newly married wife..." I grazed my teeth against his jaw, and his hand reached my hair, fisting and tugging my head back abruptly. I smiled, the flames now an inferno of unstoppable desire. "I'd like my husband to fuck me right here, right now."

A growl tore from his throat, and my back was against the wall before I could inhale my next breath, his tongue assaulting mine with a kiss so hard it left no room for doubt of exactly what his intentions were. Hard and desperate hands clawed at my dress, pulling it up and around my waist, strong fingers grabbing my panties.

My skin burned. My core throbbed. I wanted him hard, raw, hot, and all at once. There was no stopping the moans that rolled from my lips as he slipped his hand between us, pulling his cock out of his pants. The anticipation that throbbed between my legs, my sex aching and needy, had me ready to tear at his goddamn skin if it meant getting him inside me faster.

"I'm not going to play with you, little cellist." With a jerk, he pulled my leg up and forced me to wrap it around his waist.

"Good." I weaved my fingers through the back of his head. "Because I won't be a happy wife if you did."

His lips crashed against mine with such force, my head collided painfully with the wall behind me. With a hard, sharp jab he rammed his cock into me, my back scraping against the rough wall. The stone could draw blood for all I cared—I felt no pain, only this intense ache that had my body desperate for release.

The sheer savagery that erupted from our hot kisses and his cock ramming into me with rapid thrusts of his hips left my mind possessed, unable to think fucking straight. It was just one haze of fuckery and fornication—two people wholly swept away by the need to ravage and be ravaged.

"God, I love you, woman," he whispered next to my ear, both his hands flush against the wall, his hips flexing and thrusting. "I want to fuck you like this every goddamn day."

I moaned, the ecstasy of feeling the delicious pressure between my thighs filling me to the brim. Every inch of his length was inside me, pounding in and out, making sure I felt my walls wrap around him, the tip of his cock reaching so fucking deep it hurt. But it hurt to the point of pleasure—an insane contradiction that could only be experienced when immersed within this high. A state of euphoria where I wanted to stay forever. With him. Alone. Let the entire fucking world burn down around us.

But it felt different now. Somehow, having him inside me, filling me, stretching me, fucking me. Maybe it was the fact that we were bound by God now, no longer two individuals, but one entity. Two hearts beating as one.

With the skirt of my dress bunched up around my waist, I too flexed my hips, squirming against him, my body primed and ready for pleasure. I was no longer the woman he took captive and held against her will. I was no longer the woman who fought against the fire his touch left on my skin, or the girl who hated that she wanted this monster. I was his wife now. His equal. My life was now his as much as his life was mine. There was nothing that divided us anymore, which made this so much more intense and profoundly euphoric.

Elijah bit down on my lip, the metal taste of my own blood bursting on my tongue. At once his grueling thrusts ceased, and he stared down at me, rolling his hips, slowly sinking back inside me.

"I want you to look at me."

"I am looking at you."

He shook his head, slipping out of me before sliding back in so damn slow, I moved my waist, wanting his hard body to push against my core. "Don't close your eyes when you come."

"Elijah—"

Impatient hands snaked around my thighs as he pulled me up against the wall, forcing me to wrap both legs around him. There was no time to think or speak as he impaled me, going deeper than he ever had before, and I cried out as the pressure and pain morphed into the most pleasurable rapture I had ever experienced.

The low thrum of his grunts and groans, and the intoxicating scent of sex had me at the brink of complete delirium. But I kept my eyes open and locked with his, perspiration beaded on his forehead, jaw ticking as he held on to his last ounce of control, waiting for me to tip over the edge.

And I did.

My body was torn in fucking half with a climax that surged through every muscle. Pleasure had my sex clenching his cock, and he cursed, his thrusts wild and erratic as he chased his own release, until his cock jerked inside me, filling me to the brim.

Our chests rose and fell rapidly as we tried to catch our breath. My body hummed with adrenaline, and every inch of my skin he touched was electrified.

He eased me down to my feet. As if he knew I had no strength left in me to stand, he snaked an arm around my waist and held me up against him.

"I swear to you now, there will never be a single moment in your life when you'll doubt my love for you. Every day I will remind you again, and again, and again."

He brushed his lips across mine, barely touching, my skin hyperaware of him and that constant sensual pull between us. Even now, post-euphoria, my body still wanted him. My lips still wanted to kiss him, fingertips caressing his chest. It would never be enough for me. There was no scenario I could think of where I'd be sated and have my fill of this man. Ever.

Elijah pulled his tie from his collar and kept his eyes

locked with mine. A gasp swept across my lips as he reached between my legs, wiping my sex with his tie.

"As much as I'd love to sit at the dinner table thinking of my cum between your legs, I don't think you'd be very comfortable." He shot me a sly grin, easing the soft fabric across my sensitive folds, one gentle stroke at a time. "But when we get home, your cunt better be ready for me. Until then," he slipped the dirty tie into his pants pocket and held his hand out to me, "let's go to dinner, Mrs. Mariano."

CHAPTER THIRTY-FOUR

CHARLOTTE

Dinner would have been great if Elijah hadn't been leering at me with those amber eyes that glimmered with promises of pleasure. I could practically see the images inside his mind. Him. Me. Us. Fucking and fornicating as if there were no tomorrow. He made sure I stayed hyperaware of his demand, that my body would be ready for him when we got to our hotel room.

I had to make a conscious effort to pretend like I was immersed in the conversation, Milana telling me all about Rome and how she loved it whenever Saint brought her here.

I heard all about their beautiful little daughter and tried to bypass any questions she had about Elijah and our very unconventional relationship.

Milana held her glass of wine, her blue eyes nothing short of brilliant beneath the elegant lights of the restaurant. "You are a very talented cello player."

My cheeks burned. "I can't believe you heard me play. That was a real sly move by Elijah."

"How so?"

"I don't...I have what some would consider a bad case of stage fright." I wiped a curl from my face. "I can't play in front of people. It's like every nerve in my body freezes when people watch me."

She smiled warmly. "Good thing we weren't watching, then. We only listened."

"Still feels weird, though. I can't explain it."

"Does it feel weird when Elijah watches you?"

Oh, that's open to more than one interpretation.

"Not as much, no," I answered simply.

"I can see you're not too keen to discuss your relationship with Elijah." She smiled, and my cheeks burned. "Believe me," she glanced at Saint, who seemed deep in conversation with Elijah, "I know everything about an *unorthodox* relationship. One that wasn't supposed to happen...under normal circumstances." She took a sip of her wine and placed the glass down. "But you and I both know there is nothing normal about these two men."

I snickered, feeling quite at ease with her. There was a softness to her, a kindness that lingered all around her—the exact opposite of her husband. Kind of like Elijah and me.

She wiped her mouth and put the napkin on the table. "I need to go to the ladies' room."

Elijah stood. "I was going in that direction myself." And nodded at me as a way of acknowledgment before falling in step with Mila, the two of them chatting and smiling.

"How are you feeling?"

I glanced up at Saint, and he shot me a half-smile. "It's been quite the eventful day."

"It was." I grinned. "I'm feeling good. Still a bit dizzy with everything happening so fast."

Saint straightened and placed his elbows on the table, leaning to the front. "I've known Elijah for years, and I have never seen him like this. How he's with you."

"That's a good thing, right?" I placed my hands in my lap, feeling a slight tremble under his intense gaze.

"He finally seems happy. And Elijah is never fucking happy." He raised a brow. "So, I'd say it's a pretty damn good thing."

"Elijah is..." I tried searching for the right word, "intense."

"That is an understatement if I ever heard one." He took a sip of his bourbon and leisurely swirled the liquid in the glass, the ice clinking against the crystal. It was easy to see that this man was pure power, the way his presence dominated a simple dinner between friends. Even I found myself nervously rubbing my palms together. But I was determined not to show it.

"I can see you and Elijah have a special friendship."

Saint nodded. "We do. One can say our friendship is built on mutual respect. I admire Elijah, a lot. He didn't have an easy life. I suppose he's told you about his childhood."

"He told me," I cleared my throat, "about his mom and Roland, yes. And my grandfather."

"Your grandfather?"

"Yes. How my grandfather saved him, took him in."

Saint frowned. "Your grandfather is Gianni Guerra?"

"Yes."

He leaned forward. "Gianni Guerra didn't have any kids."

"Oh," I tucked a strand of hair behind my ear, "according to Elijah, he did. Some woman he fell in love with, but he left her without knowing she was pregnant."

Saint stared at me, his eyes filled with confusion. Surely, he would have known this story if they were such good friends?

"Apparently, he was trying to protect her from, you know, getting caught up in the world he found himself in."

Saint tapped his finger on the table, a pensive expression on his face. "Well, that's really interesting. I didn't know that." He tapped his finger some more. "Gianni Guerra was a hitman for the mafia." He said it as if it was just another normal conversation between two normal individuals eating a regular dinner. "His reputation paints him as one of the Cosa Nostra's best contractors. I swear to God, I think the entire goddamn mafia attended his funeral."

I frowned. "His funeral?"

"Judging by the attendance alone, one would have thought he was mafia royalty."

I shifted to the edge of my chair. "Gianni Guerra is dead?"

"Yeah. He died about four or five years ago, I think. It's actually quite sad that a legend like him had to die the way he did. He got stabbed during a drunken brawl at one of the Bernardis famous whore parties."

Blood turned to ice in my veins, my heart nothing but a solid rock that weighed a ton inside my chest. "Stabbed," I whispered, "during a drunken brawl at a... a whorehouse?" The words tasted bitter on my tongue as I repeated the words Saint had just said—words Elijah had used when he told me my father was dead.

"Yes," Saint confirmed, his eyes studying me before shifting in his seat. "I do apologize. That was quite tactless of me, talking about your grandfather's death in that manner."

"Elijah told me Gianni was in prison somewhere in Northern Italy."

Saint straightened, his eyes narrowed. "Prison? No. Gianni is dead."

My thoughts raced in a thousand different directions, trying to sort through the memories and stories Elijah had told me. My skin was cold, my spine frozen solid while I was sure my stomach would drop to my feet at any moment. "Why..." I sucked in a breath, "why would Elijah tell me Gianni is in prison when in fact...he's dead?"

"I don't know."

"I mean, are you sure? Is there a chance that you might be confused, maybe thinking of someone else?"

"No. I'm absolutely one-hundred-percent sure. Gianni Guerra is dead. I know that because I was at his funeral, standing right there beside Elijah."

"Oh, my God." I couldn't form one coherent thought, my mind racing through every possible reason Elijah didn't tell me the truth—that was, if Saint was telling the truth.

"Charlotte." Saint shot me a pointed glare. "Has Elijah ever mentioned someone by the name Ellie?"

"Ellie? Yes, um..." I placed a palm on my forehead, "Ellie is his sister. She went missing when he was a child."

"Jesus Christ." He tossed his napkin on the table, his cutlery clanking against the plate. "I fucking knew it. Goddammit!"

"What?" My pulse raced impossibly fast, my palm

sweating as my skull prickled with warning. "What is going on?"

Mila's laugh broke through the tension, both Saint and I looking at her and Elijah making their way back to the table.

"Charlotte, listen to me." He leaned closer, his expression hard and painted every shade of seriousness. "Do not say anything to Elijah about the conversation we just had. You hear me?"

"What is going on right now?"

"I'm serious, Charlotte. Do not say a word to him." He leaned back, shooting a glimpse in Mila and Elijah's direction as he straightened the lapels of his suit. "I'll arrange a meeting tomorrow, but until then. Do not say. A goddamn word."

CHAPTER THIRTY-FIVE

ELIJAH

Dinner dragged on forever. For the entire time I sat there, all I could think about was my new wife. How I desperately wanted to pick her up, carry her to our suite, and fuck her from the foyer to the goddamn porch. We should be on our honeymoon, fuck and fornicate like animals —but instead here we were at the dinner table with friends, drinking wine and pretending to be invested in the conversation while she knew my dick was hard, and I had no doubt her pussy was wet.

Saint, the bastard, he knew what went on inside my head, purposely dragging out the conversation and making dinner longer than it had to be.

Milana and I made our way back to the table, and I noticed Saint seeming more on edge than he usually was.

I helped Milana with her chair before sitting down myself. "Did we miss something?"

Charlotte cleared her throat before taking a sip of her wine.

"No," Saint started. "I was just telling Charlotte about Rome's largest fountain, *Fontana de Trevi*. You simply have to take your new wife to toss a coin in the fountain."

"Oh, yes," Milana exclaimed. "Tossing a coin into the fountain will assure your return to Rome. Whenever we are here in Rome, I never leave without throwing a coin in the fountain. Saint and I are going there tomorrow morning, as we're leaving for the US the day after. You two should join us."

"I'm not sure—"

"That would be lovely," Charlotte interrupted before glancing in my direction. "Elijah and I would love to join."

There was a brief moment when Saint shot my wife a knowing look—something I would have missed had I not been so observant. "Of course," I confirmed. "I'd love to show Charlotte around more."

"Then it's settled." Milana smiled, excitement beaming from her expression.

"Great." Saint stood and fastened his suit jacket. "This has been quite the eventful day, and I still have a few business matters to attend to before I can call it a night." He held a hand out to Milana. "Come, *segreto*. I'm sure the newlyweds would like some privacy."

"Charlotte, it was so nice to meet you," Milana said as she took Saint's hand. "And don't forget that coin tomorrow morning."

Charlotte and I both stood, and I moved to slip my arm around her waist. "We'll see you tomorrow."

Saint and Milana walked in the other direction, and I turned to face Charlotte. "Is everything okay?"

"Of course."

I touched her chin, studying her. "You seem a bit pale."

Charlotte placed the back of her hand against her forehead. "I'm not feeling too well."

"Are you okay?"

"Yeah. I think I just need to get some sleep. Today was filled with a lot of...excitement."

"Okay. Let's get you to bed." I took her hand, and we walked out of the restaurant toward the elevator. From the corner of my eye, I noticed a man standing at reception, glancing our way. There was something about him that had my instincts flare up. There was a look in his eye I didn't trust—the way his gaze drifted from me to Charlotte. Within a second, I had memorized every visible feature of that man.

Caucasian. Large frame, around six-feet-four. Light-brown hair neatly cut, and beard trimmed. We were too far away for me to see the color of his eyes, but judging by the way it didn't stand out and grab attention, my guess was either brown or green. Maybe a mix between. Nothing about him posed any threat in that moment. There was just...something.

We reached the elevator, and as Charlotte stepped inside, I stilled next to the concierge who held the door for us, leaning close and slipping money into his pocket without anyone noticing. "The man at the reception desk. I need to know who he is."

The concierge nodded, and I stepped inside as he pressed the number to our floor.

The door closed, and I pulled Charlotte closer. Her body went rigid against mine, and I couldn't help but wonder if there was more to her not feeling well all of a sudden.

"Are you sure you're okay?"

"I am." She leaned closer, but I could still feel the tension radiate off her. "I'm really just exhausted."

"Maybe you should stay in bed tomorrow. I can cancel with Saint and Milana—"

"No," she snapped. "Don't cancel with them. I want to go. I'm sure a good night's sleep will have me all better in the morning."

The elevator chimed, and the door opened. "Why don't you have an early night? I have a few things I have to take care of in the office."

She smiled, but it didn't reach her eyes. "Okay."

About to walk off in the other direction, I grabbed her hand and pulled her back, kissing her hard. The way she kissed me back, her body relaxing into mine, reassured me that she was okay—that I could focus my attention on the man who had my instincts blazing. "I love you, Charlotte."

"I love you, too."

Our fingers entwined as she stepped back and turned to make her way down the hall. God, she was the most perfect woman I had ever laid eyes on. And now I had the honor of calling her my wife.

It was a risky fucking move I pulled tonight. But for her, there was no risk too high. There was nothing I wouldn't do for her—to keep her safe. The Bernardi family was a powerful one in our society. Every one of them were cruel motherfuckers and would stop at nothing to get what they want. And what they wanted was Charlotte. They knew she was the key to all of this, and if they had her, their secrets would be buried along with Gianni. But they were making a vast goddamn mistake if they thought I'd ever let them near her. She was mine, and I'd have to be dead before I'd ever allow anyone to take her from me.

Charlotte

I GLANCED over my shoulder at Elijah fast asleep next to me. It was early hours in the morning when he eventually came to bed. He climbed in behind me, kissed my shoulder, and whispered into my ear, "Are you awake?"

I was but pretended to be asleep. It was so damn hard to do as Saint had said—to keep quiet and not mention anything to Elijah. I wanted answers, and more than anything I wanted Elijah to tell me that he didn't lie, that Saint had it all wrong. My heart was bleeding for the truth not to taint what I felt for Elijah.

I lay awake that night for hours thinking about what Saint had said. Was I a fool for doubting Elijah? For believing a man I hardly knew over the man I now called my husband?

The same man who kills people for a living.

The same man who kidnapped me.

I repeated the conversation with Saint over and over inside my head. It couldn't have been a coincidence that Saint described Gianni's supposed death almost precisely the way Elijah had described the death of my father. What did Saint have to gain by lying to me?

What does Elijah have to gain by lying to you?

There were too many questions, too many variables, and the more I tried to fit the pieces together, the less anything made sense. There had to be a way for me to figure out what the hell was going on.

I gently eased off the bed, trying my best not to wake up Elijah. He stirred, and I stilled, waiting for him to turn on his side.

My feet hit the plush carpet, and I barely breathed as I grabbed my nightgown and sneaked out of the room. The halls were extra cold. Maybe it was just my racing heart and frozen nerves, my desperation for none of what Saint had said to be true.

Entering the lavish dining room, I spotted Elijah's laptop on the six-seater oak table. I glanced down the hall, wondering if I had time to do some research of my own while I waited for Saint to tell me what the hell was going on.

Of course, it was password-protected, and I sighed as I leaned back in the chair staring at the screen. I thought of a few possibilities of what it could be.

Ellie.

The Musician.

Password, one, two, three, four, five.

All predictable and highly unlikely. But then I thought about the music box, the one Elijah bought Ellie, but never got the chance to give it to her. And then it occurred to me...

The music box.

Edelweiss.

The song Elijah said he heard me play for the first time.

Hastily, I typed in the word, and the browser opened. Inching to the edge of my seat, I typed in the name Gianni Guerra, my pulse racing at a thousand miles an hour. Every two seconds I would look at the arched entrance of the dining room, expecting Elijah to walk around the corner at any moment. This was why I never did shit I wasn't supposed to do—except marrying my kidnapper on a whim. But that wasn't the point. The point was, I didn't do stupid shit because it made me feel like I was going to have a heart attack at any moment and go straight to hell.

The search came up, and there was only one article toward the end of the page that mentioned Gianni Guerra's name.

SON OF NOTORIOUS MAFIA BOSS SPOTTED AT FUNERAL

Julio Bernardi was spotted making an appearance at suspected Mafia hitman Gianni Guerra's funeral last Saturday.

JESUS. Saint was right. Gianni Guerra was dead, and the article was dated three years ago. Ice erupted through every vein, my heart hammering against my chest and spine at the same time. It was like someone sliced me wide open, and I was bleeding out, unable to stop it from happening.

What else was Elijah lying about? And most importantly, why?

I typed in the name Ellie Mariano and clicked enter just

as I heard footsteps coming down the hall. My heart leaped up my throat, and I slammed the laptop shut before shooting upright and darting to the front of the table.

Elijah strolled in. "What are you doing in here?"

I could feel every drop of blood drain from my body, yet my cheeks burned and sweat trickled down my back. "I... um," I lifted myself onto the table, "I was waiting for you."

"You were?"

Christ. What the fuck do I do now?

You improvise, Charlotte. You survive.

Pushing back the nerves that had my skin ice-cold, yet palms clammy, I slid the skirt of my nightgown up my legs and over my thighs. "I'm feeling guilty about last night, not being able to spend our wedding night doing what we do best."

Elijah's irises darkened, almost as black as the sweatpants he wore which hung low around his waist showcasing the prominent V which I was sure had magical fucking powers, making my fingertips itch to trace along the sensual clefts. His roped muscles were physical proof of how strong he was, and the way he leveled me with his dark gaze proved just how much power he wielded over me. Everything about him was alluring, intoxicating, and utterly hypnotic. I could feel it in my bones how this potent attraction crackled between us. It was undeniable, and too strong to fight.

He stalked toward me already wearing the mask of a predator, his expression wicked and eyes hungry. My body shivered as he placed his palms on my knees, abruptly jerking my legs open.

I gasped, and he moved in between my thighs, wrapping an arm around my waist and pulling me to the edge of the table. My sex started to throb the moment he rubbed his hard length against my panties.

With a gentle finger, he touched my chin, staring down hungrily at my mouth. "I'm starting to think I created an insatiable little wench."

I placed my palms on his naked chest, his skin warm to the touch. "I think you might be right."

"Well," he slipped his hand between us and pulled out his cock, "I can promise you, you'll never hear me fucking complain."

This might have started as a way to cover up what I was really doing here, but my body was reacting to his as if I didn't doubt him at all. As if I hadn't just caught him in a lie about Gianni Guerra.

Elijah had a hold on me, completely enthralled me in a way that left me incapable of fighting the sensual allure that oozed from his pores. I couldn't ignore the glimmer of dark promises in his eyes as he studied me.

So, I let him fuck me right there on the table as if nothing was wrong. I allowed him to move inside me with hard, fast, relentless thrusts. Kissing my neck, nipping at the skin of my shoulder before sucking my nipple into his mouth, Elijah played my body like a goddamn instrument. Possessed and utterly consumed, I forgot about the lies, the doubt, the questions. I forgot about the fucking world, not caring about anything but how he made me feel.

Elijah was my cocaine. My drug. Being fucked by him had me in a haze of pleasure and rapture—my skin electrified and mind numb. The racing thoughts desperately searching for reasons Elijah lied were quieted by our moans and the sound of him penetrating my wet cunt over and over again.

God, it was a filthy ballad of lust—proof that primal instincts were far more potent than reason and common sense.

I leaned back on the oak table, surrendering to the euphoria as his fingers dug into the skin of my waist, pushing and pulling my body to match his thrusts. I was high on him, on the scent of sex, and the anticipation of an orgasm that would tear me in fucking half. And the moment my climax stirred inside my belly, I closed my eyes and relaxed every muscle. Rather than chase the pleasure, I allowed it to burn and build, my blood simmering as my body climbed slowly, leisurely, reaching the plateau. And then finally, it exploded, and I shattered into a million pieces, my sex pulsing as my orgasm ripped through me.

He continued to fuck me, impaling me until he too found his release. But this time he didn't come inside me. Instead, I felt the warm squirts of his cum on my cunt and thighs. I glanced down to watch him jerk his cock in his palm, milking it for the last drop of jizz.

"Jesus Christ," Elijah said as he looked down where his cum stained my skin and dragged a finger through it. "I have never seen anything as hot as my cum covering your cunt."

I moaned when he inserted that same finger inside me, my sex sensitive and still throbbing.

"You are truly mine, in every sense of the word. And there is no better sight than seeing you like this, my sweet cellist. Utterly spent and thoroughly fucked."

"I am," I whispered, the lies slowly starting to penetrate the haze. "I am truly...fucked."

CHAPTER THIRTY-SIX

CHARLOTTE

The water was too hot, but I didn't care. I didn't feel the burn, how it scorched my skin. All I felt was this numbing ache inside my chest, like a disease that stemmed from Elijah's lies. No matter how hard I tried to think of possible reasons he'd lie to me, none of them made it feel any better. It made me wonder what else he was lying about, causing me to dissect every word he had ever said. But everything just came down to this one monumental thing.

I loved him.

I loved him so much I married him on a whim, an impulse that convinced me that nothing would ever change the way I felt about him, which meant I might as well take the plunge and marry him, which I did. And now here I was, not even twenty-four hours later trying to keep my heart from bleeding out. My soul was cracked, my insides torn from the sharp edges of his lies. I could barely stand up straight, every muscle weakened by the pain that throbbed inside my chest.

The only thing that got me out of the shower, dressed, and in the car next to Elijah was the thought of meeting Saint and Milana—hopefully getting answers as to what the hell was going on. Deep down I prayed that there would be a logical explanation as to why Elijah lied to me. Something that would justify his deception. I just wanted the pain to go away, to be able to look at him and not feel betrayed.

During the drive to the Trevi Fountain I glanced out the window, the streets of Rome going past us in one big blur. There was nothing beautiful about any of it today. Everything was colorless and glum. The magic was gone, the splendor faded to gray. It was impossible for me to see beauty in anything while my heart ached with doubt. How could one appreciate the brilliance of Rome when everything you felt inside was black and broken?

It was only when I stood in front of the Trevi Fountain that I was able to push back the pain and heartache for a moment, to experience the fountain's magnificence. Just like the Colosseum, its architecture was unique and spectacular. The sound of the water was calming, and I stood in front of the fountain entranced by it all. The sculptures, the horses, every inch of it held a piece of history—most of it never to be known by man, solidified within the stone. I could only imagine the tales and secrets it held...*like my husband.*

Elijah wrapped his arms around me and pulled my back against his chest, his warmth enveloping me. I closed my eyes, loving and hating it all at once. My heart screamed with torment, breaking more and more with each passing second. The love I had for Elijah was crushing me from the inside, and I could hardly take a breath.

"Oceanus," Elijah said against my ear, "he stands in the

center of it all. His chariot being pulled by two sea horses, one wild and one docile, representing the opposing spirits of the ocean."

"It's beautiful."

We glanced up toward the top of the fountain, four statues standing tall and majestic. "They symbolize the effect of rain on the Earth. Abundance of Fruits. Fertility of Crops. Products of Autumn. Joy of Prairie and Gardens." The way Elijah spoke, it was as if he understood the history, lived it, felt it inside him. His voice transported me, and I was lost within the enchantment of it all. I didn't want it to end because while I was here, caught up in the moment with him, I was able to focus on the love between us rather than on my own pain.

"Here." He opened his palm, revealing three coins.

"Why three?"

He let go of my waist and stepped in next to me, sweeping his gaze across the crowds, consisting primarily of young couples throwing coins into the fountain. "It's believed that if you throw in one coin, you will return to Rome." He handed me one coin. "Throw in two coins, and you will fall in love with an Italian." He grinned then held out the second coin. "Throw in a third coin, and you will marry the person you fell in love with." He placed the third coin in my palm.

God, the torment was unbearable. I loved this man with all my heart, and whenever he showed me this side of him, romance seeping through his words, it reminded me how utterly ruined I was in love, and how deeply I had fallen for him.

"Now, you need to turn around and toss the coins over your left shoulder with your right hand."

"Okay." I smiled, and as I turned, Milana and Saint came walking toward us, and I instinctively held my breath when Saint met my gaze, a knowing look passing between us.

"Wait for me." Milana held up her coin before stepping in next to me.

"You only have one?"

She glanced at Saint. "I only need one."

It was insane how in love these two were. They were both besotted, and quite frankly, if I had met them a few months back, I'd have been nauseated by it.

I closed my eyes and rubbed the coin between my fingertips. A silent prayer filled my thoughts as I held my breath, my heart beating impossibly fast.

Please, God, help me survive this man.

Milana and I tossed our coins at the same time. The noise of the fountain drowned out the sound of our coins that plunked into the water. I wanted to come back here to Rome. I wanted to visit the Colosseum and be reminded of how Elijah and I got married there. How we consummated our marriage against its stone walls. My heart yearned to have those memories without dark lies to taint it.

I closed my hand around the other two coins, clenching my jaw as I bit back the tears.

Elijah cocked a brow, the winter breeze ruffling through his black hair. "You have two more coins."

"No." I held it out to him. "I only need to throw one."

Our gazes locked, his eyes showing me the soul of a man who loved deeply—a sullen contradiction to the lies he had told.

THE VILLAIN

Elijah reached out, wrapped his fingers around the back of my neck, and pulled me closer, placing a tender kiss on my forehead. It took every ounce of strength I had not to cry. Tears stung my eyes as the lies poisoned my soul. The last time I was this broken was the day my mom died. It was the first time I lost someone so important to me—and today, I was afraid I'd lose another.

"Elijah," Mila interrupted. "Saint tells me that no one knows the history of the Trevi Fountain better than you do." She placed a hand on his elbow. "Since my husband and I clearly don't share the same love for ancient architecture, I was hoping you could tell me a bit more."

To me, it was obvious what she was doing—especially when she glanced back at Saint as if she acknowledged that she was doing what he expected. Distracting my husband to give Saint and me some privacy so I could fall deeper into the despair of deception.

Saint stepped in front of me, the collar of his black winter coat turned up to ward off the cold. "How are you holding up?"

"I'd say that's a shitty question."

He glanced up at the gray sky, avoiding eye contact.

"You dropped a bomb on me last night, Saint. And then you expected me to keep quiet."

"I couldn't risk Elijah knowing."

"Knowing what?"

Saint shifted and glanced around us. "First, I need to know exactly what Elijah told you."

"About what?"

"About everything. Every fucking little thing, I need to know."

I slipped my hands into the pockets of my beige trench coat, pulling my shoulders upward. "I don't even know you. How do I know this isn't all bullshit?"

"Do you know him?" Saint stepped closer—a dominating force that caused me to inch back. "Do you really know Elijah?"

I scoffed. I wanted to say yes. I wanted to shout from the fucking rooftops that I knew Elijah better than anyone else. That he had shown me a side to him that no one had ever seen. But the truth was, I couldn't. I couldn't say without a doubt that the Elijah I knew was true. "Fine." I conceded. "When Elijah first took me—"

"Took you?"

I shifted from one leg to the other. "Elijah and I didn't exactly meet the old-fashioned way."

Saint lifted a brow but said nothing and allowed me to continue.

"He said that Gianni Guerra was my grandfather."

"Yeah." He wiped at his nose—red from the cold—then glanced at the crowds before looking back at me. "I did some research, and it turns out that part is true. Gianni Guerra did have a daughter."

"My mother?"

He nodded, and a sliver of relief flooded through my chest knowing at least one thing Elijah told me was true.

"What else has he told you?"

"That Gianni is in some prison, waiting to testify against the Bernardi family. And that I was in danger, because the Bernardis know if they have me, Gianni wouldn't testify. That's why he had to take me."

"To protect you?"

I nodded.

"What else?"

My thoughts were frantic, trying to search through every memory, every conversation we had. "Just that he had to watch over me for three years, did everything he could to keep the Bernardi family from finding me."

"So, he stalked you?"

"Observed was the word he used."

Saint rubbed his temples. "Anything else?"

"I don't know. Everything that happened the past few months is like a giant goddamn blur." I was frazzled, trying to sort through my thoughts. "Um, there was Josh."

"Josh?"

"Yeah, this guy back in New York. He worked for Elijah, I think, but then Elijah shot him, saying that he was a traitor."

"When was this?" Saint didn't seem surprised at all at the mention of Elijah killing someone.

"Um"—I scratched the side of my neck—"it was the night of the attack at Elijah's apartment. Someone was shooting at us. I don't know who it was, I just remember Elijah saying that they found me."

"The Bernardis?"

Shrugging, I replied, "I guess so."

"This doesn't make sense." Saint paced in front of me, staring at the ground as he seemingly tried to piece it all together. "This happened the night you flew from New York to Rome?"

I nodded. "Not like I could remember anything. Elijah drugged me. One minute I was in the back seat of the car freaking out, and the next I woke up on your yacht."

Saint stilled. "He phoned me that night. He said Plan A had been compromised."

"I remember him phoning someone, yes. That was you?"

"Yeah." He frowned, his eyes hard and expression stern. "Listen, Charlotte. The Bernardi family, they're not after you."

"What do you mean they're not?"

"It's not you they want."

"If it's not me, then who?"

Saint pulled up his shoulder as if warding off the cold, his expression sullen. "It's him they want. Elijah. He's the target, not you."

"What?" My voice was nothing but a whisper.

"Elijah knows too much about what Gianni did for the family. Julio Bernardi wants Elijah killed before his dad's trial." His jaw clenched. "Elijah is a loose end they've been trying to tie up ever since Gianni died. Hell, there's even talk that Gianni's death was planned to look like a drunken brawl."

My heart sank to the soles of my feet, my stomach twisted into a thousand painful knots. I was sure the ground cracked beneath my feet, swallowing me whole. "Why would Elijah lie about that? Why would he say I'm the target when it's him they want?"

He bit his lower lip. Clearly, whatever it was, he was having a hard time putting it into words.

"Saint."

"Elijah is...well—" He rubbed the back of his neck. "Elijah is not...himself."

"What are you saying?"

"I don't have all the specifics. I didn't think this was a problem anymore since it's been years—"

"Saint, what are you talking about?"

"I knew something was off when James informed me that Elijah had brought you to the yacht. Elijah never does anything that's not part of the plan. And you," his gaze cut to mine, "you weren't part of our plan, Charlotte."

"What plan?" Jesus, my head was spinning.

"The plan to have Elijah hide from the Bernardi family until we got it taken care of."

"Jesus Christ, I think I'm going to pass out. Nothing is making any goddamn sense."

Saint grabbed my arms, pinning me with a glare that screamed warning. "Listen to me. Elijah was in that car."

"What car?"

"The car, with his dad."

I narrowed my eyes in question. "He was with his father during the accident?"

"Yes." Saint let me go, and my legs almost gave way beneath me. "He was small, five or six, I'm not sure. All I know is he was in that accident and barely made it out alive himself."

"Elijah never mentioned this."

"He wouldn't have, because according to Elijah...he never was in that car."

My pulse raced. "What?"

Saint licked his lips and inched closer. "Elijah doesn't remember anything about the accident. He doesn't remember being in the car with his dad."

"Oh, my God. Elijah has amnesia?"

"Or something." He pulled his hand through his hair,

grabbing the ends. "I honest to God thought this was all in the past. His father, Ellie—"

"His sister?"

Saint's pained gaze met mine, the despondent expression on his face sending chills through every bone in my body. "You know about Ellie?"

"He told me about her. How she disappeared, not knowing whether she was still alive or dead."

"Jesus Christ," Saint cursed before settling his sullen gaze on me. "He didn't have a sister, Charlotte. Ellie doesn't exist. She never has."

"No." I couldn't believe it. "No. No. No."

"Yes," Saint insisted. "Ellie was never real."

That was the moment I was certain the Earth had split in half, sucking me into the dark center of chaos. My head spun with thoughts that were nothing but a jumbled mess, my mind refusing to believe what Saint just said. "That's insane. He told me about her, told me about how his abusive stepdad hurt her."

Saint shook his head. "It's not true."

"It has to be. I...there." I couldn't form a single coherent sentence as my thoughts raced. "He has this music box that he bought her, but never had the chance to give to her. Saint, he has a sister. Why...why would he make her up?"

"His injuries together with the trauma of losing his father somehow caused Elijah to create Ellie inside his head. Like an—"

"Imaginary friend?"

"Something like that. As I said, I don't have the details. All I know is what my father has told me in the past. That when Gianni rescued Elijah from that wretched house, his mind was..." Saint wiped his palm down his face. "His mind was broken."

My legs grew weak, and I wanted to collapse right there and be trampled into nothing but dust. Saint grabbed my arm and helped me sit down on the nearest bench, the cold winter air slicing through the skin of my neck. "His mind is...broken?"

He sat down next to me, staring out in front of us. "It's been more than twenty years. My father and I, we were sure the therapy helped. That Gianni managed to get through to him and somehow—"

"Fixed him?" The words tasted bitter on my tongue.

"Something like that, I suppose."

"I can't believe this." I placed my palm in front of my mouth, unable to think straight. "What else has he made up?"

"We can't be sure."

I leaned back, my mind in a state of complete anarchy as I tried to recall every conversation Elijah and I had. One in particular stood out. "He told me that the night Gianni rescued him, he killed his mom with an overdose. Is that true?"

"No," he answered, clipped. "The night Gianni found him, Elijah was hiding in the bedroom closet. He saw everything, how Gianni shot Roland and injected his mother to make it look like a homicide and suicide. The trauma of witnessing that gruesome scene was enough to cause some short-circuit inside his head, his mind fabricating what really took place that night."

"Jesus," I sighed, tears stinging my eyes as I watched Elijah and Milana in the distance. Elijah glanced my way, shooting me the most handsome fucking smile, and it knocked the wind right out of me. My heart was nothing but pieces of pain—the toxic lies and rancorous truths, it was unreal. I didn't want to believe any of it. I wanted all of this to be nothing more than a horrible nightmare, to wake up and realize that my husband was the man I fell in love with. That the man who stole my heart so unapologetically was real, true, and not some broken version of the man I thought I knew.

"How do I know what you're telling me is the truth?" I didn't look at Saint, but I wanted him to be the liar in this story. I needed him to be the villain and not Elijah.

Saint held out a business card, and I took it from him. "Dr. Angus Hillebrand. Who is this?"

"That's the psychologist who knows Elijah's case. He's expecting your call."

Saint stood, and on cue Milana turned and strolled in our direction, her hand hooked into the crook of Elijah's elbow as they chatted with smiles on their faces. They seemed like two people who didn't have a care in the world.

Saint turned to face me. "You can come with us."

I glanced up at him. "What do you mean?"

"Come with Milana and me, and we'll take you back to New York."

I stood. "What about Elijah?"

"Leave him to me. I know how to deal with him."

Tears slipped down my cheek, the cold air causing the salty liquid to sting my skin. "We can't just leave him—"

Screeching tires sounded, both Saint and I looking in the direction of a speeding car pulling up close. The door opened, and Saint's low voice cracked through the air as he screamed, "Mila!"

Adrenaline surged through the ice in my veins as I stood frozen, unable to move as I watched a man lean out of the car, gun in hand. It happened in slow motion, Elijah and Milana running toward us.

Saint grabbed his wife and pulled her down to the ground, Elijah still running in my direction. I couldn't move. I couldn't think. Time stood still, yet my pulse raced, and all I heard was the sound of my own heartbeat as it tried to rip through my chest.

An arm wrapped around my throat, and the eerie silence got shattered with the sound of my own screams, fear pulsating through my veins.

I grabbed at the strong arm that choked me, my nails scratching and clawing as I got dragged toward the car. "Elijah!" I cried.

"Charlotte!"

I watched as he ran toward me, and I kept fighting the man pulling me against him, thrashing and screaming. Too much was happening at once, and I struggled to focus, adrenaline throbbing inside my head.

The man tightened his hold around me, and he yelled something in Italian. I didn't care what he was saying; all I cared about was breaking free.

I scratched harder. Clawed deeper, but he didn't let go. Desperate to get away, I lifted my foot and kicked down, aiming for his leg, his foot, anything just to hurt him so he'd let me go.

By the way he cursed, his arm loosening just a little, I knew I got him somewhere, and I jerked out of his hold, my feet ready to run. But Elijah's screams cut through my chest, every muscle in my body instantly frozen.

"Charlotte, stop!"

I stilled, my spine ice and the back of my neck cold. The man grabbed my arm and yanked me back, pressing the cold muzzle of his gun against my temple. I shuddered as fear clamped down on my chest, squeezing the air from my lungs.

Women screamed, men cursed, and children cried around us as people scattered. It was chaos, the air rancid with panic.

Elijah had stopped, holding his hands in the air, and I closed my eyes, biting my tongue as the threat loomed behind me.

"Don't hurt her," Elijah pleaded. "Put the gun down."

"You get in the fucking car first."

I suppressed a sob, tears slipping down my face.

"I'll do whatever the fuck you want, man. Just don't hurt her."

"Hurry the fuck up! Get in the car before I kill both of you right here."

I opened my eyes and watched as Elijah kept his hands in the air, slowly walking toward the black SUV. "If you hurt her, I swear to God—"

"Shut the fuck up!" The man pressed the muzzle harder against my head, and I shut my eyes, holding my breath as a whimper rippled from my throat. "Get in the motherfucking car!"

"Okay, just let her go." There was a tremor in Elijah's voice—something I had never heard before. The sound of fear laced around his words, and it instilled a kind of terror inside me that I had never experienced before.

THE VILLAIN

"Elijah," I whispered, keeping my eyes closed as panic gnawed at my bones with every pounding heartbeat.

The man tightened his hold on my arm. "On second thought, I think she'll join us."

"No!" Elijah yelled...and then everything went black.

CHAPTER THIRTY-SEVEN

ELIJAH

I knew what fear felt like. I spent most of my childhood living in fear, constantly feeling the terror of sheer panic. Feeling your muscles tighten and your stomach turn while you struggled to breathe wasn't a new experience for me. But this...this was beyond fear. It was like the dread of hell had been ignited in my veins, horror boiling in my blood as the devil himself held a knife to my throat.

They had pulled a bag over my head, but not before I witnessed the bastard hit Charlotte over the head, knocking her unconscious. I lost my shit in the back of that fucking car, wanting to tear their motherfucking hearts out without seeing a goddamn thing. Even after they stuck a needle in my arm, I still fought and cursed them to hell, wanting their blood to stain my hands...until there was nothing.

Next thing I knew, I woke up, tied to a goddamn chair in total darkness with a rope tied through my mouth. It smelled like sewer and rotting flesh, the air damp and humid.

I couldn't see a thing, and I tried to call her, tried to say her name, but the damn rope made it sound like nothing but the desperate groans of a man ready to slaughter an entire fucking village to get to the woman he loved.

I pulled at my wrists and felt the plastic cable ties cut my skin. But I didn't feel the pain. I didn't care if I had to saw my own fucking hands off. All I cared about was making sure Charlotte was okay, that these fuckers didn't hurt her more than they already had.

The light flicked on, and it blinded me, causing me to shut my eyes. The rope was pulled from my mouth, the harsh fibers cutting my lip.

"Where is she?" I demanded, my voice echoing in the darkness while I still struggled against the bounds around my wrist. "What did you do to her?"

"She's right here."

I blinked rapidly, my eyes adjusting to the light. "Jesus," I breathed when I saw Charlotte across from me, tied to a chair, still unconscious with her head hanging down. There was blood on her coat, and my heart wanted to crack through my ribs as panic soared.

"Charlotte!" I cried. "Charlotte, wake up."

"She'll wake up soon enough."

My attention snapped in the direction of the voice just as Julio Bernardi revealed himself, stepping out of the corner.

"You son of a bitch," I spat at him. "Let her go."

"Not yet. I need something from you first." He grinned, and the scar above his upper lip curled. "Give me what I want, and I'll consider letting her go."

"I know you want her, but it will be a cold fucking day in hell before I'd let you harm her in any goddamn way."

"Oh." Julio paused. "I don't want her."

I recoiled, narrowing my eyes, not trusting this son of a bitch one little bit.

Julio frowned. "You thought I wanted her?"

I didn't respond, my mind racing.

"Oh, no, Elijah." Julio cackled. "How wrong you are. I don't want her. I never wanted her." He mimicked a gunshot in my direction with his fingers. "It's you I want."

Me? What the fuck was he talking about?

"Well, not you, but rather something you have."

"Then what the fuck is she here for? By having her here you're only pissing me the fuck off."

He laughed, those mouse-colored eyes of his filled with amusement. "You know how long I've been searching for you?"

"I don't give a fuck," I bit out, still pulling at the cable tie around my wrists.

Julio pulled his fingers through his shoulder-length hair, auburn strands falling back to fan his ugly motherfucking face. "I'm pretty sure when it comes to her," he walked up behind her, placing his filthy hands on her shoulders, "you give quite the fuck."

"Take your fucking hands off her."

"Or what?"

"Or I'll cut your motherfucking hands off right before I tear out your goddamn liver."

Charlotte stirred, moaning softly.

"Oh," Julio smirked, "look who's waking up."

"Keep her the fuck out of this, Bernardi!"

"You know," he leaned down, bringing his face closer to her, "all this time I was searching for you, I never thought I'd get two for the price of one. Yet here we are. The man raised by Gianni Guerra, and the dead man's granddaughter."

"Elijah," Charlotte whimpered, lifting her head, dried blood covering the side of her face.

"Charlotte!" I jerked, yanked, and fucking pulled at my tied hands. "Charlotte." I cut my glare to Julio. "Let her fucking go."

Julio leaned closer, pressing his face against her cheek, taunting me. "Get away from her!"

"Give me what I want."

"I don't fucking know what you want!"

Julio bit his lip as he straightened, and his amused expression turned to stone. "I have spent years looking for you. I'm not wasting another fucking second." He pulled a gun from his back and held it against Charlotte's head. "Tell me where it is."

"Jesus Christ." Every muscle in my body was coiled tight, my insides wrapped in barbed wire as I stared at the glint of a gun held against Charlotte's head.

She blinked and cringed, moaning. "Elijah."

"I don't know what you fucking want!" I screamed at Julio. "Tell me what you want!"

"Gianni's diary, that's what I want!" Spit erupted from his mouth. "I want his motherfucking diary."

"Listen to me," I pleaded like a desperate fucking idiot willing to give his last breath in order to save his wife. "Gianni didn't have a diary."

Julio shifted. "Everyone knows he kept a list." He waved the gun around. "A fucking manifest of names."

Stunned, my eyes widened. "That's what you've been after all this time? His fucking pocket Bible?"

Julio's eyes widened. "He kept the list of his victims' names in his pocket Bible? How fucking ironic."

"Why do you want it?"

Julio lifted a brow. "You know how we hate loose ends. Knowing that list is floating around is just too risky. I need it so I can fucking burn it."

This was the opportunity I had waited for, finding something I could use to my advantage, turn this entire situation around so it played out in my favor.

I glared at him. "If you hurt her, you'll never get your hands on that Bible." I made sure my threat was laced with confidence and unbreakable determination. "If anything happens to her or me, I can guarantee you that the next person to see that fucking list carries a badge."

"Don't fuck with me, Elijah."

"No!" I snapped. "Don't you fuck with me. You underestimated me, you fucking son of a bitch, and that was your biggest mistake."

Charlotte's fearful gaze locked with mine, tears slipping down her cheeks. God, I could see her trembling. But I pushed my own fear back, determined to show Julio he no longer controlled this fucking situation. I did.

Julio glared in my direction, studying me, and I could practically hear the fucking wheels turn inside his head.

Sweat trickled down my back as I anxiously waited for Julio to make his move, which would determine what I would do next.

He rubbed his jaw with his thumb and forefinger, his pensive expression pissing me the fuck off. "You're right. I did underestimate you. I had every fucking contractor search for you, but no one could find you after you escaped New

York. Not even the infamous Musician—who cost me a fuckton of money, I might add. How did you do it? How did you manage to escape us all this time?"

A laugh ripped from my throat, mocking him. "Of course the Musician couldn't find me." I cleared my throat, smiling. "You stupid fuck."

"I would advise you to watch your mouth since I'm the one with the gun here."

"Heed my warning, Julio. If you hurt Charlotte in any way, you better be sure to kill me. Otherwise, I will come for you, and I will peel your motherfucking skin off inch by inch right before I cut out your tongue. I will kill you, Julio. But it will be a slow, agonizing death. I swear to God."

Julio glowered at me, and for a brief second, I saw fear flash in his eyes. I'd seen that look enough times to recognize it. This fucker was weak, a piss-poor excuse of a man who pretended he had the balls to rule the world.

He wiped at his nose. "I promise you, Mariano, this will end with you taking your last breath."

Gunshots went off around us just as someone burst through the old door, dust and pieces of broken wood exploding into a cloud of smoke. Mayhem erupted, my ears ringing from the fired shots that echoed through the confined space.

Men came storming in, and Julio raised his gun. That was the moment I prayed. I fucking prayed to a God I was sure didn't exist until right now. I didn't care if I made it out of this alive, as long as she did. As long as Charlotte was saved—that was all that mattered to me.

Another gunshot fired, and Julio fell to the ground, blood gushing from his chest. It would have been an exquisite sight, something to savor if it wasn't for my instinct to get Charlotte far away from here—to make sure she was safe.

Charlotte screamed, the sound scraping against my spine. I wasn't sure if I yelled or not, but the moment I felt the ties around my wrists get cut I launched from my chair. There was no other sound but Charlotte's cries, the adrenaline in my veins demanding I protect her.

"It's okay." I grabbed her the moment one of the men loosened her wrists, and she slammed into me, sobbing against my chest, shuddering. "You're okay. You're safe."

Thank you, God. Thank you. That was the only thought that repeated itself in my head, my heart on the verge of bursting.

"Elijah." Charlotte grabbed my shirt with her fists, clutching me so fucking tight. "I was so scared."

"I know, baby. It's okay. You're safe now." I hugged her tighter, weaving my hands into her hair, relief flooding my system. Nothing else fucking mattered. Nothing. It was only her. Her safety. Her protection. Her security.

Saint walked in, fastening the buttons of his coat. "You two okay?"

"God, yes." I didn't let go of Charlotte. "You got my message?"

Saint lifted a brow. "Obviously."

I took a deep breath. "Remind me to give that concierge a huge motherfucking tip."

"I'll give it to you, my friend. Your instincts are spot on."

After doing a little background check on the man I noticed in the hotel's reception the night before, I came up empty. I couldn't find anything on that man. Nothing. It was as if the man didn't exist, and that was highly un-fucking-likely. Everyone had a trace. Everyone. Not finding anything on that man set off all the alarm bells.

Unable to ignore my instincts, I instructed the concierge to call me when this man left the hotel. If he didn't get hold of me, he was instructed to send the man's name to Saint with my message. *"Ghosts don't exist."* I knew Saint had the means and the resources to figure out who this man was. Everyone had a story, no matter who you were.

Saint patted me on the shoulder. "Our ghost led us here." He glanced at the ground by the door where our ghost's dead body bled out. "You're lucky I figured it out."

"Never doubted you for a second."

Saint smirked. "Because you know I'm smarter than you."

I rolled my eyes, clutching Charlotte tighter.

Saint glanced from her to me. "Get her out of here. Once she's safe, and I'm done here," his expression hardened, "you and I, we need to talk."

I knew that look. I also knew that whatever Saint wanted to talk about, I wasn't going to like it. But that was a problem for another time. Right now, all that mattered was Charlotte.

I eased back, gently wiping her hair from her face—strands of raven curls sticking to the crusted blood on her cheek. "We need to get you checked out."

She nodded, wiping at her tears. "I'm okay."

"I just want to make sure. It's a nasty hit you took."

Her hands trembled, and her body shook. "Are you okay? Did they hurt you?"

I couldn't help but smile. "After what you've just been through, you're worried that I'm hurt?"

"All I thought about was you, praying they wouldn't hurt you."

"I'm fine."

"You sure?"

I cupped her cheek. "Yes. And I'll be even better after I get you out of here."

Charlotte snuggled into my side, and I slipped my arm around her shoulders, keeping her steady as we walked out.

A loud crack sounded, and my ears popped, followed by the sound of Charlotte's screams. My body went numb—my legs, my arms, everything but this searing pain that spread like fire through my insides.

My thoughts went quiet. Silent. My body falling...falling...until it all went dark.

CHAPTER THIRTY-EIGHT

CHARLOTTE

I stared out the window, the doctor's voice echoing in the background. He was still talking and explaining, but I didn't hear a thing. I had stopped listening when I heard the words *'traumatic brain injury,'* and *'damage to the inferior medial frontal lobe.'*

Was this what an out-of-body experience felt like? Your mind drifting far from where your body was. Escaping. Fleeing. Eluding reality.

"Mrs. Mariano?"

I blinked.

"Mrs. Mariano?"

"Yes." I lightly shook my head and glanced at the files in front of me.

"Are you okay?" Dr. Hillebrand asked. "I know this is a lot to take in."

"I'm fine." I swallowed. "Please continue."

"It's what we call confabulation. It's like a type of memory error where gaps in memory are unconsciously filled with fabricated or distorted information. A patient who confabulates is basically confusing things they've imagined with real memories. In Mr. Mariano's case, he filled the gap of the accident." The doctor shrugged. "He filled the gap his father's death left with an imaginary sister."

"Ellie," I whispered, my heart torn in two, reminded of the pain I saw in Elijah's eyes every time he talked about his sister. How could one feel so much for someone who didn't really exist? How could she not be real?

Dr. Hillebrand leaned back in his seat. "My guess is when Mr. Guerra died, the trauma of losing another father figure caused your husband to confabulate certain things. Certain things that involved you, Mrs. Mariano."

I sucked in a breath. "So, nothing was real?"

"On the contrary, to him everything was and is still very real. A person who confabulates has no idea that the memories he has aren't real."

I clenched my jaw, pushing back the tears. "What do I do? Do I tell him?"

"It's been my experience that trying to convince a patient that his memories are false only does more harm than good."

"Then what are you saying?"

"What I'm saying is in your husband's case these fake memories are so deeply embedded inside his mind. And my guess is the reason for that might be the fact that there are so many similarities. Ellie is a lot like the stepsister he had, Harley. It's as if he took the image of Harley and created Ellie. And with you, the fact that you are the granddaughter of the man who raised him, the fact that you play the cello—it's all connected to Gianni Guerra. It all fills that gap. I'm

THE VILLAIN

sure if you dig a little deeper, you'll find even more similarities."

"*Edelweiss*," I said under my breath.

"*Edelweiss?*"

I inhaled deeply. "He has this music box he bought for... um, *Ellie*. The song it plays is *Edelweiss*." I swallowed the lump in my throat. "It's also the song I played on the cello the first time Elijah heard me play."

"See, another similarity." The doctor placed his pen on the desk. "If you start searching for it, you will find a whole lot more."

I straightened in my seat, trying my best not to break down. "What are my options here, Doctor? What do I do?"

He shrugged. "I can't tell you what to do, Mrs. Mariano. But what I can say is if you stay with him, you'll have to live with the fabricated memories your husband created." He paused, and his expression softened. "His reality will have to become yours."

My gaze cut back to the window. There was always that split second of silence between hearing something and having your mind make sense of it. A fraction of time when there was nothing. No sound. No thought. No reaction.

I'd experienced a few of these moments in my life. Moments when I no longer felt my heart beat or my lungs expand. Moments when I wasn't alive, I merely existed, lingering in space within the absence of gravity. Yet, I was here, sitting in this chair, staring at the man across from me whose glasses would slip down his nose every five seconds, prompting him to push them back in place. The wall behind him proudly displayed the degrees he'd accumulated over the years, and judging by the wrinkles around his eyes, the grooves on his forehead, gray hair, and sharp widow's peak, he was at least sixty.

His finger tapped on the file in front of him, the sound oddly in tune with my pulse throbbing in the side of my neck. So many things had happened during the last few weeks, my life forever changed because of one man who came like a thief in the night, snatching me from my world and forcing me into his. A man who, despite my inhibitions and instincts, had me falling into his arms as if it were the only place I belonged. A man who claimed to have been seduced by my music only to have me seduced by the magnetism of a wicked darkness that dripped off him like liquid temptation.

I should have known better. I should have guarded my heart more fiercely, fought harder. But I didn't, and there were so many reasons I gave in so easily. Maybe because deep down I was intrigued by a man who felt so passionately about my music—music I was too afraid for the world to hear. Perhaps the knowledge of me being the object of his obsession fucked with my head and made me feel flattered in some twisted, fucked-up way. Or maybe I was just tired of being alone, desperate to have someone else to lean on other than myself. Perhaps that was what I thought Elijah could offer me. After all, who better to provide security and protection than a hitman who owned as much power as he exuded with every breath?

But now, as my mind slowly digested what I had just heard, word by word filtering through that one single breath of silence, I realized with a sinking feeling in my gut that I had made an ill-informed decision. I acted on my most vulnerable instincts, and now I stood on the brink of ruin with no hope of being saved.

Not by him.

Not by anyone.

Elijah lied. So many fucking lies and half-truths, I didn't know where the truth ended and the lies begun. But it was too late now. I flung myself into this black hole, and there was nothing I could do to escape the darkness.

I smoothed my palm across my belly, the two-thousand-dollar silk shirt unable to hide the poor, struggling New York cellist I once was.

The man across from me cleared his throat. "I know this must be a huge shock. But I can assure you there is light at the end of this tunnel."

"No." I looked up and straight at him, swallowing hard as a tear slipped down my cheek, my insides being ripped apart with every breath. "There is no light in any of this."

His thin lips pressed together, his gray mustache curving at the edges. He knew as well as I did that there was no end to this dark tunnel, and therefore no hope of any light.

I got up and straightened my skirt. "Thank you for your time."

He pushed his glasses back over the bridge of his nose and stood. "Of course. If there is anything I can help with, you have my number."

"I appreciate that. Have a good day."

He shot me a sympathetic smile. "Good day...Mrs. Mariano."

EPILOGUE
CHARLOTTE

I hated hospitals. The somber mood. The smell. God, the smell was the worst. The potent scent of antiseptic was almost bitter, with undertones of artificial cleaners. The fluorescent lights were harsh and merely highlighted the dreary beige colors that did nothing to brighten an already somber ambiance. Ever since my mother died, I couldn't stand the thought of hospitals, not to mention being inside one.

The beep of the heart monitor reminded me that he was still breathing. They'd kept him in an induced coma since he tried to rip the IV out once he started to regain consciousness. For his body to heal, he needed rest, and to remain calm.

"My guess is Gianni knew." Saint crossed his legs as he sat down in the chair next to mine. "Gianni knew he had to make Elijah's reality his."

Just like the doctor said.

"Yeah." I sighed. "Probably."

"Have you decided what you're going to do?"

I bit my lip. "No. But right now I just want him to wake up and to know that he's okay."

"Doctor said he should wake up any moment now. The bullet missed his spine, so they're confident he'll walk again."

I didn't respond. I just stared at Elijah, who lay so still on the hospital bed. If it weren't for the beep, I'd question whether he was alive or not. I had been playing that scene over and over inside my head, and every time I relived it, I could feel the bone-chilling fear of watching Elijah fall to the ground. Julio had managed to pull the trigger of his gun before he took his final breath, and almost took my husband with him. I remembered the crack of the gunshot followed by the pained growl that tore from Elijah's throat. There was so much blood, it pooled around him, spreading through the crevices and cracks of the tiles.

I remembered crying out, but I couldn't hear myself. There was this eerie sound inside my head—the ringing in my ears mixed with the heavy pounding of my heart. And as Saint pulled me off Elijah, I cried and screamed for God not to let him die. To spare my husband's life. The lies, the unanswered questions, none of it mattered. All that mattered was him, his life, his every breath. God, I prayed he wouldn't take his last breath. I would have done anything if it meant saving him. Everything that was wrong with our relationship evaporated. It disappeared, leaving only that which was right and true between us. The one reason I would have traded my own life for his...the fact that I loved him more than anything in this entire world. No matter what, I loved him.

"I made a promise that day." I kept staring at Elijah. "When Julio shot him, I made a promise that no matter what, I would take care of him, and love him every day of my life if

THE VILLAIN

God would spare him and not let him die." I looked at Saint, who sat silently next to me. "I made a promise."

Saint's chest visibly rose and fell as he took a deep breath. "You didn't know the extent of his condition."

"It doesn't matter. There are no exclusions when it comes to a promise like that, Saint."

"No one will blame you if you leave, Charlotte. In fact, if you asked my opinion, I'd say leave. Go live your life."

"I'm not asking your opinion."

"Still, it's a tough decision. You need to do what's right for you."

"*He's* right for me. Being with him is right for me."

Elijah stirred, and I shot to my feet, rushing to his side. "Elijah?"

He moaned. "Charlotte?"

"Yes. It's me." I choked on a sob, tears stinging my eyes. "I'm here."

I took his hand and weaved my fingers through his. "How are you feeling?"

He shifted and grimaced. "Like I got shot in the back."

Both Saint and I snickered. "That's a crappy joke," I said.

"Too soon?"

"Way too soon."

Saint slipped in next to me, fastening his suit jacket. "You look like crap."

Elijah grinned. "Thanks. You don't look bad yourself."

Saint took Elijah's hand and squeezed. "It's good to have you back, man."

"How long was I out?"

"Couple of days."

"Julio?"

Saint squared his shoulders. "Burning in hell right now."

"Good."

"Okay. I need to make a few calls." Saint glanced at me. "But I'll be around for a bit longer."

I acknowledged his vague offer for support with a half-smile and watched him walk out.

"Are you okay?' Elijah's voice was soft, weak.

"I'm fine. Are you in pain? Do you need me to get a doctor?"

He shook his head on top of the wrinkled beige pillowcase. "I'm okay. As long as you're here, I'm good."

My heart cracked and bled some more. As much as my heart had been sliced and broken over and over again during the last few days, I wondered if I'd ever know what it felt like to not carry this massive hole inside my chest.

"I'm glad this is over."

"Yeah, me too." I pulled the chair closer and sat down beside the bed, still clutching his hand.

"With Julio gone, you're finally safe. We don't have to hide anymore."

"Yeah," I whispered, biting back my tears.

"It's just, I wonder why he thought you'd have Gianni's pocket Bible. But it doesn't matter." He let go of my hand and cupped my cheek. "Thank God I got there in time. If he had hurt you, I never would have forgiven myself. I failed Ellie. It would have killed me if I failed you too."

I could have told him the truth. I could have told him that his memories were wrong, distorted, and fabricated. That he was there with me in that room with Julio the entire time, that Saint and his men found us. I could have told him that his mind had confabulated that memory, his shooting

THE VILLAIN

creating another traumatic event that manipulated his already broken mind. I could have told him everything. That Ellie wasn't real, and merely a figment of his imagination which his brain had convinced him was real. But I didn't. I held it all inside, keeping it locked inside my own thoughts. I was at that very familiar crossroad again.

Every dream has its sacrifices. You either make those sacrifices and live with the consequences, or live without the dream.

My dream was him. Elijah. No matter what, I loved him. I fell in love with him exactly the way he was, and his mind had always been broken, which meant I loved that broken part of him as well.

His reality will have to become yours.

I nestled my cheek deeper into his chest. "You didn't fail Ellie," I whispered. "Who knows, we might still find her."

"We?"

I glanced up at him. "Yes. We. If she's out there, we'll find her."

His chest rose and fell, my body moving with the gentle motion. "I love you, Charlotte."

"I love you too, Elijah...more than you'll ever know."

This is the end of Elijah and Charlotte's story.
Thank you for going on this journey with me!
XOXO

———

Searching for your next **dark, kidnapping** romance?

RISE OF SAINT is filled with secrets, lies, a **forced marriage**, and is a scorching **hot enemies-to-lovers romance.**

RISE OF SAINT

Available now.

Become a member of my VIP Club by signing via my website:

www.authorbellaj.com

Members get exclusive sneak peeks, future release updates and more.

OTHER NOVELS BY BELLA J.

Dark Sovereign
Alexius
His Wife
Unraveled

Vows and Vengeance Duet
The Devil's Vow (Book 1)
The Devil's Vengeance (Book 2)

The Sins of Saint Trilogy
The Rise of Saint (Book 1)
The Fall of Sin (Book 2)
The Sins of Saint (Book 3)

The Twisted Duet
Blood and Lies (Twisted Duet, Book 1)
Blood and Vows (Twisted Duet, Book 2)

Underworld Kings
Cruel God

American Street Kings
Depraved (American Street Kings, Book 1)
Defiant (American Street Kings, Book 2)
Deranged (American Street Kings, Book 3)
Destroyed (American Street Kings, Book 4)

OTHER NOVELS BY BELLA J

Reckless
To Touch You
To Hate You

All the way from Cape Town, South Africa, Bella J lives for the days when she's able to retreat to her writer's cave where she can get lost in her little pretend world of romance, love, and insanely hot bad boys.

Bella J is a Hybrid Author with both Self-Published and Traditional Published work. Even though her novels range from drama, to comedy, to suspense, it's the dark, twisted side of romance she loves the most.

Printed in Great Britain
by Amazon